Praise for Robert Olen Butler

A Good Scent from a Strange Mountain

'The book has attracted such acclaim not simply because
it is beautifully and powerfully written, but because it
convincingly pulls off an immense imaginative risk… Butler
has not only entered the significant and ever-growing canon
of Vietnam-related fiction (he has long been a member) he
has changed its composition forever'
– Claire Messud, *Guardian*

'Deeply affecting… a brilliant collection of stories about
storytellers whose recited folklore radiates as implicit
prayer… One of the strongest collections I've read in ages'
– Ann Beattie

'*A Good Scent From a Strange Mountain* is remarkable…
for how beautifully it achieves its daring project of making
the Vietnamese real'
– *New York Times*

'Butler's achievement is not only to reveal the inner lives of
the Vietnamese, but to show, through their eyes, how the rest
of us appear from an outside perspective'
– *Chicago Tribune*

A Small Hotel

'With mesmerizing detail, Butler excavates layers of memory and illuminates moments of both tenderness and alienation'
— *New Yorker*

'Skillful… Absorbing… Wise and painfully realistic… A novel of ideas, an interrogation of the limitations and uses of language'
— *New York Times Book Review*

'Intelligent, deeply moving… remarkably written… *A Small Hotel* is a masterful story that will remind readers once again why Robert Olen Butler has been called the best living American writer'
— *Fort Worth Star Telegram*

'A sleek, erotic, and suspenseful drama about men who cannot say the word love and the women they harm… Butler executes a plot twist of profound proportions in this gorgeously controlled, unnerving, and beautifully revealing tale of the consequences of emotional withholding'
— *Booklist* (starred review)

'A brief, intense portrayal of the collapse of a marriage… This may be the oldest story in the world, or at least in the monogamous world, but Butler… seeks to give it new life by anatomizing the feelings and perceptions of each of the principals… in *A Small Hotel* he has performed an unusual and worthy feat. The puzzle may have only three pieces, but each of these has many facets, and the way they eventually fit together delivers a surprising charge'
— *Washington Post*

Also by Robert Olen Butler

The Alleys of Eden
Sun Dogs
Countrymen of Bones
On Distant Ground
Wabash
The Deuce
A Good Scent from a Strange Mountain*
They Whisper
Tabloid Dreams
The Deep Green Sea
Mr Spaceman
Fair Warning
Had a Good Time
From Where You Dream: The Process of Writing Fiction
(Janet Burroway, Editor)
Severance*
Intercourse*
Hell
Weegee Stories
A Small Hotel
The Hot Country*
The Star of Istanbul*
The Empire of Night*

* Published by No Exit Press

PERFUME RIVER

ROBERT OLEN
BUTLER

NO EXIT PRESS

First published in the UK in 2016
by No Exit Press, an imprint of
Oldcastle Books Ltd,
PO Box 394, Harpenden,
Herts, AL5 1XJ, UK

noexit.co.uk
@noexitpress
© 2016 Robert Olen Butler

ISBN
978-1-84344-889-1 (Hardcover)
978-1-84344-945-4 (Trade Paperback)
978-1-84344-890-7 (Epub)
978-1-84344-891-4 (Kindle)
978-1-84344-892-1 (pdf)

2 4 6 8 10 9 7 5 3 1

Typeset in 13pt Minion by Avocet Typeset, Somerton, Somerset
Printed and bound by CPI Group (UK) Ltd, Croydon, CR0 4YY

For Kelly

PERFUME RIVER

What are Robert Quinlan and his wife feebly arguing about when the homeless man slips quietly in? Moments later Robert could hardly have said. ObamaCare or quinoa or their granddaughter's new boyfriend. Something. He and Darla are sitting at a table in the dining area of the New Leaf Co-op. Her back is to the man. Robert is facing him. He notices him instantly, though the man is making eye contact with none of the scattered few of them, the health-conscious members of the co-op, dining by the pound from the hot buffet. It's a chilly North Florida January twilight, but he's still clearly overbundled, perhaps from the cold drilling deeper into his bones because of a life lived mostly outside. Or perhaps he simply needs to carry all his clothes around with him.

Robert takes him for a veteran.

The man's shoulder-length hair is shrapnel gray. His face is deep-creased and umbered by street life. But in spite of the immediately apparent state of his present situation, he stands straight with his shoulders squared.

He sits down at a table beside the partition doorway, which gapes into the crosswise aisle between checkout counters and front entrance. He slumps forward ever so slightly and puts both his clenched fists on the tabletop. He stares at them.

'You should've put your curry on it,' Darla says to Robert. So it's about quinoa, the argument.

'Instead of rice,' she says.

She has continued her insistent advocacy while his attention has drifted over her shoulder to the vet.

Robert brings his eyes back to her. He tries to remember if he has already cited the recent endorsement of white rice by some health journal or other.

'All those famously healthy Japanese eat rice,' he says. She huffs.

He looks at his tofu curry on the biodegradable paper plate. He looks back to the vet, who has opened one fist and is placing a small collection of coins on the table.

'I'm just trying to keep you healthy,' Darla says.

'Which is why I am content to be here at all,' Robert says, though he keeps his eyes on the vet.

The man opens the other fist and begins pushing the coins around. Sorting them. It is done in a small, quiet way. No show about it at all.

'Thanks to their fish,' she says.

Robert returns to Darla.

Her eyes are the cerulean blue of a Monet sky.

'Fish?' he asks. Uncomprehendingly.

'Yes,' she says. 'That's the factor…'

He leans toward her, perhaps a bit too abruptly. She stops her explanation and her blue eyes widen a little.

'I should feed him,' he says, low.

She blinks and gathers herself. 'Who?'

He nods in the vet's direction.

She peeks over her shoulder.

The man is still pushing his coins gently around.

She leans toward Robert, lowering her voice. 'I didn't see him.'

'He just came in,' Robert says.

'Feed him quinoa,' Darla says. She isn't kidding.

'Please,' he says, rising.

She shrugs.

This isn't a thing Robert often does. Never with money. He carries the reflex attitude, learned in childhood: You give a guy like this money and it will go for drink, which just perpetuates his problems; there are organizations he can find if he really wants to take care of himself.

Giving food is another matter, he figures, but to give food to somebody you encounter on the street, while rafting the momentum of your daily life – that's usually an awkward thing to pull off. And so, in those rare cases when it wouldn't be awkward, you can easily overlook the chance.

But here is a chance he's noticed. And there's something about this guy that continues to suggest *veteran*.

Which is to say a *Vietnam* veteran.

Something. He is of an age. Of a certain bearing. Of a field radio frequency that you are always tuned to in your head.

Robert is a veteran.

He doesn't go straight for the vet's table. He heads toward the doorway, which would bring him immediately alongside him.

He draws near. The man has finished arranging his coins but continues to ponder them. He does not look up. Then Robert is beside him, as if about to pass through the doorway. The vet has to be aware of him now. Still he does not look. He has no game going in order to get something, this man of needs. It has truly been about sorting the coins.

He smells a little musty but not overpoweringly so. He's taking care of himself pretty well, considering. Or has done so recently, at least.

Robert stops.

The vet's hair, which was a cowl of gray from across the room, up close has a seam of coal black running from crown to collar.

Robert puts his hand on the man's shoulder. He bends near him.

The man is turning, lifting his face, and Robert says, 'Would you like some food?'

Their eyes meet.

The furrows of the vet's face at brow and cheek and jaw retain much of their first impression: deeply defined, from hard times and a hard life in the body. But his eyes seem clear, and they crimp now at the outer edges. 'Yes,' he says. 'Do you have some?'

'I can get you some,' Robert says.

'That would be good,' the man says. 'Yes.'

'What do you like? I think there was some chicken.' Though he hasn't invoked the preternaturally healthful quinoa, he catches himself trying to manage this guy's nutrition, an impulse which feels uncomfortably familiar. He's trying to get him healthy.

'It needs to be soft,' the man says. 'I don't have very many teeth.'

'Why don't you come with me,' Robert says. 'You can choose.'

The vet is quick to his feet. 'Thank you,' he says. He offers a closed-mouth smile.

Standing with him now, about to walk with him, Robert recognizes something he's neglected: This act is still blatant charity, condescending in its anonymity. So he offers his hand. And though he almost always calls himself – and always thinks of himself – as *Robert*, he says, 'Bob.'

The vet hesitates.

The name alone seems to have thrown him. Robert clarifies. 'I'm Bob.'

14

The man takes Robert's hand and smiles again, more broadly this time, but struggling to keep his toothlessness from showing. 'I'm Bob,' he says. And then, hastily, as if he'd be mistaken for simply, madly, parroting the name: '*Too*.'

The handshake goes on. The vet has a firm grip. He further clarifies. 'I'm *also* Bob.'

'It's a good name,' Robert says.

'It's okay.'

'Not as common as it used to be.'

Bob looks at Robert for a moment, letting the handshake slow and stop. Robert senses a shifting of the man's mind into a conversational gear that hasn't been used in a while.

'That's true,' Bob says.

Robert leads him through the doorway and along the partition, past the ten-items-only register, and into the buffet area. He stops at the soup warmers on the endcap, thinking of the man's tooth problem, but Bob goes on ahead, and before Robert can make a suggestion, Bob says, 'They have beans and rice. This is good.'

Robert steps beside him, and together they peer through the sneeze guard at a tub of pintos and a tub of brown rice. Good mess hall food, Robert thinks, though thinking of it that way jars with a reassessment going on in a corner of his mind.

Of no relevance to this present intention, however.

Bob declines any other food, and Robert piles one of the plastic dinner plates high with beans and rice while Bob finds a drink in the cooler. Robert waits for him and takes the bottle of lightly lemoned sparkling water from his hand and says, 'Why don't you go ahead and sit?'

Bob nods and slips away.

Robert steps to the nearby checkout station.

A young man, with a jugular sunburst tattoo and a silver ring pierced into his lip, totals up the food, and Robert lets his reassessment register in his mind: From the clues of age in face and hair, Robert realizes Bob is no Vietnam veteran. As old as the man is – perhaps fifty or fifty-five – he is still too young to have been in Vietnam. He missed it by a decade or so.

Robert pays.

The clerk gives him a small, understanding nod.

'Do you know him?' Robert asks.

'He comes now and then,' the young man says.

Beans and rice and fizzy lemon water in hand, Robert turns away.

He steps into the dining area and sets the plate and the can before Bob. The man has carefully laid out his napkin and plastic utensils and has put his coins away.

He squares around to look up at Robert.

He is not the man Robert first thought him to be. 'Thank you,' Bob says.

Robert knows nothing about him.

'It's a good meal,' Bob says.

'You bet,' Robert says, and he moves off, thinking: *It would have made no difference. I would have done this anyway.*

He sits down before Darla.

She leans toward him and says softly, 'I'm glad you did that.' To her credit, she does not ask what he's bought the man.

She sits back.

Her plate, once featuring the spicy Thai quinoa salad, is empty. He looks at his remaining tofu curry. He picks up his fork and begins pushing it around.

She says something he does not quite hear.

He stops pushing.

There are other voices in the dining area. Conversations. He thinks: *Can it have been that long ago?*

But of course it can. Even consciously thinking about it, Vietnam yields up no clear, individual memory. Images are there – faces and fields and a headquarters compound courtyard and a bar and a bed and a river – but they are like thumbnails of forgotten snaps on a cellphone screen.

'More,' Darla says. As part of other things she's been saying, no doubt.

Robert looks at her.

She narrows her eyes at him.

'It's probably cold,' she says, nodding at his food.

'Probably,' he says.

'You can get some more,' she says.

'I don't need anything,' he says.

She shrugs. 'Shall we go?'

'Coffee,' he says. The word is a nanosecond or so ahead of the conscious thought.

She cocks her head. He went back to the stuff a few months ago after she'd wrangled a year of abstinence from him. She was reconciled to it but the one-word announcement sounds like a taunt, he realizes.

'Bob needs some coffee,' he says.

'Bob?' She twists at the word in her snorty voice, assuming he's referring to his coffee-seeking self in the third person. She occasionally calls him *Bob* when she thinks he's behaving badly.

He doesn't explain. He rises. He approaches Bob. The man is hunched over his food, wolfing it in.

Robert is beside him before he looks up.

'You a coffee drinker, Bob?'

'I surely am,' he says.

'How do you take it?'

'With a splash of milk.'

'I'll get you some.'

'I appreciate it, Bob,' Bob says.

Near the buffet, Robert begins to fill a cup from a percolator urn. Framed in the center of the urn is the bag art for today's brew. An upsweep of mountains dense with tropical forest, the vista framed in coffee trees.

Somewhere along the highway to Dak To, they'd laid out the beans to dry. He is passing in a jeep, heading to an assignment that will quickly be changed, sending him upcountry. A pretty-faced girl in a conical hat, leaning on her coffee rake, lifts her face to him. And he sweeps on past.

The cup is nearly full.

He flips up the handle.

He splashes in some milk.

He returns to Bob.

The man thanks him again, briefly cupping both hands around the coffee, taking in its warmth before setting it down.

'You a Floridian, Bob?' Robert asks.

'I'm from Charleston, West Virginia,' he says.

'Good thing you're not up there for the winter.'

Bob nods a single, firm nod and looks away. 'I have to go back,' he says.

'Perhaps when things warm up.'

'No choice,' he says. 'I've got responsibilities.' His face remains averted. He isn't elaborating. His beans and rice are getting cold.

Robert still has the urge to make this encounter count for something beyond a minor act of charity. Learn a bit more about him. Offer some advice. Whatever. And this is all he can think to ask: 'What sort of responsibilities, Bob?'

Bob doesn't look at him.

He doesn't eat.

He doesn't drink.

Robert has made the man go absolutely still. But Robert sloughs off the niggle of guilt, thinking: *He's probably been asserting these responsibilities to himself for the whole, long slide to where he is now, knowing there's nothing left where he came from, knowing he'll never go back.*

Robert puts his hand on Bob's shoulder for a moment and then moves away.

He does not sit down at their table. Darla looks up. She glances at his empty hands. 'No coffee?'

He shrugs.

She nods and smiles. 'Finished with dinner?'

'Yes,' he says.

She gathers her things and they put on their coats. She leads the way across the floor. Darla may well glance at Bob as she passes, ready to offer him an encouraging smile. She would do that. But Bob looks up only after she's gone by.

He fixes his eyes on Robert's and upticks his chin. He says, 'You know my old man, is that it?'

Robert takes the odd abruptness of the question in stride, answering a passing 'No' as he follows Darla out of the dining area.

And that is that.

~

Darla and Robert are finished in town, and he drives toward home on the parkway. The two of them do not speak. This is not uncommon after dining out.

They live east and south of the Tallahassee city limits, on an acre of garden and hardwood and a dozen more of softwood, and the quickest way carries them first along a commercial scroll of strip malls and chain eateries, lube joints and furniture stores, pharmacies and gas stations. Robert finds himself acutely aware of all this. He turns south at his first opportunity, and then, shortly, he turns east again, onto Old Saint Augustine Road.

Darla humphs, though for all their years together she has alternately used this dismissive sound as a sign of approval. It is up to him to know which humph is which.

Old Saint Augustine is easy to interpret. Canopied in live oaks and hiding its residences and smattering of service commerce behind sweet gums and hickories and tulip poplars, this is a road from the state's past, a subject he occasionally teaches at the university and Darla occasionally is happy to hear him discourse upon. Though their silence persists tonight.

She switches on the university radio station.

This same ostinato of orchestral strings presses his face to a window on a TWA 707. The Rocky Mountains crawl beneath him. He is flying to Travis Air Force Base, north of San Francisco. From there he will go to war. And this music is playing in his head through a pneumatic headset. Beethoven's Seventh Symphony. The first movement has tripped and stomped and danced, making things large, as Beethoven can do, but confidently so, almost lightly so. A little bit of the summer pastoral spilling over from the Sixth Symphony. And now, in the second movement, the largeness of things is rendered into reassuring repetitions. Can Robert believe this of what lies ahead of him, this grave contentment the music would have him feel?

He is not to be a shooting soldier. He will do order-of-battle work, rather like research, rather like the things he learned to love in his recent four years at Tulane. Wherever they put him, he will be bunkered in at the core of a headquarters compound. It would take an unlikely military cataclysm – or a fluke, a twist of very bad luck, a defiance of an actuarial reality of warfare that is obscured by Cronkite's nightly report – for him to die.

He is young enough to feel confident in that reasoning. It is September of 1967. Four months before the military cataclysm of the coming Vietnamese New Year, Tet 1968. And if he does survive, he believes he will earn a thing he has long yearned to earn, foreshadowed only a few days ago in a bar on Magazine Street. His father shed tears over his tenth farewell Dixie, Robert's fourth. Silent tears. William Quinlan has always been a quiet drunk. A quiet man, about feelings he could not command, feelings better felt by women. Robert still thinks, as he flies away to music his father could never understand, that he knows what the tears were about.

In the car, however, this ostinato is solemn and insistent. More than solemn. It aches. He feels nothing like contentment as he races through the corridor of oaks. It is forty-seven years later.

He glances at Darla.

Her face is pressed against the window.

~

Down a pea gravel drive they emerge from a grove of pine and cedar. They stop before the house they built in 1983 from early-twentieth-century Craftsman plans, with a shed-dormered gable roof, a first floor of brick, and two upper floors of veneered stucco and half-timber. For a decade Darla's parents withheld every penny of their considerable resources from the struggling young academic couple, disapproving of the politics that brought the two of them together, and then, upon their deaths, they surprised their daughter with a will that split the parental wealth in half between her and a brother as conservative as they. She got the sprawling Queen Anne estate on Cayuga Lake and enough money to keep it up, along with the expressed hope – just short of a mandate – that their 'daughter Darla and her family come home.'

The parents' death itself surprised her. It was by late-night car crash on the Taconic Parkway, both of them apparently drunk. Darla immediately sold the Queen Anne and she and Robert built this new house, to their shared taste, having lately taken their places at Florida State University. At the time, their son Kevin was eleven. Their daughter Kimberly was five.

Tonight, with Robert's Clinton-era S-Class Mercedes sitting next to Darla's new Prius, they enter the house and put away their coats and go to the kitchen and putter about, she heating water for her herbal tea and he grinding his Ethiopian beans to brew his coffee, and for a long while they say nothing, not uncommon for this early-evening ritual, which occasionally feels, for both of them, comfortable.

Then, when their cups are full and they are about to go off to their separate places in the house to do some end-of-evening work, Darla touches Robert's arm, very briefly, though only as if to get his attention, and she says, 'What did you two talk about?'

'Who?' he says, though he knows who she means.

'The homeless man,' she says.

'The weather,' he says.

She nods. 'Did he say how he copes?'

'We didn't get into that.'

'I hate to shrug him off,' she says, though in an intonation that mutes the 'hate' and stresses the 'off.' She therefore does not need to add 'but we must.'

They say no more.

They are both on sabbatical this spring, and they go to what have been their separate studies ever since the house was finished.

Robert's is on the third floor, where the Craftsman plans called for a gentleman's billiard room. His desk faces the fireplace in the north gable, with its hammered copper hood. Dormers and window seats are to his right hand and his left. His books line the room in recessed shelves.

Early-twentieth-century American history is his specialty and he is writing a biography of a journalist, publisher, and agitator for pacifist and socialist causes, John Kenneth Turner. Tonight, he is working on a paper for a history conference. 'The Prototype of the Twentieth-Century Antiwar Movement in the U.S.: John Kenneth Turner, Woodrow Wilson, and the Mexican Invasion.' A mouthful of a title that he sits for a time now trying to simplify.

Darla's study is off the first-floor hallway between the living room and the dining room. Her desk looks west through the casement windows, across the veranda, and out to the massive live oak behind their house. She teaches art theory. By certain scholarly adversaries at other schools, her research is considered to be interdisciplinary to a fault. She is known for her book *Public Monuments as Found Art: A Semiotic Revisioning.* Tonight she is trying to finish the rough draft of a paper, which, indeed, she will present at a semiotics conference. 'Dead Soldiers and Sexual Longing: The Subtexts and Sculptural Tropes of the Daughters of the Confederacy Monuments.' The title seems just right to her.

They are focused thinkers, Robert and Darla. They would, if pressed to consider the matter, attribute some of their focus to the mutual respect they have for each other's work. They need give each other not a single thought once they are sitting in these long-familiar rooms.

But the last sip of Robert's coffee is cold. And he thinks of Bob.

He wonders what the man is doing right now. There is some shelter or other in Tallahassee, surely. Bob is there. Perhaps he is thinking, still, of Charleston, thinking of whatever it is he feels responsible for. Or perhaps Robert was right about that sudden stillness in Bob. Perhaps the man is merely hunkered down for the night in this life he's drifted to, trying to figure out how he got here.

~

After the man and his wife passed and vanished and Bob got reacquainted with the food and the coffee before him and after he ate and drank and sat for a while at the table, he has once again forgotten what he knows about what can set him to thinking, forgotten this to his severe detriment since he does not want to deal with the inside of his mind, with the thinking machine revved up, not ever, but especially not at the very same time as having to deal with finding a place to sleep, now that he's missed the deadlines for the shelters and the missions and the lighthouses and the mercy houses and the promised lands and the heavenly refuges. But tonight he has forgotten what he knows about *the situation*.

So as soon as he remembers, he stands and goes out of the New Leaf Market and it's too late, the situation is upon him: It was light and now it's dark. It happened while he wasn't watching. It happened quickly.

It launches him along Apalachee Parkway. And for a long while he just focuses on pushing his body hard to get away. Push and push. That's all there is. Too much. The ache in his legs and his back starts it all aching in his head again. He doesn't know how far he's come, how long he's been walking. A couple of miles. Maybe more. Then a landmark tells him he's making progress, even as it stirs up issues. Tillotson Funeral Home passes, its phony columns floodlit like the capitol building, its marquee making some dead body famous for being dead. Some stiff named Henry tonight. Henry something or other, the second name not even worth Bob noticing. This guy doesn't matter. Some Henry who was breathing and then he wasn't.

The dark continues to nag at Bob. Its suddenness happened early, this being the first week of January. It left a bad chill behind, which is why he's been walking east as fast as he can. In January he cannot simply vanish into the urban woodlands of Tallahassee, follow a bike trail and then veer off into the woods and find his things in a place only he knows about, through a culvert and along a drain bed and up a bank to a mark on a tree here and a mark on a tree there and a few more marks and a fallen oak and a hollow beneath, a place that was good for him all autumn long and he could go there anytime no matter how his flailing mind was trying to fuck with him, and he could get his stuff and he could find a place to sleep in the woods.

All of this is rushing in Bob again, filling his head with

words, but he never thinks it's somebody else's voice.

'It's me. It's just me in here.'

He says this aloud.

He's not crazy. He knows to look around right away to see if anybody heard him and nobody has. Bob's doing fine, with only cars whisking past, no people, no one to hear. He even has the presence of mind to walk against the traffic in the stretches without sidewalks. He's not crazy. He can even circle back to his previous thought, the one before the little digression that was worth mouthing.

'I could always find my way in the woods,' he says. 'You were okay with me there. Not that you'd let on. But you didn't fool me. I knew you were okay with me there.'

This he addresses to his father. But Bob's not crazy. Bob doesn't think the old man is there with him on Apalachee Parkway to hear. The old man is just a memory to him, maybe hiding out in Charleston and yellowing from his liver or maybe spotlighted this very night in front of some funeral home, but he's nowhere nearby to hear. Nevertheless, because he's not crazy, Bob shuts his trap and does his talking in his head *where you always are, but when I'm strong – and I'm strong tonight, I know I am, in spite of the situation – I can make you behave, in my head I can take us into the woods, just you and me, and I can make it be the summer of '71, a certain day in August and I've gone and turned twelve and that was when I learned about the thing you didn't want me to know. That I was okay by you. Though it was only with the Mossberg .22 in the crook of my arm, that I was okay with the Mossberg going quick to my shoulder and I kill some animal or other that you didn't even see and it makes you drop into a shooting crouch and lay out some covering fire and then you stop and you look me wild in the eyes and inside you're going* Who the fuck are you? *and then you focus and you answer your own question in your head, you don't want me to see it but I do, I listen into your head and you go,* You're Bobby, you're my son and you can shoot, by God, I been gone away a big chunk of your life to shoot in some big woods – in some fucking jungles in Vietnam – and I come back and by damn you can use a rifle just as good as any of the boys I been with *then you look where I shot and you throw a camouflage tarp over the crack that just opened and shut in your head, and you jump up, but you're not talking, not saying a word, of course not, you're not looking at me but I know what's just passed between us, no matter how you try to camouflage it, I know this thing about the two of us.*

'Goddamn you, I know it,' Bob says.

I know it here in the woods even though I will doubt it when we get back home tonight, you will have your way with my head when you've got us in our single-wide and you're in your La-Z-Boy and you've got your bottle, and your silence is just your silence, and I better stay out of arm's reach while you're sitting there dealing with whatever it is you came home with a couple of years ago. Your situation.

Like Bob has a situation. Like now. Like this long, cold walk he's on tonight, trying the one thing he knows to try, concerning a place to sleep. A church building along the parkway, maybe thirty minutes by foot east of Walmart, an hour and a half from New Leaf, and longer still from the Hardluckers' center of town, and as he pushes on east, Bob can't stay in the woods in his head with his father for all that time, in fact his mind has already grabbed him up and galloped into that trailer park along the Kanawha, out past

27

the West Virginia State campus, out where he's not okay with his father at all, and even if Bob summons up enough energy to at least drive his mind forward to when he's older, to when he's near as tall and rangy as his dad and he can easily fend off the old man when he wants to reach out and give his son a slap – it wasn't about that really, those slaps were all open-handed, always, Bob knew all along there were worse fathers by far – even when Bob skips forward, his mind only roars louder, because his real fear had to do with whatever it was inside his father that only the old man could see, the things he never talked about. Bob was afraid those things were inside himself already, no matter if his father found them in a jungle halfway around the world, because the two of them were the same, father and son, they were stretched tall in body in the same way, they had the same hands and eyes, and they were the same by that shared thing in the woods, when they were okay together. And the okayness only made everything worse because that was never spoken about either, just like the Vietnam jungle stuff. The good things between them and the bad things that could come to men like the two of them were all one in the same unspeakable place. And so Bob tries to just walk. He just strides hard and lets the pain of the pavement pound through his joints and back and temples and gums and he focuses on what's ahead.

A pastor out here at Blood of the Lamb Full Gospel leaves the outside door to the groundskeeper's storage room unlocked on cold nights. They have a food pantry, but this far out of town they do hard-luck families mostly, not the individually lost. Out here, sheltered floor space next to a John Deere is a private little bit of charity by the good pastor that often goes unused, its being attractive only to a Hardlucker without a car. Which makes it a pretty good bet to be available to anyone ready to walk six or seven miles. Especially since the space is needed most when it's the most daunting to walk, in the cold or the rain.

Two nights ago it was cold and Bob had the place to himself. It was a hard walk. Tonight it's cold again, but at the moment, with some things talked over, he feels pretty good. Pretty damn good. He's got today's newspaper folded in his pocket, a full copy abandoned on a table, waiting for him as he finished his coffee tonight. There's a light in the storage room to read by. He's not afraid to read the news. The meal and the coffee are sitting well in him, so his thoughts turn to the man who gave them to him, the man with the same name as his, the rangy older man with the John Wayne jaw: *You said it first, my name, and I thought for a second you somehow already knew I'm Bob and it turns out* you're *Bob, and my father is Calvin, my father isn't Bob, if you were my father I'd be Junior and I don't know what I'd think about that, I think I wouldn't like it, not at all, my father is Calvin, Cal, my mother is Marie, and what did you mean, Bob, about my having responsibilities in Charleston? Did you know me there? You another of my old man's cronies are you? What do you want me to do about it?*

'I never met you before in my life,' Bob says.

He stops walking.

He's not feeling so good now.

Things are suddenly getting a little out of hand.

He realizes that.

This was a good man he met. Bob the stranger.

He needs to stop his mind.

He needs to sleep.

The church isn't much farther.

29

He walks on and the streetlights are gone, they've been gone for a while and the dark is even darker but Bob hasn't noticed till now. Still, it's all right, he's reconciled to the dark for this night, and up ahead now is an upspray of light as if rising from the earth, beaconing a message on another marquee, before the Blood of the Lamb Full Gospel Church: **GOD ANSWERS KNEE-MAIL**

Somehow this calms Bob for a time. Hardly from the sentiment. But he's not only not crazy, he's pretty smart. His mother was smart. Cal was too, in a shrewd sort of way. When Bob's mind is flailing with deep issues, to hear deep issues turned into banality is a kind of mental speed bump for him. He slows down.

He gives the sign the finger as he goes by, and he finds he can focus now for a time, and he keeps his eyes lowered as he passes the central spire and the fake front columns on the stuccoed facade. He keeps his face down and he moves through the side parking lot and around back and to the separate community building and around to the back of that and to the door and he's glad now it's almost over. He will sleep. He can sleep.

He is at the door and he puts his hand to the knob and he turns it and the knob yields and then the door and he steps into a darkness smelling of cedar mulch and motor oil, and he stops, and he waits a moment for his eyes to adjust and he sees a swift movement of shadow out of the corner of his eye and hears a guttural bark of a voice and he hears nothing more, not even the clang of the shovel against his forehead.

~

In bed now, Darla inserts her iPod earbuds, and she and Robert switch off their lamps. Their Kindles have their own light.

The tinny spill of Bach from his wife's ears fades quickly from Robert's awareness. Soon, however, he is reading the same few sentences over and over. He turns off his book.

'Good night,' she says, aware of the vanishing of his light in her periphery.

'Good night,' he says, though they have long ago agreed that the formality of his reply is unnecessary, since her head, at this point, is always full of music and she cannot hear him.

Nor do they kiss.

They are so very familiar with each other. And that familiarity has become the presiding expression of their intimacy.

Robert sleeps.

And he wakes.

He has been dreaming, but he does not remember a single image of the dream.

Not that he tries.

It is enough that he is awake.

The room is dark.

He turns his face toward Darla. He can make out – more kinesthetically than visually – the topography of her. She is lying on her side, facing away.

He gently pulls back the covers, eases his way from the bed so as not to disturb her, puts on slippers and robe, and he goes out of the room and along the hallway and down the stairs. He pulls his topcoat from the vestibule closet, enters the wide dark of the living room, and passes through the French doors and onto the rear veranda.

He stands at its edge. The moonless sky is clear and the stars are bright. His bare ankles are cold but his chest is warm. He once would have snuck a smoke here. He didn't need Darla to persuade him to abandon cigarettes, even an isolated, openair smoke or two. His father's burr-grinder cough did that.

Now he simply puffs his breath into the starlight.

His oak stands before him in vast silhouette, its lower horizontal branches thick as most trees, thick as water oaks and pin oaks. On other nights, with or without cigarettes, he felt that his scholarly discipline, his life's work, his very mind were made manifest in this tree. After all, it stood there through early-twentieth-century America, breathing oxygen into that era's air. It even likely witnessed the birth and death of the Confederacy, perhaps even Andrew Jackson's war on the Seminoles, Old Hickory's ruthlessness thwarted by the tribe's guerrilla elusiveness.

But on this night, as Robert folds his arms across his chest and squares himself to the oak, he feels the presence not of the ghosts of history but of Bob. Bob the illusory Vietnam veteran. He evoked Vietnam over Robert's quinoa at the health food store and then, being illusory in that regard, couldn't vent the war away. So it has settled back into Robert himself. For this, the veranda, facing the oak tree, is the wrong place to be tonight: a tree sits in the center of Robert's Vietnam.

He unfolds his arms, thinks to turn, to retreat to bed. But he does not move. Instead, he wakes and it's dark and a woman is beside him, naked and small, and she is waking too and the room is still heavy with the incense she has burnt for her dead. Robert has lingered with her, fallen asleep with her in a back street on the south bank of the Perfume River in the city of Hue. It is 3:40 in the morning, January 31, 1968, and they have woken to the sound of the North Vietnamese rockets and mortar rounds coming in from the mountains to the west.

Robert blinks hard against the memory.

He will not let certain things in.

He pats his pockets now, by reflex, as if he will find a cigarette, and he turns his face a little, breaking with his live oak.

But the woman lingers, still naked, in the dark of the room, lit through the window by a distant flare from across the rooftops.

And now he is throwing on his clothes. Hue was supposed to be different, traditionally spared by both sides. The targets of the North's New Year's offensive were thought surely to have been revealed in the fighting that commenced this time yesterday. Surely it was all coordinated.

He is dressed and he and the woman are standing beside the bed.

Her name is Lien. Lotus.

She hands him something heavy. Metal. He knows the thing. It is a French .32-caliber pistol that belonged to her father.

Do Robert and the woman speak?

Of course they do.

He loves her.

But he will not remember more of her now.

And he is down the back stairs into the dead-fish stench of the alley and the AK-47s are popping from across the river. The Viet Cong. Or maybe even the North Vietnamese regulars. Though his job has been to count – men, weapons, from all the field intelligence that comes in – he thinks: *We don't know jack shit about them, for all our counting.*

He goes out into the street, and far down, under the streetlamps along the river, he sees the men moving. The men he counts. He thinks: *I am a dead man.*

He turns and runs in the direction of MACV, the US compound, half a dozen blocks away. He rushes past storefronts and the passageways into rear courtyards and past the smells of mildew and dead fish and the smell of wood fires and from all directions now comes the din of weaponry, of small arms and RPDs and the whoosh and suck and blare of rockets, the sky flaring across the river, beyond the Imperial Palace walls – they are hitting Tay Loc, the city airport to the north – and now he sees men before him, as well, a squad of dark-clothed men a block up the river and gunfire is crackling everywhere and now a needle-thin compression of air zips past his head and he lunges into an alley mouth and he is running hard and figures are coming to doorways and he thinks the local communist cadres are emerging, he thinks again that he is dead, and there is only darkness around him and the alley slime underfoot and he pushes hard, and if he is to die he'd rather not see it happening, so he doesn't look right or left or feel any of the bodies coming out. He just runs and he runs and he is out of the alley and he is in a pocket park and standing before a great, dark form.

A banyan tree.

It is old and it is vast. Its aerial roots are thick as young trees and nuzzled together into their own dense forest, propping up a billowing dark sky of leaves, and there is a deep inner curve to the roots, and a turning, and in the direction of the MACV compound there is heavy small-arms fire now and he hears the AK-47s and he hears an answering M60 machine gun and the M16s and he knows what to do.

He enters the tree.

He moves into the turning and he puts his back to its roots and he sits and he draws his legs into him and he is in the dark. He can see around the out-curving columns of roots. Bodies appear, nearly as dark as the night, moving quickly past with a metallic rustle of weapons, and he pulls his head back, squeezes into himself. He closes his eyes and smells a dank wet-earth smell and something fainter beneath, an almost-sweetness, and a little sharp thing in the nose, and he thinks of the girl's incense and the dead she prays for. He knows this tree has killed another to live. These roots around him, holding him in the dark, began long ago by wrapping themselves around another tree, the strangler roots, embracing a living tree until it vanished, until it was dead inside the growing banyan. Rifles flare nearby and he presses back into the killing embrace of the banyan.

He holds the French pistol in his right hand, flat against his chest. He expects to die here.

Robert steps from his veranda.

He is panting heavily.

He has not let this happen for several years.

He moves across his lawn now, approaches his tree. He places both hands hard upon its trunk to stop their trembling.

He leans heavily there, waiting for this to pass.

But still he thinks: *I was not meant to be here. I was not meant to live this life I've led. I was meant to die long ago. Long long ago.*

~

Darla wakes, opens her eyes. Her lids are heavy, a precious, fragile state for her in the deep middle of the night. She is on her back, and above her is only indecipherable dark. She lets her eyes close. The bed has stirred and it continues to stir. Her eyes open again and their heaviness has vanished. She turns her face and watches her husband's form adjusting, arms and now legs and now arms again. She realizes he is doing this as unobtrusively as he can. He was once much worse, returning from whatever it is that he does. He is trying. She would speak,

35

but she does not want a conversation that would wake her up once and for all. If there is something on his mind and he is choosing not to volunteer it, it can wait till morning. She turns on her side, putting her back to him.

And she sees him for the first time. It is May 8, 1970, four days after the Ohio National Guard killings at Kent State. He sits alone at a bistro table in a corner of a coffee shop in downtown Baton Rouge. She figures she has him pegged: the stretchy slacks and the button-down, short-sleeved sport shirt could simply be the sartorial momentum of the LSU student dress code, only recently rescinded, but something else about him – perhaps the longer hair on top of his head and the new growth on the sides; perhaps his quiet, two-handed focus on his coffee; perhaps just that surge of intuition about a guy your pheromones tell you you'll fall for – something – makes her figure they are PX clothes and a military whitewall haircut abandoned at last and a cup of better coffee than he's had for the past two or three years. He is an ex-soldier.

Behind her, on Fourth Street, some of the thousand people who just marched on the state capitol are drifting by, stoked and chatty with righteousness. Enough of them are also crowded into the shop to justify Darla receiving her cup of coffee and then approaching this man with green eyes and disparately dark hair and a jaw as smooth and hard as monument marble.

He looks up at her, though slowly, as she draws near, as if he were reluctant to shift his attention from the coffee.

She plays her hunch. 'It looks like you've wanted that cup of Community for a long time.' She learned quickly, as a New York girl first-year grad student, about the local coffee, ground and roasted on the north side of town.

'I've been away,' he says.

Darla looks around the crowded room as if checking the available seating. She knows it makes no difference; she'd be doing this anyway. Still, even though she has for several years been quite comfortable with her female empowerment in this new age, she chooses to portray, with the search, a practical reason for the question she is about to ask. She nods at the empty chair across from him. 'May I?' she asks.

'Of course,' he says.

She puts her coffee cup on the tabletop and sits.

He stirs now in the bed next to her.

She stops this memory.

She is no longer sleepy. She needs to count bricks in an imaginary wall. She needs to take deep breaths and let them out slowly.

She thinks: *What prompted this bit of* recherche du temps perdu? *Not a small French sponge cake. Not even Community Coffee. Perhaps my Thai quinoa salad, though for its overspiciness rather than its latent nostalgia.*

She can't even muster an irony-arched half smile for herself. She would like to dismiss the past with this sort of smartypants joking. But that is a lifelong impulse she has lately come to see as cowardly. The fact is she clearly remembers falling in love with him. Loving him. Loving him and loving him.

And now that she is sitting before him in a Baton Rouge coffee shop with only a small tabletop of a French sidewalk café separating the two of them, and now that she is gazing directly into those eyes of his, they remind her of the emerald green of a Monet forest. She thinks to remark on this. Even in those first few moments with him. She also thinks, however, to mask her desire by immediately noting that it was the pigment that drove Monet mad. But instead, she says, 'Did you march?'

He blinks those green eyes slowly, as if trying to understand.

Given her hunch about what he is or recently was, she hears herself as he might: the question could be a way of asking if he is a soldier. They are being routinely spit upon these days.

She clarifies. 'To the capitol. Over the war.'

'Ah,' he says in a tone that suggests he was unaware of the event. 'No.'

'Surely you knew,' she says. 'We went right past that window. A thousand of us.'

'I figured it was a Greek Row picnic,' he says.

For a clock tick or two she believes him. The green eyes show nothing.

Then they come alive. Widen and spark, and Darla and Robert laugh together.

His eyes.

She looks toward him in the dark in the bed.

She realizes she has not been noticing those eyes for some time. She makes a note in her head to look him carefully in the eyes today.

And it occurs to her now, for the first time, after all these years: *My god. I'd actually expected an observation about the pigment of his eyes driving Monet mad to hide my desire. It would, in fact, have cried out my desire. His eyes were driving me mad.*

Did she ever go on to openly make that observation about their color?

She tries to remember.

She cannot.

She thinks not.

I never did tell him, she thinks.

And then: *Thank god. He got me into his bed quick enough as it was.*

But she did tell him. It was on their fifth wedding anniversary, spent in bed in their apartment in Baton Rouge, making love in the morning but then spending the rest of the day – wisely, necessarily, they thought – reading for their PhD oral exams. They did so, however, naked together in bed, the heat turned up high, as it was a chilly February day. In the late afternoon, as the light from the window was fading, just after Robert switched on a nightstand lamp, she told him about his eyes, thinking perhaps he and she might touch again for a time on this special day. She told him about their color. Told him that she'd planned to cut him down at once, however, with her line about Monet. Perhaps at the moment of her confession Robert's head was too full of the academic rhetoric of history. Her head was too, after all. For he simply smiled a little and offered a bland *How sweet* and he resumed his reading and she resumed her reading and they did not touch again for a few days, and when they did, the incident was forgotten.

Darla is counting bricks in an imaginary wall, pausing at each hundred to take a brisk, long breath and then letting it out as slowly as she can, trying to ignore the unconscious, restless body in bed beside her, trying simply to sleep.

Shortly after her third hundred, Robert turns heavily onto his back and sighs. Darla hesitates briefly – just long enough to realize how there is no good reason to hesitate, even briefly, to follow this impulse – and so she seeks his hand at rest between them and lays hers gently upon it. She thought he was probably asleep, and he is, but she keeps her hand on his until, just past her fourth hundred, she falls asleep.

~

When Robert wakes, there is a thin etching of gray dawn along the vertical edges of the blackout blinds. Darla's hand is long gone from his and he has missed the gesture. He is lying on his back and she is to his right, on her side, facing away. He is capable of a gesture similar to hers. He could lay a hand gently on the point of her hip now, as she sleeps, and then take it away again after a time without having to raise any issues or expectations between them. He has done so, with her sleeping, within the past week. But this morning he has woken to find Jimmy in his head and he needs to deal with that first. Gently, very gently, so as not to wake her – for she can be a light sleeper sometimes, an aggrievedly light sleeper – he turns onto his side with his back to her.

For some years now it has taken Robert a little bit by surprise whenever he thinks of his brother. But the prompts this time are instantly clear: Robert's venture to the veranda without the purgative focus of a cigarette, particularly on a night of Beethoven's Seventh; the consequent memory of his flight from the North Vietnamese soldiers in Hue, of his refuge in the banyan tree; his taking refuge, as well, from the army, for an occasional night, in the arms of a Vietnamese woman.

Robert long ago recognized the irony of all this. In some sense he actually ran and hid before Jimmy did.

But it wasn't the same.

Even now, almost forty-seven years later, he feels compelled to repeat the litany of differences: More than a few Americans at MACV, officers and enlisted men alike, had local women to go to now and then; the communist offensive on five other provincial capitals the previous night had convinced everyone in Hue that the city's traditional exemption from serious attack, tacitly accepted by both sides, still pertained; Robert's break from the army was not even AWOL, much less desertion. And Robert had not run from the war. He did not even run from that night's battle; he sought cover and would later emerge.

He would later emerge.

And a price would be paid for not running.

Robert shuts down this line of thinking.

He does not want to emerge from the banyan. Not this morning. Not ever again. There is no need. He has long since reconciled himself to those few days in 1968.

So much time has passed. Generations. For Christ's sake, he's had his own children and grandchildren since.

And the irony about his act being akin to Jimmy's is superficial. A conceit. Jimmy did run. From the war. From far more.

Not that Robert blames Jimmy.

Not for his politics, certainly.

Not for decades.

Robert eases onto his back once again, expecting that thought to send Jimmy on his way, but instead he and Jimmy are sitting in overstuffed chairs angled toward the settee where their father is in a familiar stage of dozing off. Sitting upright, head sinking, he will soon – barely lifting his face and without opening his eyes – pivot slowly into fetal repose on the velour.

It is Labor Day, 1967. Robert is on home leave with orders to Vietnam. He graduated in June of '66 from Tulane and struggled through that summer with what to do. He went off to LSU on a graduate school deferment, but he dropped out as soon as the fall semester was finished and he enlisted.

Robert is wearing his dress greens. Glad for his father to see him in them. His father was a nineteen-year-old hard-stripe corporal in the infantry under Patton in Germany, about to become a platoon sergeant when the war ended.

But the conversation has been odd. Minimal. Tangential. Almost sullen, for his father's part. Pops is a quiet drunk. But sober, he can talk. He has the gift of gab. Even smart gab at times. He isn't well educated but he's well read. Their home has always been filled with books, and he even hounded any traces of Third Ward Yat out of his sons' speech. Still and all, Robert understands: About real feelings his father also is a quiet man. He gets drunk on his feelings and clams up.

And Robert figures there are other things going on to shut Pops down, figures the old man and Jimmy were probably fighting before Robert arrived and the fight simply has overridden everything. His little brother, fractiously self-assertive and needy as usual, has simply jumped in between him and their father.

Robert, in his bed, closes his eyes to the oak beam running above him in the ceiling as if it were about to fall and split the bed in two. He is tempted to slide forward a couple of hours, to the abrupt ending of the family's Labor Day afternoon in New Orleans.

But he does not.

He remains in the moment when he and Jimmy are themselves quiet, almost placid-seeming, with each other, as they sit watching their father fade into sleep in the front room of the family's double shotgun in the Irish Channel. When Pops bought the house – after he was promoted to stevedore foreman at the Seventh Street Wharf – he opened the common wall of the semidetached, here in the living room and in the back, at the kitchen, making a unified home of it. Robert was ten, Jimmy was eight.

As their father begins to snore, the brothers look at each other. It's been more than a year since they've been together. Robert made his decision about the war on his own. The previous summer Jimmy was hitchhiking out west, and he spent Thanksgiving and Christmas somewhere in the Northeast with a girl he'd met on his travels.

Without a word or a nod, the brothers rise and go out the front door and down the porch steps. Clay Square lies before them, the de facto front yard playground of their shared childhood. Two years apart, they were playmates and then enemies and then friends and then largely indifferent to each other, as they sought their own independent selves, and now neither of them is sure about the other. They are ready to be what they will become on this little walk together, as Robert goes to war and Jimmy enters his senior year at Loyola after months of faux vagabondage during the Summer of Love.

They pause at the sidewalk and scan the broad, oak-edged sward of the park. The boys have too much history between them there, too much contending and screaming and too many tears and bloodied noses, long passed but with the affect still clinging to the place, and they turn south on Third Street, heading toward the river.

'So you've done this,' Jimmy says.

'This?'

'The US Army in Vietnam.'

Robert looks at Jimmy.

He is visibly Robert's brother, with the same jaw, their father's jaw, but Jimmy is paler in hair and skin, missing their mother's touches of darkness, which she got from her own mother, who was Italian. In spite of the confrontational quickness of his remark, Jimmy isn't looking at Robert. He's keeping his eyes ahead, down the street.

Robert says, 'I did the *army*. It was up to them where they sent me.'

'That's a cop-out,' Jimmy says, though he still doesn't look Robert's way and his manner is matter-of-fact. 'Did he put you up to it?'

Robert knows who Jimmy means. Pops. As of this Labor Day weekend in 1967, they have both always called him that. But Jimmy invokes him now as an impersonal pronoun.

'No,' Robert says at once, taking the words literally to make the answer simple. No, there was no overt conversation, no request or exhortation or plea.

Jimmy says, 'This isn't his war, you know. Even if he wants to make it that. Ho Chi Minh is not Adolf Hitler. Far from it.'

'I told you this isn't about Pops.'

'It's an evil war,' Jimmy says.

Robert says, 'Did your girl of the summer put you up to this?'

Jimmy stops walking abruptly.

Robert stops too, turns to him. He expects a fight now. But even though Robert is a step in front of him, Jimmy keeps his eyes down the street.

They stand like that for a long moment.

Robert senses his brother grinding toward a choice. A fight is one option, clearly.

Now Jimmy looks him in the eyes.

From years of experience, Robert knows how to read his brother's face. It surprises him now. Nothing is there that fits the way Jimmy began this conversation. No furrow, no flare, no twitch. Nothing that fits his temper.

'My feelings are my own,' Jimmy says, and his voice is actually soft. Robert cannot remember the last time he heard this tone in his brother.

'I believe you,' Robert says. Though he's not sure he does. But he makes his own voice go soft as well.

'I bet he's proud of you,' Jimmy says. He is still managing his tone.

'I don't hear any sarcasm in that,' Robert says.

'There isn't any.'

'Is she a flower child?' Robert says. 'Teaching you gentleness?' He regrets it at once. No matter that he's starting to hear Jimmy's tone as an affectation, a lie. It's still a better way for them to talk, surely.

Jimmy doesn't answer. His cheeks twitch slightly and release, twitch and release. He's grinding his teeth.

If a woman is indeed gentling his brother down, the attitude deserves nurturing. So he makes himself a little vulnerable to his brother, offers an admission. 'He isn't showing it.'

Jimmy stops working his jaw. 'I don't follow,' he says.

'Pops,' Robert says. 'His approval. He was never going to actually show it. We both know that.'

Jimmy furrows again, briefly, and grunts a nod of sympathetic recognition.

'My decision was my own,' Robert says.

Jimmy nods again, in assent, looks away, beyond Robert to the square. They are silent for a few moments. Then Jimmy says, still looking into the distance, 'She's bringing it out in me.'

Now Robert doesn't follow.

Jimmy turns his face to him, sees his puzzlement. 'Gentleness,' Jimmy says. 'She's only bringing something out in me that's already there.' He pauses, then adds, 'And she's not a flower child.' This last, however, comes out devoid of gentleness. Not quite angry, but sharply firm. Still, in an earlier time, Jimmy would be in full-flighted umbrage now.

Robert says, 'I didn't mean to insult her.'

'It wouldn't be an insult anyway, if she were,' Jimmy says.

Robert thinks: *If you didn't take it as an insult, you wouldn't have hardened up in the denial.* But he doesn't let it out quite that way. He says, 'I was just asking. Trying to assess what degree of criminal you both think I am by putting on this uniform.'

'I thought you were asking to source my gentleness.'

'Those two things often go together these days. The gentleness and the judgment.'

'We're judging a government.'

'By embracing another,' Robert says. 'North Vietnam's oppressions are even institutionalized. Read a little history. No government, no country in this world has spotless hands.'

A quick clench comes to Jimmy's face, furrowing his brow and tightening the margins of his eyes. But he unloosens at once. His forehead stretches tight in willed calm.

Robert finds this oddly touching. His brother is still working hard to please his girlfriend.

'I won't argue Vietnam with you,' Jimmy says. 'Personally, I can't stand the politspeak and jargon and sloganeering. I can't stand the drug-addled vapidness either. But I'm sorry for the war coming to our family like this. I am.'

'It will come to you, as well.' Robert says this softly, not as a willed effect but from an ache that he is surprised to feel this keenly. He has even brushed aside his brother's implicit rebuke. Talk was starting that graduate school deferments were about to vanish. The war could come quite personally to his brother next May.

Jimmy does not answer. But he does not look away. He and Robert hold their gaze for a long moment. Then, as if they'd spoken of it and agreed, the two of them turn and continue south on Third Street.

They will not speak again about the war. Not on this day. Not, as it turns out, ever again.

In his mind now, in his bed, Robert has had enough. The room is cold.

He wants his first cup of coffee.

He draws back the covers.

He sits, puts his feet on the floor.

But he has come this far on Labor Day, 1967, and the rest of it must play through him so he can drink his coffee with the past relegated once more to the past.

Much of that final scene is a blur. It wasn't about him, after all. He was simply a witness, standing apart. He's not even sure where they all are in the house. He can see only Jimmy and Pops. They're shouting at each other. Likely they're in the kitchen, because Mom walks out, brushing past Robert. He should follow her. But he doesn't.

He stays, though for a long while only in body. He tunes out the words, as Jimmy is drawn by his father into the politspeak he said he despises. High-decibel politspeak that goes on and on.

Until abruptly the voices cease.

For a moment the room rings with silence.

Robert takes notice.

Jimmy and Pops are standing close, facing each other. And then Jimmy begins to speak, but softly.

Robert listens. He misses some of the words, but he gets the gist. It's about a murderous war. It's about those who defy their country. Then Jimmy's voice rises and Robert hears clearly: 'Those are the real heroes.'

And William raises his right hand and slaps his son across the face. Jimmy's face jerks away from Robert's view.

The gesture has been flash-powder fast and William's hand has vanished. Robert's mind is lagging way behind. He saw what happened, recognized it. But Jimmy has quickly brought his face back to his father's, and for a moment Robert doubts his senses, wonders if he saw correctly. For all his bluster and working-class manliness, Pops has almost never used his hands on his sons.

And it happens again. Robert sees a movement at William's left shoulder and hears a sharp sound and Jimmy's face jerks this way, showing itself to Robert. Pops has struck him with his other hand, and he barks a single word: 'Cowards.'

Robert's body is startled into immobility while his mind revs up to understand. And it comes to him: It's General George Patton, Pops's beloved high commander. It's Patton's infamous gesture in a field hospital in Sicily in 1943, slapping a shellshocked soldier across the face as a cowardly malingerer. The press got hold of it and Eisenhower stepped in, reprimanded Patton, took him out of combat command for a crucial year. Pops has spoken more than once about the bum deal this war hero got for a righteous act. Pops absorbed this gesture over the years. His muscles memorized it. And finally what seemed a familiar circumstance reflexed it.

All this tumbles through Robert's head as more words are spoken from across the room, as Jimmy then moves away, as he passes Robert, whose body is still inert. Nothing in Robert's thoughtful understanding of the situation suggests what action his body might take.

Jimmy is gone from the room. He will continue out of the house. He will not return.

It's all over. The end.

But for Robert in his father's kitchen, and for Robert in his own bedroom, what ended was simply that Labor Day in 1967. Jimmy would go on to his senior year at Loyola. It would be ten months before he'd go to Canada.

What Robert does not see at the time and what he does not see now is Jimmy's face after the second slap. The blow brought Jimmy's eyes to Robert's. But at that moment Robert was seeing only what was in his own head: an imagined image of Patton slapping a mind-blasted soldier in a hospital ward; Pops sitting somewhere with a beer, bemoaning Patton's unfair fall from grace.

Robert missed Jimmy's eyes fixed on him, missed what they asked.

And so he puts the incident away, as he always has: Everything happened very quickly; there was nothing to be done; it was all about these other two men anyway.

Robert rises from the bed.

Soon, in the kitchen, ready for the morning in khakis and cardigan, Robert burr-grinds his coffee beans, trying to return fully to this house, to the winter morning, to a day of work ahead in an America of a century ago. To do so he considers this Ethiopian he is grinding as if he were a Starbucks Foundation Endowed Professor of Coffee writing a monograph on these complex beans, washed and sun-dried in a cooperative in the village of Biloya, grown in deep shade more than a mile high in the surrounding mountains by a thousand farmers on less than two acres each, a coffee comprised of a dozen heirloom varieties, Kurume and Wolisho and Dega and more. Roasted last week in Durham, North Carolina, just a little past medium, the beans just beginning to turn dark.

As he waits for the water to pass through the filter of his Technivorm Moccamaster at exactly two hundred degrees, however, he marvels: *All this stuff in my head is prompted by that man in New Leaf. Not even him. My first mistaken impression of him. He has nothing to do with Vietnam.*

'You were restless last night,' Darla says.

He turns to her.

She stands in the doorway in black running tights – she still has fine legs, this Dr Darla Quinlan – and red fleece jacket. She holds her watch cap, her hair pulled back and bunned up, the pull of her hair smoothing the wrinkles in her face enough for them to nearly vanish at this distance. If he were nearer, he would touch the bottom of her chin with his fingertip, lift her face just a little, and even her incipient jowls would vanish.

'No more than usual, I think,' he says.

'Perhaps not,' she says.

'Sorry I disturbed you.'

'It's not about me. I wondered if you were all right.'

'I am.'

They look at each other in silence, each feeling the wish to have more to say but unable, for the moment, to think what.

'Tea first?' Robert finally asks.

'I like to run first,' she says. But she does so without a trace of a dumb-shit-you-should-know-that-after-all-these-years tone. Robert wonders if that means she's considering putting the running preference aside.

'Just this morning,' Robert says. 'It's cold out.'

She hesitates, but says, 'That makes it better to take the tea when I return.'

They fall silent a moment.

'You'll be working by then?' she asks.

'How long will you be?'

'I don't know,' she says. 'I didn't sleep well.'

'Sorry,' Robert says.

'It wasn't you. I knew you were restless because I was already awake.'

'Does it make you run longer or shorter, not sleeping well?'

'Longer, usually.'

'Tough girl,' he says.

'Tough girl,' she says.

'We'll see,' he says.

She angles her head to indicate she doesn't quite understand.

'Whether I'm working when you get back,' he says. They are silent again, but not moving.

'I can stay,' she says.

'You should run,' he says.

'All right.'

She puts her cap on. She turns. She turns back. 'You could have a second cup. You love the new beans.'

'The second cup goes to my desk,' he says, though without a trace of a tone – or even a trace of a feeling – that she should know that after all these years.

Darla goes.

How is the silence of this kitchen consequently different because she is out running somewhere on the dirt and macadam remnants of a WPA road instead of still sleeping upstairs? Somehow different. Felt several times lately by Robert, like a newly, faintly arthritic knuckle. He cannot say why.

He takes up the coffeepot, and now, in order to work, he has to try to put Darla out of his mind along with Bob and Jimmy and Lien and Dad and the others who hover around them.

Perhaps because his work often leads him to consider the smallest semantic details, he hears the shift in his mind from his earlier memory to this present moment: Pops stopped being Pops somewhere along the way. He is Dad now. And to his face, there was rarely an occasion to address him with a name at all. *Dad* to his mother, when they spoke of the man.

But this is exactly the hovering of others he needs to resist. Semantics – his *mind* – snagged him on his father just now, so he thinks it will be a simple matter of the will to return to this kitchen and his coffee and the scholarly day to come. But a woman slips into him. To his surprise, it is not Darla.

Lien. She came to him last night beneath the oak tree, across all these years, and he left her last night just as he left her when the Tet siege began. Now, she comes to him as she always did, silently, gently. Borne not on a thought but a river.

The sunlight flares from the water and he turns his face to her, pressed chastely against him in the narrow bow of her uncle's sampan, the man out of their sight line behind them, beyond the bamboo thatch shelter in the middle of the three-plank boat. He is their chaperone, working the long sculling oar, bearing them on the river past the Citadel, past the coconut palms and the frangipani, toward Ngu Binh Mountain. Robert and Lien met only a few weeks ago in her cousin's tailor shop, where she works. He came again and again as if to consider a tailor-made suit until finally she said, *I am happy Robert never choose*, and she invited him to float with her upon her river in this season that gives it its name. And indeed the water all around them fills him with a ravishing sweetness possible only on the cusp of rottenness. The blossoms of fruit orchards upriver – litchi and guava, breadfruit and pomegranate – have fallen into the water and decayed in their passage to the South China Sea. The sunlight flares from the water and he turns his face to her and she turns her face to his and they hold each other in this gaze, before they have ever kissed, ever embraced, weeks before they will make love, and the perfume of this river fills them both, and she says to him, *Mr Robert, your eyes are the color of water drop on lotus leaf,* and he says, *Miss Lien, your name means 'lotus,' yes?* and she turns away from him, glances over her shoulder toward her uncle, to make sure he cannot see. Then she looks at Robert again with her eyes the color of a black cat turned auburn in sunlight, and she leans to him, and they kiss.

He has not had this memory – has feared and resisted this memory – for years. He knows how to let go of it. He reinhabits this: Lien offers him the French .32-caliber pistol that belonged to her father, and he takes it and he turns and he heads out her door and down the stairs and into the war. This is a memory he can put aside without needing his willpower.

He closes his eyes.

He smells the coffee he has brewed.

He opens his eyes.

Once again he takes up the carafe. He pours his Ethiopian in small circles, listening intently to the purl of it, leaning in, flaring his nose to its smell, isolating the notes of peach and blueberry and cocoa. He thinks, reflexively, to carry the cup to the living room, as he often does, to sit in the reading chair that faces the French doors to the veranda. But the oak tree is framed in those doors.

He sits instead on a counter chair at the kitchen island.

He puts his back to the casement window looking out to the veranda. This will be only about the coffee. He puts his hand to the mug handle.

The telephone rings.

He straightens sharply, inclined not to answer, short of its being Darla on her cellphone, in distress out in the woods. The answering machine is within earshot, in the hallway between kitchen and living room. At the second ring the machine's synthesized woman's voice says, 'Peggy Quinlan.'

His mother, on her cellphone.

Robert looks at the clock over the kitchen sink.

Barely past seven.

She has insomnia. She has unreasonable worries about Dad. She has reasonable irritations with him. She gets lonely, even with him always around. She never thinks what time it is.

Another ring and the answering machine announces her name again.

The coffee is hot.

Robert will let the machine answer. He can call her in a quarter of an hour.

He puts both hands around the mug, warms them there. He will take his first sip when things are quiet again.

Shortly the machine answers and his mother's voice, strained and short of breath, says from the hallway, 'Robert, pick up if you're there. Your father has fallen. We're at the hospital. He's broken his hip.'

Robert releases his cup of coffee, rises.

He crosses the kitchen, feeling he's moving too slowly. He's adjusting to this thing. His father turned eighty-nine in November. He's had trouble with his heart. A broken hip is bad.

His mother has gone silent.

He reaches the kitchen door, and just before the machine cuts her off, his mother says, 'Okay. Call me as soon as you get this. I need you, Robert.'

His parents are less than an hour away, forty miles north, in assisted living in Thomasville, Georgia.

He enters the hallway, passing Darla's study, glancing through the open door to the empty desk across the room, the oak tree beyond, and he stops at the telephone table opposite the vestibule.

He picks up the phone and dials his mother's cell.

'Thank God,' she says. 'Where were you?'

'How is he?'

'Not good, honey. Not good. The doctor is very concerned.'

'We'll talk when I get there,' Robert says. 'You're at Archbold?'

His mother does not reply. Then her beat of silence turns into a choked-back 'Yes' and she begins to cry.

'It's all right, Mom. He's a tough guy. I'll be there.'

'Hurry,' she says.

And Robert does. He pours his coffee into a thermos and dresses and writes a note to Darla. He tapes it to the front door: *My father has broken his hip. I'm in Thomasville. Don't worry. Work well.*

He turns onto Apalachee Parkway.

His mind roils with anticipated scenes at the hospital and he cuts each one off, tries to think of things he can manage. Like whether and how to make the connection, in his paper, between John Kenneth Turner's partisanship in the Mexican civil war and factions of the Vietnam antiwar movement siding with the North and lionizing Ho Chi Minh. Easy things like that. Things not having to do with family.

In this struggle of mind, Robert seeks distraction, so he turns his eyes to the Blood of the Lamb Full Gospel Church, which he is approaching. Here he routinely finds ironic amusement on a marquee that presumably intends to persuade the fallen to enter therein and learn the absolute truths of the universe, but doing so with messages that veer in tone between fortune cookies and one-liners from a born-again Milton Berle. But this morning his eyes slide past the new message to a Leon County EMS ambulance parked in front of the church, and then to a pair of white-coated men lifting a dark-clothed blur of a third man from a wheelchair into the back of the vehicle, and then past them to a fourth man, tall and nattily topcoated and standing stiffly upright, watching nearby and seeming, given the context, to be the pastor himself, the benighted editor in chief of that marquee.

And the church has passed and Robert thinks of his father, how he would share his son's amused disdain for the man in the topcoat, how his disdain, unamused, extended as well to Mama's priests. Robert wondered if that would be so even now, as his father finds himself on the cusp of some absolute truth of the universe, a truth you could learn for certain only by dying.

~

In a room over a clothing and leather goods shop on Baldwin Street in Toronto, Canada, Robert's brother Jimmy is waking. He lies on his side, at the edge of his bed. The panes of the window before him are groved in fern frost. He owns the building, has owned it for thirty years. The shop is his. These winters are his, finally, more or less. The room is cold but he's been sleeping with the covers sloughed down to his chest.

He pulls them up now to cover his arms, his mind filling: windowpanes overgrown with ice; an upstairs room in a two-story brick row house; he and Linda clinging close in a sleeping bag on a futon, the ice lit by the streetlight on McCaul. This was their first winter in Canada, spent only a few blocks from where he now lies thinking. The house was rented by an earlier wave of American resisters and deserters and the women who fled with them. They'd turned it into a commune and a crash pad for other exiles newly arrived. He and Linda had crashed there the previous summer but were permanent by that winter night, the night they celebrated the occasion of their meeting, eighteen months earlier. They had done so with a sweet lovemaking – slow and quiet, as there were two other couples asleep in this room – and with a trembling from the cold that never quite stopped, even after they'd spent themselves and lay clinging.

Jimmy blinks at the daylight brightness of this ice before him now.

He closes his eyes.

He thinks: *That was the closest we have ever been. In that moment.*

This is perhaps true.

His mind declines to fill with details of subsequent events, from only a few weeks later: Linda's hand on the commune founder's arm, sounds behind a closed door, the smell of him on her skin. Nor with the subsequent principled conversation he and Linda calmly had, after a few hours of shouting, about the liberated soul, male and female, alike and equal, about a new age and a new culture and the freedom of love. Which was like their principled conversation in San Francisco during the Summer of Love, about war. And like their principled decision,

57

as his student deferment expired the following spring, for them to begin anew together in this place. This cold place.

All of that so long ago.

They've stuck to their principles.

He is weary now. In the legs, in the hips, in the groin, in the chest. In the eyes.

He opens his eyes once more to the ice on the window.

And he sees only the floaters. The lifelong accumulation of all the little crap between him and the world. Sometimes he can see through them as if they aren't there. Sometimes they are all he can see.

He is glad he will be with Linda tomorrow in their home on Twelve Mile Bay. Next month they will have been married twenty-four years, at last for more than the number of years they were together unwed.

He hunches his shoulders and draws the covers closer. He owns the building but the room is cold.

He'll have Heather call someone to look at the furnace. And he sees her now, sees not floaters, not ice, not the scenes of principled compromise between him and his wife, but sees Heather sitting before the iMac in the back room downstairs, just yesterday morning. He stepped into the doorway from the front of the shop and she realized he was there and he could see a little smile come to her face. A smile because he was there, because it was him. And she did not care if he could see. She smiled to her own purpose, her own intentions, her own unvoiced willingness, before she let him know she knew he was there.

Then she touched command-S and swiveled in her chair, and her skin was as white as a new snowdrift, though the smile she gave him directly was meltingly warm, and her usually heavy-lidded dark eyes widened with the smile. She was somewhere in her thirties, a single mother of an early-teenage girl, but his head filled with the talk of Heather Blake: how she thought it was very cool, very very cool he'd been a hippie; how her benighted parents had despised the hippies but she longed for that life, because as free as things seemed to be in her generation – and God help us how free it was for teenagers today – it was free only in blow jobs and loose talk; how the spirit wasn't free, how it took an old spirit to be free, a mature spirit, like his. All of which talk had accreted over the couple of months she'd worked for him. Never a pointed discussion. But bit by bit. Yesterday morning, confronting Heather's smile and the history of this talk, he sagged heavily against the doorjamb. But he simply asked, *How's the website going?* She laughed. As if she read his mind. As if she were saying, How silly you are. But she said, *It'll be back up within the hour.*

Jimmy is still lying on his side, facing the window.

The principles they spoke of, he and Linda, their freedom to love, those were never undone. Not even on their wedding day. Not overtly.

And the marriage has lasted. Canada has lasted.

He is keenly aware of two things now. The stalks and leaflets of the fern blades on the window seem hoary but alive, even though they are an illusion, merely a cold replica of a living thing. And the bed. He is aware of the bed.

He eases from his side onto his back.

He turns his head.

The bed is empty.

Not that she is gone, Heather Blake. She has never been here.

He lifted himself from the doorjamb yesterday morning and stood straight and thanked her for her internet expertise, and he turned away from that little cocking of the head she gave, as if she'd expected him to say something else. Lately she always seemed to be waiting for him to say something else. But he turned and went about his business.

Through the years he has acted three times on the principle of personal freedom that he and Linda agreed upon. Briefly acted. The incidents were discreet but never intentionally hidden; they simply were never spoken of. That deceptionless silence also was decided between them. There'd been no need to say anything; their daily lives, each with several separate friendships and separate responsibilities in their business, especially during the two decades on Twelve Mile, made that easy. The commune founder seemed to have been a brief thing for her. Jimmy is not sure if or how often she has exercised her privilege, since.

But why exactly is his own bed empty now?

He does not quite regret it. If he has regrets, he could still act. But he does briefly wonder why.

The answer, he senses, lies in the image of the fern frost lingering deep in his chest like a nascent cough. Long ago he and Linda left their parents' religion – left all religion – behind. But for the past few years there have been things Jimmy's been trying to work out in some other way. Most recently he has been telling this to himself, which, indeed, he does again now: *It is only science of the past hundred and fifty years that has shaken our belief in our consciousness surviving death. But elemental science gives us examples that confirm the ancient and abiding paradigm. The caterpillar, for instance, does not even have the sensory mechanism to perceive the butterfly it will become; but it will be transformed nevertheless.*

He is sixty-eight.

He coughs, drily, from the chill he carries inside him. Surely the pale nakedness of Heather Blake would be a more certain hedge against death.

And yet it isn't, somehow. The young feel they are immortal. *Must* they, to care so much about fucking?

He is to have lunch with his leather tanner today. But Jimmy wants simply to drive the three hours home. The lunch is mostly a social meeting. Maybe he can pull the meeting forward to a morning coffee.

And he does.

So shortly after one o'clock he turns off the Trans-Canada Highway onto Twelve Mile Bay Road. For nearly a week there has been no snow and the road is clear, the drifts and plow-spew mounded up on both sides of the narrow pavement, tunneling him home. After seven miles he takes the fork onto Harrison Trail along the north side of the bay, and six miles farther he turns off Harrison toward the water and into his ten acres, thick with snow-swathed white pines.

He emerges from the tree line, and off to the right is the south-facing, two-story, board-and-batten, Italianate house he and Linda restored from a century's worth of battering by Lake Huron winters. The place is a homely architectural idea, especially in its simplified farm version, a box with a low-pitched hip roof and a runt of a front porch. A Birkenstock of a house. But perhaps even because of that, it has always felt right to them, and they've made it their own.

He took their Volvo to Toronto and he parks in their adjacent garage. Linda's Forester is gone. He hoped to catch her at the house before going out to the barn. He didn't even have a thought of what they might do. Just sit together for a while. Talk about small things.

He walks the hundred yards west along their asphalt connecting drive to the leatherworks, their converted and expanded three-bay English barn where they still make their own highend handbags and purses, satchels and briefcases, portfolios and backpacks, sketchbooks and journals and Apple appurtenances. The car, the two SUVs, and the pickup of the four women who work for him are aligned before the barn. There are no marked spaces on the asphalt skirt but most days the order of the vehicles is the same, the spacing even. His Gang of Four is meticulous in everything.

As he approaches, the low roiling of his mind subsides. There should be laptop satchels and messenger bags ready for edge finishing. When the pieces are intended for shelf stock it's understood Jimmy will always do the finishing himself. As he's become successful and volume has increased, he's let all the other work go to his gang. But this near-last thing, this labor-intensive thing, subtle to the eye but a hallmark of a quality bag, this he has kept for himself on as many of the bags as possible: the application of his special formula of beeswax and paraffin wax and edge paint layered and heated and sanded half a dozen times and sometimes more, sealing the leather tight from rain and snow and the moisture-laden air itself. He has occasionally wondered, but never tried to calculate, the number of hours of his life that he's been sealed inside the doing of this thing. Jimmy's Zen, the women of the leatherworks call it.

He steps through the middle bay door.

As soon as it's shut behind him, before he deals with people, he pauses and takes in the smell of the new leather, thick in the air from a recent shipment of top-grain sides. The leather that he buys, from the man he saw this morning, is special:

trench-cured, packed tight in rock salt and buried in the earth for three months; and bark-tanned, bathed with oak and hemlock. Gamey still, this smell, fatty, faintly briny, but with an undercurrent of a smell like hazelnut. He closes his eyes to concentrate on that deep-current scent, a promise of the settled, sweet-fumy leather smell to come, something his customers will want to put their faces against, to breathe in.

He opens his eyes.

In this central barn space, the women, knowing his ritual, are looking up from their stations, waiting for him. Two of them have been cutting pattern pieces, skiving edges – the skiving the only thing done by machine on the best of their bags – and the always laser-focused Mackenzie twins have been hand-stitching.

'Good afternoon, Gang of Four,' he says.

'Good afternoon, Jimmy,' they say in unison.

All but Mavis immediately return to work.

She leaves her patterns, steps around the table, and approaches him.

She has worked for him for a dozen years, living alone for ten of them, during which decade she was a divorcée from a man and lean of build, but two years ago she married a woman and she filled out with happy fat, which she has since been pleased to keep. In those ten previous years she would not have been the one to rise to greet him, but she is the one before him now and smiling.

'How are you, Mavis?' Jimmy says.

'Fine,' she says.

'Have you seen Linda this morning?'

There is a brief stopping in her. This registers on Jimmy, barely, but he assumes – though the assumption is as slight a thing as the stopping itself – that Mavis is simply trying, given the intense focus of her work of a few moments ago, to distinguish this morning from yesterday morning.

'No,' she says.

A beat of silence passes between them.

For his part, this silence is not in expectation of more from Mavis but in idle curiosity over where Linda might be.

Mavis, for her part, is moved to elaborate. 'I didn't expect her and didn't think to look for her.'

'Ah,' says Jimmy.

Another beat of silence and she says, 'We've got some bags for you.'

Jimmy thinks to call Linda on her cell. Or to go into the house and see if she left a note. But instead he says, 'Good,' and he moves off to the far end of the central bay to his worktable and his pots of wax and paint, his trimming tools and heating wand, his sander and his various favorite buffers – the tine of a deer antler; pieces of sheep wool and blue denim and brain-tanned camel hide.

He works a while, and in his concentration he does not even register the buzz of the intercom and the murmur of Mavis's voice, and then she is standing before him. This he is aware of, and he lifts his face.

'Linda is home,' she says.

He's a little slow to react and Mavis is very quick in turning away, so his acknowledgment is nodded to her retreating back.

But he goes out at once.

As Jimmy nears the end of the connecting drive, he sees Linda emerge from the front door and come down the few steps of the porch, her focus on him. He approaches.

It was not so long ago that he began to think she was starting to seem her age. Not that he could quite say why. She is still white-oak-hard and sturdy and upright, a thing she was when he first met her on a beach in Alameda with flowers in her hair and flowers painted beneath her eyes and with her breasts bare in solidarity with some other young women on the shore. He would soon feel the toned hardness in her body when they were in each other's arms, hard enough that he was surprised at how gentle she was with her hands and in her voice and with her mouth. And in her eyes. They were as dark and fetching as a seal pup's, but her brows were thick and severe in their arch. In heart and mind, as well as body and face, she was so very much a child of that era. An era of militant gentleness, judgmental tolerance. Over the years, paradox continued to shine through her, and it masked the inevitable weathering and wrinkling and sagging of her body. Masked them utterly. She still seemed to him young. She remained interesting. And so the source of this recent sense of her aging was surprising and hard to identify, and it came clear to him now only in its abrupt absence: She is striding to him and there is a thing about her that those of the Summer of Love would have called an aura. An aura. Yes. He is, in this moment, acutely aware of an aura about her, of energy, of something like youth, and he realizes that for the past weeks, months even, it was something else.

And as she draws near, she says, sharply, 'How do you think your mother got our home number?'

'Did she?' he says, thinking: *So that's the transformed aura. Anger.* Thinking too that the discovered phone number might be a simple thing, an oversight on his part committed sometime along the way; perhaps it did not occur to him to register the number as unlisted when they moved up here to Twelve Mile.

65

She sets her arms akimbo. 'She left a message on the machine.'

'What did she say?'

'You need to hear for yourself.'

They head off toward the house, side by side.

'You're home early,' she says. 'Did Guy cancel?'

'No. We had coffee instead.'

'I was at Becca's. She's not good. She and Paul may be through.'

Her anger at his mother seems to have dissipated quickly. She's put the whole thing off on him now, and he's okay with that. He says, 'Is somebody dead?'

'Dead?' She looks at him.

He realizes she's still thinking about their friends. He's asking, of course, about his mother's message.

They go up the porch steps.

He concedes to her agenda. 'This is nothing new, is it?' he says.

They've reached the door, and they pause. She gives him another look. He's confused her again.

He clarifies: 'Becca and Paul.'

She shrugs. 'Not yet,' she says.

Now it's he who's lost the thread.

She reads it in his face. 'Dead?' she says. 'No one's dead yet.'

He leads her inside and into the front parlor, which they've filled with Mennonite furniture. He approaches the sideboard.

He stands hesitating over the answering machine.

He could simply erase the message. Right now. Erase it and change the number. His mother knows his wishes in this matter. It has always been best for all of them.

But he touches the play button.

Her voice wheedles into the room. *Darling Jimmy. It's your mother. I'm sorry. I can't tell you how much I regret how things went between us. Between your father and you. I've always loved you, my son. He has too. That's important to say. He has too. I don't mean to push my way now into your life when I know you're trying so hard… Not trying. Succeeding, I'm sure, in your new homeland. I don't mean to… I'm sorry. But your father is in a bad way, physically. The doctor is very very concerned about him. He may not live long. Whatever that might mean to you. At least just for you to know.*

This all came out in a blathering rush, and then she fell silent, though she did not hang up. Perhaps she heard herself. Perhaps she knew that all she could do next was ask directly for something he'd long ago made clear he had no intention of giving. Not that his father wished to hear from him, even if he was dying. His mother was no doubt doing this on her own. He could hear her breathing heavily. *The machine will cut her off soon*, he thinks. He waits.

But before this can happen, she says, *Your brother loves you too. We all do.*

She pauses again. Then: *Does your phone give you my number? Maybe not.*

And she speaks her phone number into the message. Jimmy has no intention of remembering it.

In case you want it, she says.

And the answering machine clicks into silence.

He hesitates.

Humming in him is an apparatus of thought he assembled years ago. For him at least, blood ties are overrated. It's only people who have a deeply intractable sense of their own identity – an identity that has been created through parents or siblings or grandparents, through those of their own blood – it's only people like that who can't imagine an actual, irrevocable break from family. But you drift apart from acquaintances. You even drift apart from previously close friends. Why? Because your interests and tastes, ideas and values, personalities and character – the things that *truly* make up who you are – shift and change and disconnect. Indeed, it's harder for friends to part: you came together at all only because those things were once compatible. With your kin, that compatibility may never even have existed. The same is true of a country. You didn't choose your parents. You didn't choose your land of birth. If you and they have nothing in common, if they have nothing to do with who you are now, if you are always, irrevocably at odds with each other, is it betrayal simply to leave family and country behind?

No.

Fuck no.

Jimmy extends his finger, touches the erase button. With only a quick sniff of hesitation, he pushes it.

~

Bob is on his back. And he starts to slide, feeling the movement first in the front of his head and then running down his body like nausea. He opens his eyes. He was upright a moment ago. Under a sky. After a talk with Pastor Somebody. After a sleep. But a cold sleep. Very cold. He's been outside somewhere. Now, though, there's a low, dark ceiling above. It's not just him moving. Everything is moving. A face looms suddenly over him. A jowly, red-cheeked face, a bulbous nose. They are moving together, Bob and this man. From the front of Bob's head: a knot of pain pressing there, pressing outward.

He tries to lift himself up at the chest.

'Hold on, sport,' the face says.

Bob lets go. Falls back. He begins to spin slowly. He closes his eyes against this.

That nose and those cheeks. A rummy. *This is the guy who did it*, Bob says in his head. *The son of a bitch who brained me.* He tries to rise up again, and even though he knows he's not prepared, he thinks, slowly, carefully, meaning each word: *I will kill you.*

A pressure on the center of his chest. He falls back. 'Hold on,' the voice says. 'I'm here to help you.'

Help?

'You're on the way to the hospital.'

The pressing in his forehead. He's stretched tight there. Thoughts congregating, trying to break through skull bone, trying to leap forth.

Bob opens his eyes, thinking he might catch sight of them. *That's crazy*, he realizes.

His mind is clear now. He believes the face.

Okay. Okay okay okay. You're not the guy.

For a moment Bob loses track of exactly what man he is trying to find or why he should care so hotly.

'Can you hear me?' the face asks.

'Why shouldn't I?' Bob says.

'Good.' The face narrows its already narrow eyes. 'I need to ask you some questions. You understand?'

'What's to understand?' Bob says. The man is an idiot. 'We have to see if your head's okay.'

'My head.'

Bob thinks he has filled those two words with sarcasm. To

the emergency tech he sounds dazed. 'What's your name?' the EMT asks.

Bob's first response is to himself: *My name. All of this about my name suddenly. Not just with this rummy. Too much about my name.* He's not sure how he got that impression. So the first thing he says aloud is, 'Why is it too much?'

The face cocks sideways.

Bob is simply trying to figure this out. Not that he expects the face to have an answer to the question.

And then Bob remembers. The other Bob.

'Do you understand what I'm asking?' the face says.

'What are you asking?'

'What's your name?'

'Hello, I'm Bob,' Bob says. 'Bob isn't so popular anymore.'

'Bob,' the face says.

'Bob,' Bob says.

'Bob what?' the face says.

'Bob what,' Bob says. 'Bob fucking what.' A sharp thwack of pain in his head. Not in the forehead. At the back of his head. From his father's hand. *Tell the man your name,* his father says. *If you're going to sneak around in the night, little motherfucker, you're going to get captured and then it's name, rank, and serial number.* Bob has followed Calvin from their single-wide. It's the middle of the night, but in a fourteen-by-sixty every sound kicks around in your head even if your bedroom is on the opposite end from theirs. All the words, jumbled and blurred but clear enough tonight about his mother's fear of his father meeting up with somebody, a buddy, somebody up to no good. Now Bob's standing in front of a man with a hippie-wild beard, an army field jacket dappled in piss-colored street-light, a First Cav patch – horse's head and diagonal slash – at the shoulder.

Name. And another slap at the base of his skull. *Bob,* Bob says. One more slap from his father: *Do it right.* Bob says, *Robert Calvin Weber.* A beat of silence and his father barks, *Rank.* Bob looks at him. *Damn straight,* his father says. *You don't have one. Lower than a buck private.* And then his father does a thing that he sometimes can do. He abruptly puts his arm around Bob, crushes him close. And he says to the man in the field jacket, *But he's a crack shot, this one. He's a goddamn killer in the making, my boy.*

'Do you remember your last name?'

The face.

'Weber,' Bob says.

'All right, Bob Weber. Where are you?'

The fuck. 'Hell,' Bob says.

And the man gives Bob *that look.* Every man jack of the Hardluckers knows that look. The look when the upstanding asshole – the Upstander – in front of you can't find or never had or gives up on or runs out of patience for a guy who looks and smells and just plain exists like you. He gives you that tightening and tiny lifting of the upper lip under just one faintly flaring nostril, that back crawl of a gaze, that little lift of the chin, all of this so slight you could easily feel it wasn't him at all, it was you, it was you shrinking, a shrinking that's been going on in smooth, small increments for a long while and you only just now can see it, like staring so hard at a clock's minute hand that eventually you can watch it move. *That look* says what you're in fact witnessing is *you* growing *smaller,* and this son of a bitch giving it to you has seen it all along.

Bob wishes he had the will to lift a hand and make a fist and punch this face. Not the will. He probably has that. The strength.

The look vanishes now. This man and Bob both know it was there and will always be lurking, but it vanishes, so the two of them can go on.

The face says, 'If you're messing with me, I need you to stop so we can know how to help you. Tell me where you are.'

Bob is weary. His head hurts. 'Seems like an ambulance,' he says.

'Okay. Where did we find you?'

Where.

The pastor crouched before him, a dense mane of shovelblade gray hair crowning his head. Bob was sitting upright, probably this man's doing. He was beneath a tree. The church community building squatted across the yard. *I'm Pastor Dwayne Kilmer,* the man said, putting a blanket around Bob's shoulders. *Call me Pastor Dwayne.* Bob's ears rang loudly and a small angry animal was trying to claw its way out of his forehead, but things were coming back to him already. *Who did this?* Bob said, raising his hand to his head. *I don't know,* Pastor Dwayne said and started to add, *In the…* But Bob interrupted, waving his hand: I was in *there.* He could not remember the name for it, though the door was in plain sight. *It was empty,* Pastor Dwayne said without even turning to look in the direction of Bob's gesture. He knew more than he was saying. *It's a sin to lie,* Bob said. Pastor Dwayne rocked backward in his crouch. *Now Brother Bob,* he began. *Do you know me?* Bob said, sharply. *How do you know my name?* Pastor Dwayne said, *You told me a few moments ago.* This stopped Bob. He couldn't remember. Then he thought of a question he needed to ask. *Who did this to me?* The pastor patted him on the shoulder. *I don't know who did it, Brother Bob. That's the truth.*

'Can you say where it was that we picked you up?'

Bob blinks hard at this question. For a moment he hears it coming from Pastor Dwayne. But it's the face.

The face is waiting.

Bob figures the face probably has some power over him for now. For ill or for good. Bob's hungry. His bones ache from the chill. He probably needs this guy to help. Bob should answer.

'Bloodied by the Lamb Hospital,' he says.

Instantly he knows he somehow bungled it. Wrong sort of place. 'Gospital,' he says.

Not right. '*Gospel*,' Bob says. 'The Bloody Lamb Full of Gospel.'

Clarity. Clarity.

The face has *that look* again.

'That's close enough, isn't it?' Bob says. 'I'm not crazy and I'm not stupid.'

The face fixes itself and says, 'Okay. Just rest.' It drifts away from Bob's view.

Bob closes his eyes. He feels the motion all around him. He is being carried along fast now. No bumps. A straight line to somewhere. And he feels his father's arm go around his shoulders, like it can sometimes do. As always, that gesture only makes Bob ache. Ache and ache. And he thinks of standing in the night in front of their single-wide, lit by street-light, standing side by side with his father, the man's arm around him, and there's a tree growing nearby, a jungle tree that sprung up there in the trailer park and nobody gets wise to it till it's too late, and in that tree is a Viet Cong, a sniper, a helluva shot of a sniper, and the VC squeezes his trigger and sends out a single round that crashes into one side of Bob's head and out the other and then into his father's head, and he and his old man die together, right there and then, standing there just like that next to each other.

~

And as that phantom sniper's bullet spins through Bob's brain, Robert passes the concertina fence at the federal prison on Capital Circle, half a mile north of the parkway, the fence a thing his mind has always known to ignore, in its evocation of a military perimeter. But it's not ignorable with the issues of this past night and this morning. His eyes know to hold on the road ahead, know to prevent even a glance to the side, but the periphery is always there for the seeing, and he is quite aware now of the four rows of razor wire spiraling along beside him, and with them Vietnam spins near, and a deep-driven voice inside Robert whispers: *You are a killer.*

He does not acknowledge it. Does not let this event play itself over, as it has done a thousand times in these five decades, in dreams, in near-sleep, in full waking obsession. It is this he fights off as he drives to his hospitalized father: Robert is huddled in the deep dark of the banyan tree. Outside are the sounds of pitched battles, none of them immediately nearby, the heaviest across the river. He wraps his left arm around his drawn-up legs, hugs them closer, and they press the pistol in his right hand more tightly against him, the fit of the weapon in his palm and the weight of it upon his chest making him feel oddly calm. Though his mind knows how foolish this is. The enemy is rushing through the city, filling it as if the Perfume River has risen and breached its banks. The tree and the pistol will soon fail him. If he is to live, he needs to think this out. Surely the North's night offensive is focused on the key military positions in the city: the airport; the South's division headquarters in the old Citadel across the river; and the place where Robert belongs, the MACV compound. If those places fall, particularly MACV, Robert is dead anyway. If they survive the night, Robert is dead if he cannot make his way back. Finding his way back will be vastly more difficult in daylight. He cannot stay where he is. He must use the cover of night to at least find another hiding place, nearer MACV.

All of this is preamble. Usually when the event coils through Robert's head like concertina razor wire, the decision to emerge has already been made. The next few essential moments travel on their own. He closes his eyes. He turns his head, cocks it, trying to focus his hearing in the direction of MACV: AK-47s, M16s, grenades launched and exploding. Robert pushes those sounds away into the background. He listens nearby. Nothing. The rush of dark-clad bodies just beyond the tree seems to have ended. He takes a deep breath. He lets go of his legs, stretches them out, takes another breath. He rises. He clicks the pistol's safety lever forward. He holds the weapon before him, ready to fire. He steps from the tree. Though his eyes are dilated to the dark, nothing is clear on this overcast night, not pocket-park sward or trees or alleyway beyond or huddled city shapes all around, everything is smeared together in the tarry night. He must find his way through. He pauses. And from somewhere behind him and to his right a white flare rises, rushing to its apogee, far enough away that its light simply dapples through the trees and so Robert can see but he cannot see, and there is movement to his left and he looks and a shape is there, half a dozen paces away and it is a man clad in shadow and instantly Robert's hand is moving and he is squeezing at the trigger and the pistol pops and jumps a little in his hand and it levels and pops again and again and the shape flies back into the dark and Robert hears the shape – the man – hears the man thump onto the ground, and Robert turns and runs.

And why should this man whose face he never saw, who surely was a Viet Cong, who surely, moments later, would have done the same to him if Robert had not shot first, why should this man thrash still inside Robert? *You are a killer,* Robert whispers again to himself from somewhere deep in the dark, somewhere invisible in the trees. But so many men have had to reconcile so much more, so many killings, so much blood that they have spilled in some far place where there was no alternative except to let their own blood be spilled, brought into this situation by their country, in the name of and for the protection of all that they and their families, now and for generations before, have held dear. And later on this day in Hue and on the next day and on the next, first in the streets and then safe among his own in the MACV compound, Robert will shoot and shoot and it is not entirely clear if he has killed again but he probably has. But this one, this one dark figure will not simply die, will not allow himself to be buried in the psyche the way most of all the millions who have died in wars have been buried inside most of all the millions of their killers. Why? Because Robert did not go to Vietnam to do this. Because he had a graduate school deferment and he let it go and so the army gave him a choice: to enter into officers' training and risk a combat assignment or enter as an enlisted man and select his own army occupation. So he chose not to kill. He went to Vietnam to slide away to the side, to land and work and fly home as one of the eight out of ten who goes to war and never kills, who never experiences any actual battle, who never fires a weapon. Who goes to war to cook or repair or fuel or type or drive or warehouse or launder or telegraph;

or goes to study and analyze, like doing the research he loves; who goes to war and sleeps and eats and drinks and writes letters and listens to music and falls safely in love in another country with an exotic girl and writes a resume and plans a future life and goes home; who goes to war to please your dad, to receive your dad's approval, to make your dad proud, to win your dad's love.

You didn't have to kill to do that.

Robert has never told his father about the banyan tree. About the man he shot in the dark.

You are a killer.

Still. Still. So many men had it figured out that way, thinking they would be one of the eight in ten who never engaged in actual combat, but ended up having the fight come to them, having an army – not just men, not just a solitary man but an army – having an enemy army come at them and their pals, and then everyone did this thing together, so many men ended up killing, ended up killing other men, ended up turning into killers, many times over. But somehow so many of those men – surely so many; just look at all the veterans who apparently are leading routine lives, more or less happy lives, lives full of all those values we putatively fought for – so many were able to figure out how their killings were outliers, were acts apart from who they really are, so many somehow figured out how to live the rest of their lives as men who are not, in fact, killers, are anything but killers.

But when Robert emerged from his tree, this was not an enemy army before him. This was one man. A solitary man. A few paces away in the dark. A man who simply was there. A man who simply moved. A man who could have been anyone. Maybe a frightened boy. The Viet Cong recruited boys. Maybe he was solitary because he was running away, ready in that moment to make some sort of separate peace, one man to another. Worse: maybe not a Viet Cong at all. Maybe no enemy at all. Maybe a man who minutes ago had been hiding in his home in the alleyway. Or hiding in another tree.

Robert had not seen a weapon.

Though that proved nothing. It was too dark. And the North's soldiers who had only recently passed through would certainly have killed Robert. What the hell was that man doing there? The great likelihood was that he was a soldier like all the rest, and for Robert to have hesitated would have been for Robert to die. Nearly a decade ago, Robert's own Florida passed the first stand-your-ground law: If you find yourself in a situation where you reasonably fear that someone is about to kill you or seriously injure you – no matter where you are – you have no obligation to retreat. You can kill. You can kill and you are innocent. You are innocent.

Robert and Darla have spoken several times about how they despise this law.

Robert has not spoken with Darla about how he has quietly invoked this law over and over to try to make that voice inside him fall silent.

He has never told Darla about the killing.

Five miles of urban-sprawl businesses have passed like white noise and now Robert crosses over the interstate. The faint quaver of the overpass, the rush of traffic beneath him, snap him back to the car, to his hands white-knuckled on the steering wheel.

'It was a fucking war,' he says aloud. And to himself: *What's wrong with you? What kind of man are you? It was the Tet*

Offensive. I killed a Viet Cong who would have killed me.

He loosens his grip.

He takes a deep breath.

He considers the gravity of his father's situation. Eighty-nine years old. A broken hip. A bad heart. A smoker's lungs. And this thought surges in Robert: *At least I didn't let him down. I went. Especially with Jimmy doing what he did. If Dad dies now, at least there is that.*

Robert doesn't quite go so far as to say to himself, *He was proud of me.* Though he lets himself assume it. William Quinlan never went so far as to say that. Not in those words. But the things he might have said, the things Robert wanted him to say, by the very nature of those things – intense, tender, vulnerable feelings unbecoming to a man of the era and of the sort that his father was – those very things kept him quiet.

And as the incident in the dark in Hue recedes in Robert, he notes that neither has his father ever spoken of the killing he himself did. He did kill. Unquestionably so. He was an infantryman. Indeed, William has rarely spoken of the war at all to his family, other than to say he was there, other than to speak generally of its grandness and its righteousness.

Robert stops at a red light.

Rarely to his family. But not never. His father puts an arm around him. And an arm around Jimmy. Robert is nine years old, his brother seven. Pops is sitting in a chair on the porch of the house on Clay Square and the two brothers are standing. He pulls them to him, then lets them go, but it is clear they are to stay where he's put them, at whisper distance. He says to them, low, *Boys, it's time.* He smells of bourbon. It's late on a spring afternoon. The shadow of their house has crossed the street and entered the park. *You know I was in the war. You should know what I went through for you. Can you imagine how scary it was? I want you to think of this, boys. I was with the Third Army under a great American general named Patton, and we were sweeping toward Berlin. We were in the outskirts of a city called Bingen. The Nazi troops were falling back. The enemy, you understand. So there was a house we thought they'd been using as a headquarters. A small house but with an upper floor. I went up. No one was there. Nothing of interest, and so I was ready to come back down the stairs.*

Their father stops now. Takes a deep breath. Puts his arms around them again, draws them closer, and he says, *Now pay careful attention.*

He lets them go, but delicately, so that they remain even nearer to him.

So I am still in the upper room and I head for the stairway and I start down. Not particularly hurrying. Down a few steps, a few steps more. Then I'm on the bottom floor. And I've been thinking maybe I should look around down here as well. But I don't. For some reason I think to hell with it and I go to the front door and I step out.

He stops one more time and says, *Now, boys, I want you to start counting seconds. You know: One Mississippi. Two Mississippi. Like that. You know?*

They nod.

And while you count I want you to imagine me moving across a little porch of this house and down into the yard and then taking a few more steps. But not many, not big. I'm going slow, 'cause everything was okay inside. Are you ready?

They are.

80

And they begin to count.

After *Three Mississippi* he says, *I'm stepping off the porch.*
Four Mississippi.

I'm barely in the yard, he says.

Five Mississippi.

I took a step.

Six Mississippi. Seven Mississippi.

Two more steps.

Eight Mississippi. Nine Mississippi.

BOOM! Pops barks the word and claps his hands together
and the two brothers jump and cry out.

Pops waits a moment. Lets them calm down. Then he
says, *An artillery round hit the house and the whole place and
everything in it was blown to smithereens. I was that close to
being dead.*

He pauses so he's sure they get it. They get it. They're still
quaking.

*As it was, the blast threw me about twenty feet and I ended
up bruised and scuffed and my head was spinning for an hour. I
was alive. Barely. It was that close, boys. You know what else that
means. You two were that close to never being born. Never even
existing. Think of that.*

Jimmy is weeping. Robert is still shaky in the legs but he's
making sure he stands up straight before his father. Jimmy
begins to tremble and the weeping turns to sobs. Pops is
looking off down the street, toward the river. Robert puts his
arm around his brother.

A horn honks.

And again.

On Thomasville Road, north of I-10, at the traffic signal
before Walmart, the light has turned green.

Robert shakes off the past.

He thinks: *All of that is done with. He will die now.*

~

On the cusp between the tumbledown houses of Thomasville's poor and the bespoke dwellings of Thomasville's moneyed, along an avenue of attendant health care enterprises – for pain, for feet, for teeth and hearts and vascular systems, for flu shots and for lab work – Archbold looms large in a six-storied complex of cream stucco walls and red-tiled roofs. Robert parks in the landscaped lot before the hospital's main entrance. As he steps from the car, his cellphone rings. He reads the screen. *Home.* Darla is back from running. He closes the car door, leans against it, and answers.

'You got my note,' he says.

'I'm so sorry,' Darla says. 'How is he?'

'I just arrived. I'm still in the parking lot.'

Darla is standing, sweating, in the foyer, just returned. It occurred to her to shower first. But she carries a memory, not so much in her mind as in her body. She stood in the doorway of the bedroom in their first house in Tallahassee, a rental near Lake Ella, and there was only darkness before her. She'd just spoken to her brother Frank on the phone downstairs. *Dead.* His voice. *Both of them.* And she'd said *Oh.* She stood in the doorway and she realized that this single word might not have been the right one. Perhaps she'd said more. But she could not remember any further words with her brother, nor any details of her passage from the phone downstairs to this doorway. She thought: *We need an extension up here.* She stood there waiting for something, but she could not imagine what. And then he emerged from the darkness. Robert. She blinked hard at him.

She thought: *I haven't been seeing him very clearly lately.* And Robert knew to say nothing, he knew instead to step very close. He smelled of Ivory soap and flannel and coffee on his breath. *He should brush better.* And his arms came around her, one at her waist, his hand coming to rest in the small of her back; the other under her arm and angling across her shoulder blades, that hand landing on her shoulder, cupping her there, and his hand on her back rose and moved farther around her and he drew her against him, and as soon as he did, she could remember what had happened, and she fell into him, fell a long way into him. Their first death. The first close death that comes to a man and a woman who are sharing a life. The first death brings all the future deaths with it. Brings all the deaths in all the world. And he held her close.

She does not remember this consciously now, as an event. Her body remembers, in the muscles, on the skin, simply as something it owes. Darla knows what the broken hip in Thomasville likely will mean for Robert, who has gone deep into his life without a close death of his own, and so she has not showered before making this call. She says, 'Shall I come?'

'Thank you,' he says. 'But no. Not yet. He's probably… I don't know. It's going to be all about Mom. It'll be about her. You don't need to come. Please just do what you need to do today.'

She says, 'Perhaps I need to be *there*. Not for her. For you.'

'Weren't you doing something? A field trip?'

'Did I say?'

'Last week. Something.'

She thinks. Then, 'Ah. Monticello.'

'You want to meditate there, yes?'

'Yes.'

'Go. Be a Southern belle.'

'Not quite.'

'Whatever you need.'

She doesn't answer for a moment. From the prompting of her body, she tries to think if she should ignore what he's saying. If she should go to him anyway. But her body also feels a sharp-scrabbling chill. He keeps the thermostat too low overnight. Always. She should turn it up before she runs, but she never seems to remember. She doesn't want to go to Thomasville. 'All right,' she says.

'I'll see you later,' he says.

'Are you sure about this?'

'I'm sure.'

They fall silent. But they do not immediately hang up. They aren't good at ending phone calls. They both hate phones, in fact. They can't read each other's body or face, which is crucial to them, to inflect their silences.

'Really?' she says.

Just enough silence has ticked by between them that it takes a moment for Robert to place the *really* into its proper context.

While he tries to, she interprets the few beats of his silence to mean he's not really sure.

'I'll come,' she says.

'No,' he says, figuring it out. 'I'm really sure. Thank you.'

And he hangs up.

I do that too, she says to herself about the abruptness of his ringing off. She won't worry anymore about him for now.

She touches the off button on the phone and places it in its cradle.

~

Robert finds his mother sitting on an upholstered couch beneath the skylight halfway down the entrance corridor. Peggy Quinlan rises at his approach and comes to him and they hug in the way they've hugged for decades, leaning to each other at the waist, cheek to cheek, patting each other behind the shoulders, as if always consoling each other. The patting is firmer this morning.

'Thank goodness you're here,' she says. 'They're preparing him for surgery. The doctor is coming down to talk to us.'

They let go of each other. She takes his hand and leads him to the couch. 'I need to sit,' she says.

They do.

Robert turns mostly sideways to face her.

'Are you okay?' Robert says.

'A little shaky. I didn't eat.'

'Ma,' he says. 'You have to eat.'

'After the doctor.'

'How's Pops doing?'

She smiles faintly at Robert.

He sees it. 'What?'

'"Pops,"' she says. 'It's just good to hear you call him that again.'

He was unaware. He's not sure it's good. 'How's he doing?'

'He's pissed,' she says. Then she quickly adds, 'I put it that way because it's how he says it.'

Robert wags his head at her. 'You can say "pissed" for yourself.' And he regrets niggling. Why make a point of this now? But he knows the answer. The artifice of her. This is not the time for her to be working on her image.

As she often does, Peggy quickly co-opts Robert's irritation with her by claiming it for her own, criticizing herself. 'Of course,' she says. 'What a silly time to hear the whisper of the priest. Piss piss piss. There. I'm pissed too.'

Though part of him recognizes her self-deprecation, antically adorned, as just another strategy of image-making, Robert gives her credit for it. 'Good girl,' he says.

'But he's more than pissed,' she says. 'He's scared, darling.'

'He's a tough guy.'

'You don't see him like I do. He's not so tough.'

This is hardly the first time she's claimed this. Robert has always doubted that it's so. He has understood her assertions about the inner life of William Quinlan simply as her taking the opportunity to project *herself* onto the blank screen of her husband.

'He's faced death before,' Robert says.

'It's not about the dying,' she says. 'It's about leaving other things unresolved.'

'Jimmy.'

'That,' she says. 'And more.'

Robert nods at this. But he does not even try to think what those other things would be. They could be legion.

Peggy waits.

Robert stays silent.

She says, 'I called Jimmy.'

'What?'

'I called him.'

'How?'

'Your grandson.'

She waits again, and Robert can only do likewise in response. He refuses to drag the story out of her. She is prone to this sort of drama.

She says, 'I asked Jake if there was a website. He found

one. It's like the white pages for Canada.'

'Didn't you already try to find his phone number?'

'Years ago. But this time, there he was. Not in Toronto anymore. A town called MacTier. It was his voice. I recognized his voice on the answering machine.'

'So you didn't talk to him directly?'

'No.'

'When did you call him?'

'This morning, though I've had the number for a little while. I knew how losing Jimmy continued to hurt your father. Even if he wasn't talking about it.'

'I'm not so sure.'

'I don't expect him to call me back. At the end I was too much on your father's side. How could I not be? But it wasn't so bad between the two of you, was it?'

'Bad enough.'

'Still.' Peggy picks up her purse from beside her and opens it and draws out an index card. She offers it to Robert.

He lets it hang there between them.

'Please,' she says. 'His number. He may listen to you.'

'I'm not sure it's a good thing, even if Dad wants it.'

'For me then.' The throb in her voice sounds genuine. Still Robert doesn't take the card.

A figure appears in Robert's periphery.

'Mrs Quinlan.' A baritone, but not as warm as you'd expect from the pitch. A scalpel-edged voice. Robert turns to it. A man in blue scrubs, young-seeming somehow but with his managed scruff turning gray and with wrinkling at brow and eyes.

Robert and Peggy rise.

She uses the moment to thrust the index card into Robert's hand.

He pockets it.

'Dr Tyler,' Peggy says, 'this is my son, Robert.'

He shakes the man's hand. It feels faintly oily.

'Please sit,' the doctor says.

They do, and Tyler perches on the front edge of a chair set at a right angle to Peggy's end of the couch.

Robert sees now that Tyler holds a plastic ziplock bag of almonds in the palm of his left hand. The man dips in and takes a few and chews them as he speaks. He lifts the bag a little, to draw attention to it. 'Forgive me,' he says. 'These are part of my prep. Good protein and good magnesium. To be at my best for Mr Quinlan.'

Peggy gives him a nod of permission, not that he was asking. 'Go right ahead.'

'I have to tell you honestly,' he says, drawing the sentence out slightly so he can look both Robert and his mother in the eyes as he speaks it. He pauses briefly, chewing his almonds, swallowing his almonds, though presumably the intent of the pause is to let these two family members have a moment to prepare themselves for the implied bad news.

It has another effect on Robert, a little to his surprise: He wants to slap the almonds from the man's hand – *eat them in the goddamn elevator on your way to the operating room if you must* – and to grab him by the front of his scrubs and shout, *Out with it.*

Tyler says, 'The statistics are not good. Of those who break a hip after the age of eighty, one in two will not live more than six months. And Mr Quinlan has two complicating factors beyond the hip. His heart issues, of course. And unfortunately, the fall has broken his right wrist. This will make rehab very difficult. We can put the bones back together. But having a man his age on his back for an extended time can lead to fluid build-up, which can lead to complications, most commonly pneumonia or congestive heart failure. We will be vigilant. But you need to know the special risks.'

He is done. He takes more almonds. Robert and Peggy understand that he's waiting for questions. Does he want them to ask the obvious one? *So will he die now?*

The doctor will evade.

But he has just said it.

Even Peggy knows this. Her question is simply, 'When will we be able to see him?'

'It depends on how things progress this morning,' he says. 'But understand he'll be on morphine at least through tonight. He won't be fully aware. You can go home and rest. Call us mid-afternoon.'

As if simultaneously hearing the same cue, they all rise. They shake hands, and Doctor Tyler is gone.

Robert and Peggy do not move, do not speak. They struggle to absorb the official version of a prognosis they both already knew well enough, from common knowledge. Now it's personal, however.

Finally Peggy says, 'I came in a cab. Can you take me home?'

'Of course.'

Her eyes are full of tears and she steps to Robert and now the two of them hug with no bend at the waist, with quiet hands upon each other's back, with no artifice or mulled memories or sense of family failures. They hold each other quietly, mother and son, and though Robert is a man capable of them, he finds he has no tears to shed.

~

At their kitchen table, Jimmy sits facing the window, the afternoon shadows bluing the snow. Behind him Linda is making chamomile tea. He stares at the darkening bluff of white pine. He's also standing in the center of his parents' kitchen in New Orleans. Robert is nearby, in his uniform, ready to go fight in an unholy war to please the man Jimmy's been furiously arguing with about the issues of the United States' bloody interference in Vietnam. An argument that has kept Robert in the room, their mother having fled, after taking care to turn off all the pots on the stove. Robert did not flee but he hasn't said a word. He's just standing there. If he's ready to go kill for their father's disastrously distorted patriotism, he should at least be ready to argue the justifications. He may have found some semblance of physical courage to decide to go – likely to vanish when the reality of the carnage is upon him – but he is an intellectual coward.

But no. That's present-day thinking. At the time, Jimmy has some crazy little hope. He and his brother talked about these very issues a couple of hours ago. Just the two of them. In the midst now of the old man's fury, Jimmy has a fragmentary hope about Robert's silence, that their own discussion – civilized compared with this present one – had opened his brother's mind.

Jimmy is weary from the fight. He is all shouted out. His father seems weary too. They have both suddenly fallen silent, standing nose to nose, breath to breath, but Jimmy finds one more point to make. Voice pitched low, the sudden quiet after all the noise making it seem even more emphatic, he says: 'The real heroes in all this are the men and women who've said *No* to their country. Instead of becoming part of an illegal and murderous war, they've gone to jail or gone into exile. Those are the real heroes.'

The blow comes quick. Jimmy doesn't even feel it the first time, not the slap itself, only a force, a pressure flipping his head to the side.

Though he knows what's happened.

He brings his face back just as quick.

The eyes before him, his father's eyes, are seething.

The next blow he feels, a flare of pain shooting up through his temples and down to the roots of his teeth, and his face turns and his brother appears and his brother's eyes are upon him and upon this pain and upon their father and Jimmy's eyes lock on Robert's, and there is only quiet around them and there is only this moment of their eyes, holding, and Jimmy realizes that in spite of the clash of their philosophies and their politics, in spite of a childhood strewn with older-brother petty cruelties – he was himself guilty, after all, of younger-brother cruelty – in spite of one of them being not just the older but the favored son and one of them being the lesser son, the redundant son, in spite of all that, Jimmy finds he now expects something of his brother, expects the bond of shared blood and shared tribulation of family and zeitgeist to pull taut and to hold.

But these eyes. His brother's eyes witnessing this defining moment with their shared father. These eyes are empty. They are dead. Behind them is nothing.

The clink now of cup and saucer before Jimmy. The smell of herb and steam and Linda. He is happy for the interruption. But he stares at the cup, decorated with roses, and he has let go of his brother's eyes and he is facing his father once more and feeling empty himself now, wondering if there will be another blow from this man, but wondering this from a great distance, and his father's mouth is moving, shaping words Jimmy does not hear.

Except for the final few: *Then you are no son of mine.* Clarity. The end.

'You okay?' Linda's voice.

'I'm okay,' Jimmy says to Linda.

She sits at the table with her own cup of tea. Usually she sits opposite him. They have always looked unflinchingly into each other's eyes to speak of important things. Now she sits to his right. *Nearer to me*, Jimmy thinks.

He appreciates this. He puts his hand on hers. She puts her free hand on top of his. But only for the briefest of moments. She rushes the gesture. She pats him there and takes both hands away, arranges her cup of tea into some imperceptibly precise position before her. She lifts the cup and sips.

Jimmy does not notice any of that. He's standing at a pay phone outside a diner on Elmwood Avenue in Buffalo, New York. He and Linda have been handed off by the New Orleans Draft Resisters to the Buffalo Resistance and they are about to enter Canada forever. It is July of 1968. Jimmy graduated from Loyola in June. It has been five months since the North's Tet Offensive showed Walter Cronkite and therefore American television and therefore, at last, any right-thinking Americans what was really happening in Vietnam. Jimmy's student deferment is no longer renewable. His induction is imminent. He and Linda are ready to leave. They will go into Canada as visitors and stay as landed immigrants and eventually become Canadians and this is their last hour in the United States.

His parents will find out eventually, he supposes. He doesn't give a damn how his father hears. But he gives a partial damn about his mother, enabler of William Quinlan though she be.

So Jimmy is dropping quarters into a phone and calling the house on Third Street.

His mother answers. He says what he must, and things clearly are hurtling toward a final good-bye. Before he realizes his mother has fallen silent not from lovingly conflicted emotion but for this other purpose, she has put his father on the phone and the man says, 'Your mother is crying.'

'I'm sorry for that,' Jimmy says.

'What the hell are you doing?' his father says.

Jimmy finds that the prospect of even speaking the words to this man makes his mouth clench. That he and his father have not spoken of Vietnam since Labor Day – have hardly spoken at all – makes him confident this is true: 'You know what I'm doing.'

That William Quinlan is making no reply confirms it. The silence ticks on, filled with long-distance static and now a distant car horn and now Linda's hand falling upon Jimmy's shoulder, squeezing gently there, and remaining, remaining as he waits for a last few words that surely will come.

And then they do, though more simply than Jimmy expected, and therefore more final.

His father says, 'Good-bye then.'

And through the thousand miles of telephone wires comes the click that was the last sound from his father through the forty-six years since.

Jimmy sees the pines, as if he has just opened his eyes from sleep.

He looks at Linda.

She is staring into her cup of tea.

Jimmy looks at his own cup.

So.

He picks up the cup. Sips.

Puts the cup down. The faint tap and scrape of china upon china.

'I wish I could help you,' Linda says.

He looks at her.

Her eyes hold on him now.

'Why do you think you need to help me?' he says. Something seems to release in her. A tension he did not notice. She nods.

'Why do you think you can't?' he says.

She sniffs. Looks at her teacup. Drinks from it.

'You and your father,' she says without looking at him. She says no more. That is answer enough for both questions.

He studies the tree line.

He senses how comfortable he and Linda are together. At last. For how many years of their marriage would this event have prompted a spirited conversation, a recitation of shared beliefs, a problem-solving debate about families and politics and ethics. A loving, respectful debate, but a debate.

Now they are quiet.

From that sense of comfort he feels he needs to reassure her. 'I'm fine,' he says.

'Truly?'

'Truly.'

'Of course,' she says, as if reassuring herself this could be true. 'After all this time.'

'Yes,' he says.

'Good,' she says.

And they are quiet for a few moments more.

Then Linda says, 'Then can I ask a favor?'

They are looking at each other again.

'Of course,' Jimmy says.

'Don't let your father's situation get you started,' she says. One debate topic has not dissipated with their long-accumulated closeness, one that began only a couple of years ago. He has already ceased to speak of the subject. He's told her he has. She doesn't need to lean on it at this moment.

Thinking these things, he remains silent for a few beats.

She clarifies, unnecessarily. 'Your recent interest in a supposed afterlife.'

Jimmy thinks: *Ah, my darling, you are still young, as you have once again begun to seem. You still have faith in nothingness.* And he hears himself beginning to debate her in his mind, where he concedes: *I envy you your faith. It is worse to wonder.*

Linda says, 'I'm sorry. That sounded harsh. Particularly under the circumstances.'

'No,' he says. 'It's all right.'

She nods. And she seems to be waiting. For what? He's absolved her for harshness. He has already pledged to keep his thoughts on this subject to himself. He says no more.

She says no more.

They drink their tea and then, side by side, carry their cups and saucers to the sink.

~

Darla parks in front of the nineteenth-century brick opera house just off Monticello's traffic circle. In the center sits the Jefferson County Courthouse, in the Classic Revival style of the town's namesake. She crosses the street and turns to her left to circle the building, her eyes on the monument for the Confederate dead at the north side. From this approach, only its eight-foot base is visible beyond the waxy, evergreen crown of a century-old magnolia.

She has come here to fight against her mind. The semiotician part – studying signs, the signifiers and the signified – is prone to jargon-driven incomprehensibility; the art scholar part – studying created objects – can easily be stricken aesthetically blind. Both parts constantly threaten to cut her off from fundamental human life as it is lived, first and foremost: in the moment, through the senses. Not that she doesn't love her mind. It is always quick, for instance, to see a good irony, such as this very distrust of her mind having itself begun as an *idea*. And it was her analytical self that challenged her to look more deeply at these monuments, issuing the challenge in this very town after she and Robert came here with friends for roadhouse food and antiques and found this relic of Old South, lost-cause passion and laughed at its excesses and, yes, at its unintended semiotics.

To give voice to this monument's signified meaning, both in its own era – the last years of the nineteenth century – and in this era, she needs time to stand and meditate on the thing. She is convinced that at the deepest level its meaning is essentially a meaning of the body. Of the bodies of this monument's creators. The bodies of the women of the Ladies' Memorial Association of Jefferson County, Florida, and of the United Daughters of the Confederacy.

As Darla approaches she is surprised to find her own body trilling a little at the longings signified in the part of the sculpture hidden behind the crown of the magnolia. But even with her empathy already engaged, in the next few moments, as the centerpiece of the memorial becomes visible, it is difficult for her to see the thing in terms other than those that make for easy, companionable, derisive twenty-first-century laughter: a monumental shaft rises long and straight there, condomed in a Confederate battle flag, showing itself to her suddenly from behind the tree like a Johnny Reb dropping his pants, his man-part ready for action, its condition even captioned in marble at the base: ERECTED 1899. Erected still, a hundred and fifteen years later, in perpetual frustration.

She draws near the monument.

She grows still inside.

This is not just about facile Freudianism.

The frustration commemorated here is real and deep and human. It is not simply the outcome of a failed political cause but of failed human connection. These were women trapped in a male-driven time and culture that both inflamed and suppressed their passions, intellectual and physical. Inflamed and suppressed and thus redirected and inflated them.

And these were women whose men were savaged and broken and traumatized and distorted and reinvented by war. It is not lost on Darla, as she stands before the western face of the monument, that she is herself part of just such a generation of women.

And without votes, without clear forms of influence, but in bodies and minds roiling with nascent independent identities and with passions that cried out for self-driven expression, these nineteenth-century Southern women created clubs. Became clubwomen. To think and feel and organize together. History clubs and travel clubs and library clubs. Improvement clubs and betterment clubs and advancement clubs. A Ladies' Memorial Association. The Daughters of the Confederacy. And in this town, as in almost every other town, a literary club. Darla could see the women of the Jefferson Country Literary

Club convening in the parlor of one of their Carpenter Classic homes on a weekday afternoon, just the women, in shirtwaists and Newport knots, sitting together, dreaming together, creating words together, writing them down, these purplish, engorged, sublimating words before which she now stood.

Let this testimonial of woman's deathless fidelity to man's imperishable valor speak to the sons and daughters of this Southland for all time to come.

Darla stops reading.

She sits up and it is very dark. She and Robert have been living together for less than a week. He is beside her in the bed. She struggles to disentangle her mind from a trivial dream and to animate her sleep-heavy limbs, but her hearing is fully awake and she recognizes a snubbing of sobs in him and then a strangled gasping and then a wrenching in the dark and his body moving. The sounds that woke her dissipate, and only a heavy, trembling breathing remains. She can make out Robert's body, sitting now, turned with his back to her.

She lifts her hand, hesitates, moves it to him, touches his shoulder.

He starts.

'Sorry,' she whispers.

He stands abruptly.

But he does not move off.

He breathes heavily, and then not at all, and then a little less heavily, making an effort to control himself.

He lies back down.

He does not explain, not even to say he's had a bad dream. Not on this night, not ever in the decades to come, does he speak of the nightmares of their first couple of years together. She's not supposed to be party to them. But surely she knows them well enough. They are of Vietnam. They are of what he has seen, what he has done.

This first time, he's been out of the army for barely four months. Is she moved on that night to think of his *imperishable valor*? No. Right and wrong are clear to her at age twenty-three: Perhaps he stood against the horrors he faced in Vietnam; perhaps he did not run. But for this to be achieved in service to a cause not only lost but utterly wrong, the act would be stripped of anything she'd call courage. His true valor could be found in his having marched with her against their own government. But in her growing fidelity to Robert Quinlan, when he dreams and awakens to his guilt, to his shame, how is she to help him? He has already done whatever it is he has done. She wrestles with all this and then with a rush she has an answer: His valor, expressed by protesting in the streets of Baton Rouge, is even greater for its first having been challenged and wrecked in this unholy war. The longhairs who duck all that and hide and then prance their own righteousness are not half so brave as he.

Darla blinks her way back to Monticello.

The longhairs. Her father's phrase.

She does not want to consider her father.

She concentrates on the text of the monument.

Let this mute but eloquent marble testify to the enduring hardness of that living human wall of Florida soldiery that stood during four long years of pitiless war – a barrier between our homes and an invading foe.

She is making a familiar argument to her father. 'You talk like Ho Chi Minh is threatening to invade Ithaca and march up our shore and into our parlor,' she says. The two of them are sitting on wicker chairs on their front veranda overlooking Cayuga Lake.

Resisting still, Darla turns from the Confederate monument and walks a few yards away, stops beneath a cabbage palm, its lower fronds burnt brown by last week's freeze.

Her father is here too.

He's blathering about the domino theory.

Why does she even bother arguing?

As he goes on, she continues for now to accede to the family tradition for discussions: You at least pretend to look at each other. But she can't believe he's insulting her intelligence by spouting this nonsense. Demanding she believe that when Vietnam turns communist it will immediately topple to Chinese control and then Cambodia will fall and then Laos and on and on.

She's heard enough. She says, 'Our country is totally ignorant about who it's dealing with.' This much she says to his face. She is ready to make the case. But the face is so familiar. Once, she voraciously studied every twitch and glint and moue of it for approval. But now Darla's First Law of Parental Physics has prevailed: Every obsessive daughterly action to find her identity through her father will eventually result in an equal and opposite reaction. The idea of speaking to this face repulses her. And his eyes make it worse. They are the blue of a clear sky starting to go dim on a late-autumn afternoon. They are *her* eyes.

So on this day, sitting on the veranda of their upstate Queen Anne with a man who is used to being the patriarchal boss, who won't listen to reason, who spews the domino theory to justify a country gone mad, she breaks with the family tradition.

She lowers her face a bit without taking her eyes off his, just to signal that what she is about to do is conscious and meaningful, and then she turns her head away. She even shifts her shoulder a little in the same direction, to make both points: She is enlightening him and she is turning her back on him. And then, as if to the forest of hemlock and sugar maple that surrounds their house, she says, 'Virtually every city and town in Vietnam has a statue of a hero. They all have one thing in common. They honor Vietnamese heroes who threw the invading Chinese out of their country. It's preposterous to argue that a unified Vietnam will turn into a puppet state for the Chinese. They have two thousand years of invasion and resistance between them.'

Markus Kallas, Darla's father, grew up in Hell's Kitchen. As a teenager he helped his storefront-butcher father create and market a sideline of Estonian blood sausage. As a twenty-three-year-old, with his father's death, he took over the business. As a thirty-year-old he began making his fortune by canning meat and finding a better way to keep it moist through the heat processing. He is old-country, old-school, and self-made. However, with Darla's words, Markus Kallas – who finds the showing of strong feelings to be unseemly in such a man as he – even Markus Kallas cannot hide an involuntary softening and beaming in his face. In spite of his daughter's odd and insulting gesture of talking as if to the trees. She's not like all the rest of that hippie crowd. She has done her homework. She even has the right kind of backbone, stiffened by study and thought. She is old-school. His political opinion does not change because of her reasoning, for he did not reason himself into the opinion, but his feeling for his daughter, in some fundamental way, does. Moments later he layers over his newly altered feeling with the seemly reserve he is devoted to, though the feeling itself will abide till his death on the Taconic Parkway.

What will abide in Darla, however, is an unaltered feeling about him, for in those few moments she was looking into the trees and she did not see what was briefly evident in his face.

So she returns to the shadow of a cabbage palm four decades later with this thought, directed specifically to her father: *After Vietnam was unified it took only three years to prove me right. The first war they fought was in Cambodia, where they kicked out a genocidal communist regime supported by the Chinese. The second war they fought was on their own northern border with the Chinese themselves. You never understood a thing.*

The veranda and the house on Cayuga Lake linger in Darla's head even as she reflexively pulls back from a road tractor wheezing its way past in the traffic circle, its semitrailer stacked with pine tree trunks. She cannot imagine her father's leaving her the Queen Anne in his will as anything but a ploy. As an effort, even from beyond the grave, to bend her to his will, his way of life, his way of thinking.

The semi is gone. The smell of pine lingers. She rouses herself. She moves back to the Confederate monument. *Focus*, she thinks. Focus.

Let the young Southron, as he gazes upon this shaft, remember how gloriously Florida's sons illustrated their sunny land on the red fields of carnage, and how woman – fair and faithful – freshens the glory of their fame.

Ah, Freud. The young men gazing upon the monumental shaft of their fathers. Encouraged to do so by their mothers and their grandmothers. The ladies of the club. Darla will certainly elicit laughs at the Semiotic Society of America annual meeting. What will the laughter of those mostly male semioticians signify? The following year she might do a paper on *that*. But her very purpose, in the paper and on this day, is to find and speak the significance of this monument that brooks no laughter.

Darla closes her eyes and listens. Listens to the overwrought voice of these women, their prose bepurpled with passion for their men. In the parlor that Darla imagines, where the Literary Club of Monticello crafts this prose, most of the women are Darla's age. Their men are dead. Their husbands. Dead from the war. But dead even if they survived. Even if they still sleep beside these women each night, three decades later. For the men have grown small. The cause in them has been lost to self-pity and pettiness, to meanness and an oppression of their women. Or even simply lost to a quotidian life after the war was over, a life of bricklayer or cabinetmaker, mule driver or lumberjack, haberdasher or druggist or barber. Or teacher.

And Darla asks: *How did these women, fair and faithful, preserve their passion?*

Not just preserve. Amplify.

And she knows. Their passion was for the dead. And being dead, those men could never disappoint.

~

On this night, at his insistence, Robert and Darla go to their studies and work, he being all right, his father being eighty-nine after all, his mother bearing up just fine. Darla appreciates the chance to massage her notes from the day. They act as if this were any other evening. But when they finally enter their bed, neither of them picks up a Kindle from a nightstand, and she forgoes her iPod as well. And as soon as they are arranged in their places – side by side with a forearm-length space between them in the king bed – as if on cue, they both stretch up and turn off their lamps and lie back.

The room is still but for a faint buzz from an LED electric clock, a relic of their first year in this house, preserved by Darla on her side of the bed.

After a time, he says, 'The children.'

'I called them,' she says.

'You did?'

'I did.'

'Good,' he says. 'It only just occurred to me.'

'I called them,' she says.

'When?'

'This morning. While you were at the hospital.'

A beat of silence.

She asks, 'Are you sure you're okay?'

'I'm okay,' he says.

'If you're not, I hope you'd say so.'

'I would.'

A few beats more.

Then Robert asks, 'How did things go in Monticello?'

'Fine.'

'Did you think like them?'

'The ladies?'

'Yes,' he says. 'The Daughters.'

'The daughters?'

'Of the Confederacy. Did you get inside their heads? Like you wanted?'

'Yes,' she says.

'What was it like?'

One more beat.

'Passionate,' she says.

And now their last waking silence of the day begins. Darla does not linger with the Confederate women. Her fading consciousness somehow veers to her grandson, Jacob, who answered the phone this morning when she sought Kevin, mistakenly dialing her son's home number rather than work.

She recognizes the boy's voice, though it sounds different to her. It's been nearly a year since she spoke with him. He was skiing somewhere at Christmas. He's twenty. Not a boy. His voice surely hasn't changed from nineteen. But there's something in him that's new. Maturity maybe.

'Is that you, Jake?' she says.

'Grandma?'

'Yes.'

'How are you? I've been meaning to call Granddad.' She hears him pause a beat, catching himself. 'Call you both.' She smiles. Jake's a good young man, not wanting to hurt her feelings.

'I wish I could put him on the phone,' she says. 'But he's at the hospital up in Thomasville. It's Grandpa Bill. He's fallen and broken a hip.'

'Oh fuck.' Jake catches himself in the curse but, in doing so, utters an almost inaudible *Oh shit*. Almost.

Darla smiles. He's still a boy.

'Sorry, Grandma,' he says.

'It's okay.'

'I'm just shocked, you know?' he says. 'Jeez. I've been wanting to talk with him too.'

'Honey, you'll have a chance. I'm sure he'll be all right.'

'Both of them,' Jake says. 'You know?'

For a moment she doesn't know. Then: Bill and Robert both. Jake's been thinking of them, wanting to talk with them. While there's time.

'They're both fine,' she says.

Fine. One has a broken hip at nearly ninety. The other has turned seventy. But fine. They're fine. Her mind is slowing now. *Lugubrious*, she'd say about her mind. The word *lugubrious* presents itself to her as a little surprise from someone. She thinks: *I'm falling asleep.*

She turns onto her side, and the movement stirs one last moment of clarity in her. The conversation with Jake was not a veer from Monticello. Robert's mortality is a matter of someone's active concern. Robert could vanish in a moment, this man who she met, who became a part of her life, only because he went to war. She is sitting at a desk, rather like her desk downstairs, but it sits in the middle of a parlor in Monticello, with her ladies of the Literary Club gathered around. She holds a quill pen over a blank sheet of paper. Motionless. She can think of no words to write, though she clearly understands she must compose a tribute to her dead husband, the Southron Robert Quinlan, veteran of a lost war, who is dead.

For Robert, as well, this silence is a waking silence. The past courses through him as spontaneously as if it were the dream imagery of incipient sleep.

Lien stands in a bower of blooming flame trees on the bank of the Perfume River, waiting for him. It's June, a rare cloudless day, fiercely hot. On Le Loi Street along the river, Operation Recovery has expunged the rubble of razed buildings and the bodies of the dead. The trees are splashed with flowers the color of arterial blood.

She vanished with the Tet Offensive. Word of mass graves of civilians was spreading through the city and it was understood what sort of people were slaughtered by the North in Hue: government officials, freethinking university teachers and students, those who could identify the embedded Viet Cong, those who had worked with and those who had lain with the enemy Americans. Bargirls. Girlfriends. Robert feared Lien was dead.

When restrictions eased and he could leave the MACV compound, he went at once to the site of the tailor shop. The building survived but the shop was closed and boarded up. When the sampan community near the central market reassembled, he walked its banks over and over, searching for Lien's uncle, trying to remember the man's face, hoping he would himself be recognized by the man.

And then, one afternoon, an old woman stopped him outside the MACV compound and said Lien's name to him and told him a day and a time and this place, and he approaches her now.

She wears a white *ao dai*, the tight-bodied Vietnamese silk dress with its skirt split up the sides from feet to waist, revealing black pantaloons beneath, a dress she has, on special nights, worn privately for him without the pantaloons, naked beneath it from waist to feet.

He holds a brown paper parcel tied in hemp cord.

She turns her face at the sound of his approach, comes forward. She makes no move to touch him but explains this with her first words. 'I do not touch you like I wish from people that see us.'

'I understand,' he says.

Her dark eyes focus on his, but dartingly: his right, his left, back and forth, as if she does not believe the one and seeks something in the other, then seeks it in the first again, hoping what she saw a moment ago has changed. Or has not changed. *Her* eyes seem anxious. Only that. Their lids are rounded some by French blood. He longs to ask her to close her eyes for him to kiss her there. Surely she can read in him the feelings that produce this longing. But he senses already he will never kiss her again.

'I was afraid they killed you,' he says.

'I hide,' she says. 'I have one place to hide and then I run away.'

'When did you return?'

'Few days before now,' she says. She seems to begin to say more – a taking of a breath, a lift of her chest – but she lets it go, does not speak.

He does not dare to ask the questions flaring in his head. Will she stay? Can they be together? Instead he feels the weight in his hand.

'I brought your father's pistol,' he says.

She takes the parcel from him, saying, 'I was afraid also they killed Robert.'

She looks again into his eyes. She studies him closely but with her own eyes steady now.

In the center of his chest he trembles. Standing before her gaze, given that he feared for months that she was dead, he is slow to fully understand the trembling. He takes it simply for passion.

'He did help you?' she asks.

Robert does not understand.

She sees this.

'My father,' she says, lifting the parcel a little.

'He saved my life,' Robert says, wishing he could believe it was as simple as that.

She nods. Her eyes are growing bright from nascent tears. He aches to lift a hand. To touch her face. But he knows what's next. It was always to come to this. Surely it was. But they've lost so many nights already. And those nights still before him in this country – eighty-seven more, the count on the calendar on the wall beside his bed – now that she is safe, now that she is here, at least some of those nights could be made to feel as if he were never going to leave her. As if she could somehow go with him.

But he already understands there will be no more nights.

'I am glad,' she says. 'My father can like you.'

'Could have liked,' he says. The man is dead. The correction is a wistful reflex. She has always asked that he correct her English. She has always wanted to be perfect in her English for him.

'My father could have liked you,' she says.

They wait.

He feels something shift in her.

'You understand,' she says. You must. You should. You will. You can't.

'That you must go?' he says.

She smiles. She has heard herself leap in her words in a way that he should not have been able to follow. But he has. They have always understood each other. And so her smile quickly fades. And the tears begin to fall.

She does not wipe them away. She does not avert her gaze.

'I understand,' he says. And he feels his own eyes growing warm.

'I cannot see this,' she says. Very gently. He knows she means his tears.

He looks away to the river to hide them. The seemingly incessant clouds of Hue keep the water the color of cheap jade. Today, beneath an empty sky, the Perfume River flows blue.

He says, 'You'll leave Hue?'

'Yes,' she says.

He thinks he is in control of himself now. He looks back to her.

'I love you beaucoup much forever,' she says.

Before they can laugh at her irony – she has used the catchphrase of the bargirls – she touches his hand, a fleeting wisp of a touch, and she turns and walks quickly away.

Watching her go, he understands his earlier trembling. It was not entirely passion. The trembling would also have had him speak to Lien about the man he killed. She was the one person who might have been able to absolve him.

But it's too late. And as he watches the white flutter of her *ao dai,* the long drape of her black hair as she leaves him, his trembling returns. Now, though, it is indeed passion. The last feeling he will ever have while his eyes are actually upon her is this ache to take her in his arms and hold her as close as he can.

In the following months, his active passion for Lien slowly faded. She was gone forever, irretrievable, this woman he'd loved. Whatever was uniquely left of her within him, he could not, would not consider. Dared not.

That was in another country. A country at war. He worked hard to see Lien as a *Vietnamese* woman. He focused on the *otherness* of Vietnamese women, on the seemingly universal kinesthetics of them – the feeling in his chest and arms and loins for their smallness, for their softness of parts and hardness of will, for the glide of them. And so all of those qualities faded from him once he returned to the States and to the women who had shaped his desire from boyhood. These Americans were the women – in their diversity, in the scale of them – who were imprinted on him. Then, in a coffee shop in Baton Rouge, Louisiana, he felt his physical desire embed itself in a long-shared culture, in a shared cast of mind, in another woman's uniqueness, an American woman. He was ready for Darla.

And now, in this dark room, on the night his father fell and began to hasten toward death, his remembrance of lost passion flows on in him like a river of Cerulean Blue and enters the sea: Darla, earlier this evening, as she emerges from her study. He stands at her door, as is their way. Whoever of them first notices that it has passed a certain hour will go to the other and wait at the door. And she emerges as she always does, with a faintly startled look as she returns to him from the realm of her mind, and she gives him a soft sigh, as if yes, the workday is through and there you are and I am glad. And he feels, as he sometimes does at this, a swell of tenderness. He felt it when he stood in her office door this evening and he feels it again now, in this moment, in this bed, and Robert wishes to take Darla into his arms and hold her as close as he can.

He turns onto his side.

She is lying with her back to him.

He pauses.

Between Robert and Darla, when did sleep begin to trump desire? It has. And thoroughly enough that even as he desires her now, this is not a question he asks himself. He simply pauses from the fact of it. Perhaps it began after a certain number of years together, after they had come to a certain bone-deep familiarity; perhaps there was a crucial time or two when he turned to her and she was sleeping and, in waking to his touch, she simply patted the beseeching hand and coiled back into unconsciousness. Or perhaps it was she who first touched him in this way. For neither of them was it understood as a general policy. But something soon shifted. Being of a certain age, perhaps they indeed preferred their sleep and respected this preference in each other. And telling themselves it was only about this or that particular night, they did not realize what else might come of it.

~

Bob knows where he is. He is inside his head and his head is a deer tick swollen fat and he dare not move or a gnarled and hairy hand – it's the hand of God, if you want to face facts, and Bob is ready to face facts – the hand of God will reach down and take his head between thumb and forefinger and He will squeeze and Bob's head will explode with blood. All Bob can think to do is put his own hands on his head and try to hold it together. He draws his arms out from beneath the sheets, and he knows where he is. A thing he must learn over and over today, it seems. He's in the eight-bed observation unit off the emergency room. He's been here before for something or other. The place smells of his mother. Her Clorox. Her sponging it on kitchen cabinets, on counters, on the sink in their single-wide. Her hands smelled like this place. Always. Softly, she would grunt and growl and wheeze at the sponging, she would weep at the sponging. He puts his hands on his head, a palm over each ear, his fingers reaching up, pressing hard until the bed can take him and he sleeps.

Then he wakes, and nearby a voice says, 'Brother Bob.' Bob begins to turn his head in that direction and the pain rushes like a breaker of blood into his right eye, crashing and foaming there.

A hand is upon his head.

This will be it. Finally. The big squeeze.

But the hand simply rests on him, and Bob focuses his eyes to see Pastor Dwayne, who is in the midst of a prayer, the details of which elude Bob. But presumably they are to fix all this.

'In the name of Jesus,' Pastor Dwayne concludes, and he draws his hand away. He smiles.

Bob's head still hurts.

Pastor Dwayne says, 'How are you doing, Brother Bob?'

'Brother Bob's head hurts like a sonofabitch,' Bob says.

Pastor Dwayne maintains his smile. Even warms it a little.

'The Lord spared you from serious harm.'

Bob says, 'Have you found out who it was the Lord spared me from?'

'I'm afraid there's no way to determine that. The man was long gone when we found you. As you well know, we freely offer that space to anyone in need.'

Bob's body wants him to sit up in umbrage, but the pain in his head checks that impulse instantly.

'Be still now,' the pastor says. 'I'm here to help you. The hospital will keep you for only twenty-three hours. That time is almost up. But I've spoken with the social worker. They'd normally find you a halfway house for a few days. I've asked if I might take you in at the church, and they've agreed, if that's all right with you.'

Bob pops a little breath in halfhearted assent. You always take the handout in front of you.

'After your head feels better, perhaps we can find you some work,' Pastor Dwayne says. 'Our Heavenly Father brought you to us for a purpose.'

Bob would dispute this now if another sea wave of pain

weren't rolling through his head. *Heavenly or not, a father just wants to fuck with you.* Bob knows the pain has helped him out. Don't push back at the old man if there's anything more to be had from him.

And so by mid-morning Bob has an inflatable futon and a reading lamp and a New International Holy Bible in a conference room off the church office, converted to a temporary living accommodation so readily that he knows other Hardluckers have preceded him in this place. Bob is wearing flannel and denim, new to him, with the smell of cheap dry cleaning layered over intractable Goodwill funk. He has showered. He used the talcum powder set out for him. He has new underwear. He knows he better not stay.

Pastor Dwayne has blessed him and encouraged him to rest and to read today and to take his pain medicine, and he has promised a nice chat later this afternoon, when he has finished his day's errands. In the meantime, Sister Loretta, the church secretary in the next room, will help him in any way he needs.

Sister Loretta, buxom and no doubt well talcumed, was standing in the conference room doorway beaming and nodding at him in assent through all of this encouragement, though now that Pastor Dwayne has gone on his way, she has returned to her desk and is presently on the phone talking to a friend. Her voice pitches suddenly lower, though Bob, bending near to the frosted glass panels edging the door, can still hear her speaking kindly of the poor unfortunate in the conference room who the pastor feels responsible for, but it's okay, the friend should come pick Loretta up at noon, as the poor man is fast asleep. She can take an hour away. Pastor Dwayne won't mind.

Shortly after noon Loretta is gone and Bob steps from the

conference room. A distant corridor rings with hammering. A man in coveralls carrying a ladder passes by on the gravel beyond the office windows and Bob steps back to put the conference door between him and any possible glance.

The footsteps on gravel recede and all is quiet. Even the hammering stops for a few moments, and Bob stays where he is till it resumes.

He crosses the room, passes Loretta's desk, and he opens the door into the pastor's office.

Bob is not a thief.

He has not been a thief for decades, and even then it was for only a few years in his late teens. He never used a gun. Never a gun. He was quiet. He was an amateur. He stopped after a couple of whiffs of jail but before he had a permanent record.

He does not enter Pastor Dwayne's office with the intent to steal anything. He does not have even a flicker of a thought to do so.

Now that he's standing in the room, the door closed behind him, the bright chill silence of the January morning pressing against the windows, Pastor Dwayne's massive mahogany desk crouching before him, Bob could not say why he's come in here. Better simply to put on the sweater and overcoat and watch cap and gloves they'd gathered for him from some donation bin and to walk away right now, while no one is looking.

But this man Dwayne has found an empty La-Z-Boy in Bob's head and has taken a seat and put his feet up. Though he's playing it smarmy for the moment. When he stood before the fresh-scrubbed and newly clothed Bob, he explained about his errands and what he expected of Bob for the day's activities, and then he stopped talking and he took a moment to look at Bob, up and down, and he said, 'I see something in you.'

Maybe that's why Bob is standing in the man's office now. *Do you know me? Who the hell are you that you know me?* Bob will turn the tables on him. Figure *him* out. *I bet I know you.*

The wall beyond the desk, between two windows looking into a tree line, holds a bronze cross up near the ceiling, and beneath are frames and frames.

Bob circles the desk and approaches.

A cluster of color photos. Dwayne and wife. Bob does not look at her face. Dwayne and his sons: young Dwayne and child boys; older Dwayne and teenagers; old Dwayne now and men. Arms around one another's shoulders.

Bob moves his eyes sharply away from the family photos, all featuring that Jesus-aping loving father, Pastor Dwayne Kilmer. Bob's gaze lands on another arrangement.

A diploma for a Master of Arts in Theological Studies from Bob Jones University.

A photo of Pastor Dwayne shaking hands with the governor of Florida, the two men grasping hands but looking at the camera, the governor a bald man with a lunging, sappy smile like the smiles of the Hardluckers you need to watch out for in the shelters at night.

A typed letter, framed in gold plate. At the top is an eagle sitting on crossed rifles, the NRA logo. *Dear Pastor Kilmer. I am grateful to you for your support in our efforts to protect our Second Amendment rights. What our opponents do not understand is that we have a First Amendment only because we have a Second. Men of God such as yourself…*

Bob skips to the signature. He cannot read it. The first name appears to begin with a great, curvy P and the rest is a tight march of undifferentiated letters that could be all *u*'s or *m*'s or *n*'s or *l*'s. Then Bob's eyes slide to the right, to what he realizes is a companion frame, and he thinks he recognizes the square-jawed man speaking behind a lectern. Back to the letter. The logo. And yes. The man's name is printed in small type beneath it. Not a P, in the signature. A fancy C. Charlton Heston. Bob's old man loved this guy. Moses the gunslinger.

Bob looks abruptly away from this wall, turns around.

He starts, as if someone has snuck in behind him.

But it's the high back of Dwayne's desk chair.

Bob circles it.

Sits in it.

He puts his arms along the arms of the chair.

He settles himself. As best he can, for his head is quickthumping in pain.

There's nothing to do for that. Just push through it.

He begins to open drawers.

Center drawer. Ballpoint pens. Paper clips. Cluttery little crap.

He's having trouble concentrating, trouble seeing things clearly. But the thumping slows a bit. Bob knows it's his heart beating in his head. It's his heart driving the pain.

He opens the top drawer in the desk's right-hand pedestal. More clutter. Brochures for the church, a bottle of aspirin, a granola bar, a phone-charging cord. In the second drawer are pristine envelopes, stamps, a stapler.

Bob hates this guy. As if he were lying to Bob's face. This bland daily shit. It's all lies.

He slams the second drawer and pulls at the bottom one. It won't yield.

Bob pushes back in his chair and looks at the drawer. It's the deepest one. Files probably. *Who gives a damn?*

But Bob doesn't like Dwayne keeping his secrets. The drawer

has a simple pin tumbler lock. And Bob still has a small skill from his teenage thieving days.

He opens the central drawer and removes two paper clips. He bends one to work as a torque wrench, the other as a rake.

He has to leave the chair. His head and his knees begin to scream at him in pain but he makes himself crouch down. He is determined now.

He draws near to the lock. He inserts the first paper clip, turns it, holds the tension, inserts the second, and he begins to rake the pins inside the lock. His fingers fumble a bit for a moment, but long ago he had a good feel for this, and his muscles quickly remember and he rakes again and once again and the last pin slips into place and the lock yields.

He opens the drawer.

Vertical files, but they're pushed to the back. Forward, lying at the bottom of the drawer, is a Glock 21 pistol, and a box of .45 auto cartridges.

And Bob thinks: *Dwayne, Dwayne, Dwayne. Pastor Dwayne. Dreaming of ISIS sending a few boys over here to Tallahassee to bust in and rape Loretta and grab you and cut off your head, but you're ready to defend your First Amendment church with your Second Amendment Glock, you're ready to protect your flock like a good father should, like a good shepherd, like a Heavenly Father.*

Heavenly Father my ass.

Bob's own voice in his own private head has clambered heavenward to the oldest old man of them all.

Sneering all the way, of course.

And another sea surge of pain swells in him and crashes behind his eyes and tumbles down his face and into his throat and into his chest.

Punishment for the sneer, no doubt.

And he hears a voice.

Not his own.

A loud voice.

A big fucking loud voice.

I'VE BROUGHT YOU HERE FOR A PURPOSE. Bob's not crazy. Bob knows he's hearing this voice in his head. But just because it's inside his own private head doesn't mean it's not a voice. A real voice. Talking to him. Every voice you ever hear when you're right there in the room with it still has to pass through your head. Even if you close your eyes and make the face and the mouth saying the words vanish, the voice remains, talking away. So where is it *then*? In your head. Your own private head. Just because it's in your head doesn't mean it isn't real.

I BROUGHT YOU HERE.

The voice pauses.

A beating pulse of pain in Bob's head.

An invitation to litany.

I BROUGHT YOU HERE.

And Bob responds: *To make me okay.*

YOU HAVE A PURPOSE.

To be okay.

I BROUGHT YOU HERE.

To you. To you.

YOU HAVE A PURPOSE.

To arm myself.

And Bob takes up the Glock 21 and its box of cartridges. He closes the drawer, and he uses his boyhood skill to reengage the lock. And he thinks: *Dwayne'll never know. He won't even miss his weapon till the Viet Cong bust in and then he'll know and he'll go* Oh shit *and they'll cut off his head.*

~

Earlier this morning, as Pastor Dwayne negotiates Bob's release into his care, Robert reassures Darla that she needn't go to the hospital today – his father would surely be embarrassed to be seen in an invalided state – and she goes off on her run. Robert is drinking his coffee at the kitchen island, aware still of the spot on his cheek where Darla kissed him good-bye. A utilitarian kiss, surely, conveying gratitude for a courtesy rendered, but it landed wetly there, as if her lips were parted. Perhaps not so surprising; she is, after all, *ardently* grateful. He can well understand her gratitude. He doesn't want to go either, for a low-grade dread won't stop niggling at him over this visit.

He takes the last sip of his coffee and carries his cup to the sink. The dread is not just about his father, but about his mother as well. And thinking of her, he thinks of the index card.

He turns from the sink and realizes where the card is. He puts his hand in his pocket and draws it out. She has written *James*. What was in her head? Is her use of his never-used formal name a rebuke of her other son? An attempt to distance herself, shield herself? But the card was intended for Robert's eyes. It's just another dramatic pose. Beneath is a phone number with a 705 area code.

This will be a day rife with choices between one unpleasant option and another. The present decision: call his brother after all these years and risk actually having to deal with him, or incur further implorings from his mother to help reconcile the family. The latter will be tedious in a familiar way. The former is disturbing in being so unfamiliar. But the prospect of a call to Jimmy at least stirs Robert's morbid curiosity. If the conversation goes badly, so be it. Robert will simply hang up the phone and that will be that till they're all four of them dead.

Robert takes the phone from its cradle near the foyer and carries it to the living room. He sits in the recessed window seat at the opposite end from the French doors to the veranda.

He dials.

Jimmy grasps the phone at the first ring.

He is sitting at his kitchen table, facing the forest. The phone was already beside him. Linda rose early and was gone when he came downstairs. Her note said that Becca was having a meltdown. Jimmy has been expecting Linda to call and check in, as the two of them were intending first thing this morning to discuss a long-overdue switch from DSL to UPS Canada. The expectation of her call was strong enough that he has not looked at caller ID.

With a voice thick with spousal familiarity he says, 'Yes?' The resultant beat of silence straightens him up in his chair. Somehow he knows it's Florida again.

Robert was expecting – was hoping – to leave a barebones message on an answering machine and put the burden of all this onto his brother. But the sudden, surprisingly familiar, surprisingly warm voice ratchets instantly into their shared past. Robert knows the warmth isn't for him. Not that this disappoints him. His brother was simply expecting someone else. For a moment Robert thinks to hang up.

But instead he says, 'Jimmy?'

Jimmy doesn't recognize his brother's voice immediately. Robert understands the next few moments of silence as *It's you, is it? What the hell are you doing, calling me?* Robert almost hangs up.

But the voice registers now on Jimmy. 'Robert?'

'Yes.'

They both fall silent.

The same impulse stirs in Jimmy that prompted him to simply erase yesterday's message. Touch the button. Keep the dead in their graves. He does not consciously consider this, but the years have worked away some of the softer rock of his brother's estrangement. It's still bouldered up in his head. But not like his mother's. So he says, 'Mom put you up to this.'

'Of course.' As soon as he says it, Robert hears the easily inferred subtext: *I would not be speaking to you otherwise.* He did not intend it.

But Jimmy does make the inference. 'You did your duty,' he says.

In the thumping finality of Jimmy's tone, Robert hears his brother's subtext – *So now that you've done it, hang up* – and Robert regrets his part in turning the call so quickly into this. They're on the phone together after forty-something years. No matter how it came to pass, why not say a few things? Robert does not hate his brother. He is not angry with his brother. Or even disappointed in him. Over the years Robert has come simply to feel nothing. As if his brother died. Died pretty young – right after college – before the two of them had a chance to mature comfortably into an adult, brotherly friendship. He's dead, and whatever grieving that entailed is long over with. No one even visits the grave anymore.

But his brother is alive at the other end of the line. So Robert says, 'This isn't about her.' He pauses, not quite knowing how to further soften things.

Jimmy says, 'Is he dead, then?'

'No.'

'Is it all overblown?'

'No. Just not dead *yet*.'

'I have no interest in seeing him. Dead or alive.'

'I suspect he feels the same way.' This didn't come out the way Robert wanted.

Jimmy does not reply. He thinks: *At least he's saying it straight.*

But Robert tries to fix it: 'Not that it means a damn thing to anyone, what he feels.' And he thinks: *That sounds sarcastic. Critical.*

And Jimmy thinks: *So much for straight.*

Robert says, 'I admire that in you, not giving that particular damn.'

'What?' Jimmy draws the word out to clearly mean *Bullshit.*

Robert considers bailing now.

But he doubles down. 'I admire it and I share it.'

'When did that happen?'

'We're neither of us twenty-two anymore.'

'You figure you actually grew out of trying to please him?'

'The price was too high,' Robert says. He has not put it this way to himself. The banyan and the man in the dark have been too close to him lately. They were big-ticket items on the bill he paid.

The words surprise Jimmy too. This is an admission he could not have expected.

The consequent silence between the brothers persists long enough that Robert finally says, 'Are you there?'

'I am,' Jimmy says.

Robert realizes he is standing at the veranda doors. He does not remember rising and crossing the room. He is looking at his live oak but has not seen it till this moment.

Jimmy is standing at the kitchen window. A hundred yards off, the white pines are jammed close, side by side, like a cordoned crowd before a burning building. For many years he understood his brother's defining act that Labor Day afternoon as a betrayal. He thinks: *Not from his point of view. It was an act of loyalty. Behind his eyes, he was being William Quinlan's loyal son. His only son. Of course the price was too high.*

'I won't come,' Jimmy says.

'I understand,' Robert says.

'You know it was different for me with him.'

'I know.'

'It was different for me because of how it was for you.' Robert might have expected this from Jimmy but not so simply or directly. Where they both now are, in mind and heart, is the result of way too much life lived incommunicado. Robert realizes they're teetering on the brink of forty-six years' worth of unexpressed blame and justification, anger and regret, jealousy and insecurity.

Jimmy has come to much the same realization.

Neither wants to tumble into all that.

Both, though, in spite of the telephonic silence swelling in their heads, are reluctant simply to hang up.

This time it's Jimmy who says, 'You there?'

'I'm here,' Robert says.

They know a little something about each other, the knowledge having been arrived at in the same way. At some point in the last few years, at some moment late at night, pajamaed and weak-willed, caught up in the technogeist and visited by a soap-operatic curiosity about the past, each began to Google names. For Robert: the lenient commanding officer at MACV in Hue, who had his own girlfriend in a back alley room and who was glad just to get Robert back alive at Tet, and who died in 1998 after two decades as an insurance executive in Omaha; Lien, who was untraceable; a sloe-eyed girl from high school; and Jimmy. For Jimmy: Mark Satin, the director of the Toronto Anti-Draft Programme; the first woman Jimmy slept with after he and Linda sensibly established how freely free love would remain in their lives; Heather, whose Facebook picture album was full of pub parties and her child; and Robert.

Jimmy says, 'I understand you teach.'

Only for a moment does it surprise Robert that Jimmy knows something about his present life. He realizes, from his own knowledge of Jimmy, that there need be nothing sentimental about this, much less affectionate.

'Yes,' Robert says. 'At Florida State University. History.'

'Sounds like where you'd go from Tulane.'

Robert hears, as well: *Not to Vietnam.*

Though Jimmy did not intend this.

Robert says, 'American history. Usually Southern. Early twentieth-century particularly.'

'I saw your bio at the school site.'

'And you make leather goods,' Robert says.

'I do.'

'Bags.'

'And other things. But bags are our specialty.'

If Robert knows about this, so does their mother, and Jimmy almost adds: *So does she own one?* But there is no way to ask that and make it simultaneously clear that he doesn't give a damn.

Robert almost says something about the glowing reviews and press coverage at Jimmy's website, about the special things Jimmy does to the leather, but Robert can't immediately shape those words concisely or clearly and maintain the appropriate tone of benignly tepid small talk.

And so they fall silent one last time.

Both men turn from the windows they are facing.

Then Jimmy says, 'You understand?'

'That you won't come to see him.'

'Yes.'

'Of course.'

'Tell her to let go of this.'

'I'll try.'

Both houses tick with morning silence. The brothers feel the vague impulse to say a little something more before they end the conversation, but neither can possibly imagine what it might be.

'Good-bye then,' Jimmy says.

'Good-bye,' Robert says.

They disconnect.

Each takes the cordless phone away from his ear and looks at it for a moment as if it were a faded Polaroid found in a shoe box.

~

Jimmy's four women workers have gone off together for their monthly lunch at Mavis's house and he is glad now to be able to sit at his worktable and have the barn to himself. Linda has not yet checked in with him. It must be going badly at their friends' house.

He has taken up his deer tine and his softest square of camel hide and has hunched into the furious burnishing of the edges of half a dozen messenger bags, filling himself with the smell of warming beeswax and edge paint, emptying himself of

Robert's voice and the family he has left behind.

But shortly he hears the middle bay door creak open and closed. He looks across the floor.

It's Linda, and he thinks: *Good. The antidote.* Whatever of Robert and Peggy and William he has not been able to burnish away will vanish in five minutes with Linda.

She is flushed from the sun and the cold and sheds her quilted coat as she approaches. Beneath, she is turtlenecked to her chin and is long-legged and slim-hipped in black dress-up jeans.

She stops before him.

She strips off her knit hat and shakes her hair down. 'Your women are gone,' she says.

'This is their day for Mavis's wife to make them venison stew.'

She obviously hasn't noticed the phenomenon.

'A start-ups tradition,' he says.

'Ah,' she says.

She grows still, her coat over her arm, her hat in her hand. She is staring at him but he has no sense that she's seeing him. She's considering something, he senses.

Becca no doubt has confided in her. Linda wants to speak of it but has probably made a vow not to. Linda takes that sort of pact seriously.

'You've got a tale to tell,' he says.

She makes a small sound, deep in her throat. Not quite a sound of assent. More meditative.

Jimmy waits for Linda to figure out what she's free to reveal.

Then she says, 'When will they be back?'

He's thinking of their friends splitting up and hears this wrong. His puzzlement must be showing. Linda clarifies. 'Your women.'

'My women...' he says, drawing out the phrase to add an unspoken *as you oddly insist on calling them*, '... usually take an hour and a half or a little longer on stew day. They make it up at the end of the afternoon.'

'And they left recently?'

'Twenty minutes perhaps.'

Linda nods and lays her coat and hat on the near edge of Jimmy's worktable, and she says, 'Then let's go sit on the couch together for a few minutes.'

'All right,' Jimmy says.

He follows her to the south end of the barn and into the break room next to their office.

'The coffee's fresh,' he says.

'I'm good,' she says, and she heads for the flannel chesterfield. He follows her.

She arranges herself sideways at one end, her legs drawn up beneath her. A long story to come.

Jimmy sits in the middle of the couch, within reaching distance, holding distance if need be. He turns toward her and waits.

She is still working something out in her mind. Then she says, 'They're finished, Becca and Paul. Forever and for the best.'

'I'm sorry,' Jimmy says.

'No,' Linda says. 'It *is* for the best. For everyone concerned.' A recent image of the couple flickers into Jimmy's head: a restaurant in Toronto, the two of them side by side on the bench seats, Paul's pugilist jaw and horn-rimmed reader's eyes, Becca's ballerina bun and Bardot pout. They are nearly two decades younger than Jimmy and Linda but the four of them are joined together by New Democratic Party politics, halibut fishing on Hudson Bay, and a couples' chemistry that synthesizes compassion and snark.

Before Jimmy can consider this image, it flickers out again with Linda reaching into his lap and lifting his hand toward her. She leans to it and kisses him on the very spot where a wedding ring would be if they were to wear them.

'My darling,' she says as she replaces the hand in his lap. But he instantly senses what is happening.

'I need to go away for a week or two,' she says.

If he objectively considers this, there is the possibility that she will, as Becca's best friend, simply stay with her or go away with her to help her through the first wave of trauma over the dissolution of her marriage. Paul is once divorced; Becca has never been.

But Jimmy understands. Linda is invoking the agreement that allowed the two of them to officially wed. A quarter of a century ago it was what they both wanted, equally, philosophically. It was how they'd sorted out the world together – before marriage and after – with regard to equality and rights and interpersonal power and the nature of love. All these things freely given and received and shared.

Jimmy has always been content with this.

He has wanted it.

But now in the center of his head he feels a hot dilation, like the frame of a Saturday movie serial sticking in the projector and its image splitting and searing and burning through.

'I'll be back soon, my sweet Jimmy,' she says.

He does not say anything.

This declaration is clearer than is their custom.

She keeps her eyes on his. Nothing intense in her gaze. This is how it has always been for them. They have always treated each other's lacunae with loving tact. It is what they want.

The conversation is meant to stop here.

They will hold hands. They might kiss. They might even make love now, here on the chesterfield, to assert their abiding connection.

But the burning is done in Jimmy's head and there is only a blank screen. A tabula rasa. And from it he asks, 'Were you the reason for the breakup?'

Minutely – but minutely is significant for Linda, Jimmy knows – minutely she flinches. Then she composes herself once more.

She takes his hand again. 'They've never meant as much to you as to me,' she says. 'You're not worried about the breakup.'

She's right about that. Nor is it the issue. But he does not say so.

'Nothing has changed between you and me,' she says, squeezing his hand gently.

Then he hears himself ask another question. 'Which of them is it?' He realizes only in the asking that he does not know, could not guess.

She lets go of his hand, but her voice remains gentle: 'I think the way we've always handled these things is best, don't you?'

Now he asks, 'Does the other one know?' But obviously not. Otherwise none of this would now be a surprise to him. He would surely have heard from the excluded one.

Linda straightens before him, taking a deep breath. Her eyes do not narrow or harden or flare, as they can do when he and she argue. If anything, they soften for him. He feels a twist of admiration over this. Then a tighter twist, of tenderness. And then a sudden chest-clamping regret.

She says, 'Are we wrong, my darling? Surely not. We have

always been so smart about this. Love on this earth is not a singularity. It is a profusion. As simple as a kind word at a checkout counter. As complex as you and I. But love always has boundaries. By the parts of us – mind, body, heart – that are involved, or not involved. And to what degree. And for how long. I feel certain this is a partial thing now before me and a brief thing. Our love for each other – yours and mine – is the bedrock for any other experience in this fleeting gift of my life. It's the same for you, isn't it? We've said so to each other. Often. Aren't we grateful for that?'

And at this she lifts her hand and touches his cheek and says, 'Whichever of us dies first, I want our lips to touch in that moment.'

She pauses, and she says, 'I love you, Jimmy.'

She waits, her fingertips lingering on him.

He can think of nothing to say.

He is not moving.

He can't imagine what's showing on his face.

She withdraws her hand.

She shifts her legs, squares her shoulders to him a bit more. She says, 'Why don't you spend a couple of weeks with that girl Heather. She would like nothing better, I'm sure.' He still can find no words.

She says, 'Maybe she'll help you stop worrying about what's next.'

~

Just before noon Robert answers the foyer phone. As he expects, it's his mother. 'Darling, he's off the morphine drip and starting to wake up.'

'I'll be there within the hour.'

Peggy rightly takes these as his last words and jumps in. 'Before you hang up. I'm out in the hallway. I need to ask. Did you try?'

'Jimmy?'

'Of course Jimmy.'

'Yes.'

'And?'

'He's not coming.'

Robert hopes that will be it.

He waits for her.

She waits for him.

Not for long. 'Why are you doing this to me?' she says. 'What did he say?'

'Do you really want details?'

'Yes.'

'There aren't many. We didn't instantly turn into chums.' Robert hesitates only very slightly before the lie: 'I don't recall the exact words.' He recalls them quite clearly. 'But it amounts to this: Nothing has changed. We all need to let him go.'

Robert waits for a dramatic sound on the other end of the phone. A stricken word. A sob even. But there's only silence.

This troubles Robert more than her usual emoting. Better for her to be angry. She needs to be fighting. He says, 'We're still toxic to him.'

'Did he say that?' This comes out sharply. Her dukes are up. Good.

'No,' Robert says. 'Not those words.'

'What words?'

'I'm not going be his proxy in an argument with you, Mom. I'll see you in an hour.'

'Toxic,' she says.

'Listen. The only way this thing could have been made right was for Pops to reach out. Not Jimmy. Years ago. At the latest when Carter gave the amnesty. Pops should have told Jimmy to come home. Told him – God forbid – that he understood, that he didn't condemn him.'

Robert has said all he intended to, and Peggy delays only long enough to draw a breath. She says, 'I am so sick and tired of the men in this family.'

Robert lets her have her big curtain line unchallenged. But she stays on the phone.

So does he, though she's no longer on his mind. He wonders at Jimmy, at how firmly he grasped his own life and held it close all these years.

'Are you still there?' Peggy finally asks.

'Yes.'

'Why? Come up here to me.'

And a short time later he is passing the Blood of the Lamb Full Gospel Church. He turns his face to it, puzzles over what that was all about yesterday morning. A man in coveralls is carrying a ladder along the side of the church building.

And then the church vanishes with a run of pine along Apalachee Parkway.

Peggy is waiting for Robert in the hallway outside his father's room. She steps toward him.

'Have you been waiting out here all this time?' he says.

'No,' Peggy says, keeping her voice hushed and flapping her hand at him to do the same. 'It's been an hour. You've always been punctual.'

'Is he still awake?' Robert accepts her tone, has kept his own voice low. A private conversation in the hall would cause an argument for her and Pops.

'*Fully* awake,' she says.

They've already been arguing.

Robert says, 'So what do you need to say on the sly?'

Peggy's head snaps ever so slightly. It always comes as a surprise, that he sees through her.

'Yes, well,' she says, 'I just wanted to remind you he's in a delicate state.'

'Of course.'

'Not just in his body. His mind. He's lost his mind.'

'The drugs,' Robert says.

'He's lucid,' Peggy says. 'Just mad.'

'Let me guess. He doesn't want a priest to come visit.'

'I won't even tell you how he put it,' she says.

'It's his choice,' Robert says.

'So please don't let him get worked up about anything.'

'I'll do what I can.'

Peggy clutches Robert's hand. Somehow it feels real, this gesture. 'I know you will.'

He takes both her hands in his.

She says, 'I'm just so afraid I'm going to lose him now.'

'He's a tough guy. He can beat the odds.'

'God knows I'll miss him,' she says. 'Even at his worst.'

Especially at his worst, Robert thinks. *His worst has kept you happily energized.* But he gently compresses her hands and says, 'The best thing is for you to go on downstairs and get some coffee and a Danish. Linger over them. I can handle Pops better if it's just the two of us.'

Peggy searches her son's face, seems to reassure herself about something, and then nods.

They let go of each other, and without another word Peggy is gone.

Robert approaches his father's hospital door.

He steps in.

At first the only sound he recognizes in the room is his father's heart, digitized into a soft monitor beep. And now the faint hiss of the air flowing from the wall into his father's lungs. Pops lies in his bed, his torso angled upward, his arms laid out on top of the blanket, the left one wrapped thickly from hand to elbow. He is watching out the window: the bright afternoon sky and the distant tops of longleaf pines.

Robert hesitates. His father keeps his watch. Always cleanshaven, as if he were standing for inspection by Patton himself, his cheeks and chin are covered now in dark scruff.

Robert says, 'Pops.'

William turns his face abruptly to his son. 'Sorry,' he says. 'I thought you were Mother.'

Robert approaches the bed, wondering briefly if his father's mind has indeed gone wrong, if he was expecting his own mother, the long-dead Grandma Quinlan. But of course he meant Peggy.

'I sent her away for coffee and pastry,' Robert says.

'Good,' William says. And then his eyes wander off, as if the exchange has set him thinking.

Why does Robert have the immediate impression he knows what's on Pops's mind? Perhaps it's the recent, vivid reminder of the daily struggle between his father and mother. That and the coffee and pastry. These stir the past in him, not as recollections, but enough to give him his impression as he arrives at his father's bedside.

What has worked covertly in Robert are two events. In one of them, a decade ago, on an otherwise routine phone call from New Orleans, his mother suddenly sounded real, sounded vulnerable in a way unalloyed with dramatic artifice. Robert had just casually mentioned that Darla was at school for the afternoon.

'She has a class?' Peggy asked.

'No.'

'For what then?'

'Whatever.'

'She's often away.'

'Away?'

'At school.'

'Of course.'

And Peggy's voice shifted now to that authentic-seeming place, though he didn't pick up on it yet. 'Does it bother you sometimes, this regular separation, when you're so close to someone? When you don't really know what's going on in their life? What they're doing?'

'Oh, I can easily guess,' he said. The tangle of students and colleagues and papers and bureaucracy.

'Your father goes off every afternoon like that,' Peggy said. Her tone pitched downward, inward. 'He's done it every day for years. Ever since he retired. No one's around to notice but me.'

She paused.

Robert was clearly aware now of the authenticity of this riff.

She went on, trying to figure it out as she'd apparently been doing for some time. 'He loves to drive his car, it's true. He's always loved to drive his cars. He's driven since he was eleven, after all. There were no licenses back then. This love grew with his bones. I understand. But it's more than that. He's going for a little drive, he says. He's going for coffee, he says. Every day. He goes away for hours. I understand I can be a burden. Just to be around me. He wants to escape. But I wonder how much coffee you can drink. I wonder if he's alone.'

Now a long silence. In moments like this, Robert usually knew when she was waiting for him to give her something back. But this silence felt different.

Then she said, very softly, 'I sometimes wonder if he has a woman.'

Another silence.

To his surprise, the notion of Pops carrying on a flirtatious friendship at his age did not strike Robert as ridiculous. So although a laugh would have sufficed, he felt the need to deny this. He began to shape a reply.

But she said, 'You wouldn't know.'

'I'm sure he doesn't,' Robert said.

'No one would know.'

Robert tried to find more words.

But she intervened, her tone breaching into avid reassurance, 'Not that I'm suggesting anything about Darla.'

'I didn't think…'

'You've got a peach there, Bobby boy. You better take good care of her or you'll have to answer to me.' And Peggy laughed a loud, sharp laugh.

And then, a few years ago, Robert and Darla drove the six hours together to New Orleans for a semiotics conference. While Darla did her panels, Robert went off to see his parents. This was a last-minute decision. William and Peggy had visited Florida the previous month. There would be no sustainable small talk left between them for a while. But Robert felt guilty to be this close and not spend a few hours. He would surprise them. If they were out, at least he'd tried.

It was a quarter to two on a Friday afternoon when he turned onto Third Street from Magazine and crossed Annunciation into his parents' block. Up ahead he saw Dad's Impala pulling away from the curb. The afternoon vanishing act. Robert could simply take his father's place at the curb and visit his mother. Or he could follow his father.

At the foot of Third, William turned uptown. Robert stayed close, not taking any chances of losing him. Over the intervening years Robert had given very little thought to his conversation with his mother about all this, other than to conclude she'd never have said those things to him in person. The disembodiment of the phone had put her into a deep-seated Catholic frame of mind, as if she were in a confessional booth, speaking to an invisible priest.

This was probably quite simple. It was about coffee and a chance to escape the bickering. But if Dad was having an octogenarian tryst, Robert wanted to get a glimpse of the woman in the affair. Mom would never need to know.

William stayed on Tchoupitoulas for as long as he could, for the whole length of the river docks, till the street ended at the zoo. This he skirted, and then he followed the levee into Carrollton, turning onto the area's eponymous main drag. He drove only a short distance farther and turned into a strip-mall parking lot.

Robert pulled into a spot down the row and watched his father get out of his car. If Dad had bothered to look around he would have seen Robert's head and shoulders among the car tops down the way, but he did not look, was not the least bit furtive. He did not move to the sidewalk along Carrollton Avenue, but struck out along the parking lot lane toward the side street.

Robert followed his father.

He was impressed by the man's vigorous stride. Perhaps the stride of a man meeting a woman. Certainly the stride of a father who, from this distance, seemed not to be aging. Who might live forever.

He crossed the side street and turned away from Carrollton. A couple of doors up was a coffee shop. Chicory Dickory, Coffee and Beignets. At least the coffee part of Dad's story was true: he went in.

Robert neared the shop, slowed drastically, approached carefully, and paused in the doorway. His father's back was to him. He was standing before a table with three other men who were standing as well, their chairs pushed away as if they'd just risen. They were all of them old. Their right arms and hands were frozen in a sharp military salute, and they were swiveling slightly at the hips so that each could direct his gesture to each of the others.

They sat.

The clock on the wall said precisely two o'clock. Immediately a waitress arrived with a tray of beignets and coffee for four. She lowered the tray and they all served themselves from it, making small talk with her, calling her by name. These guys were regulars.

Robert pulls a chair to his father's hospital bedside. He's aware now of how he knows what his father was thinking. Coffee and pastry and the irony of Peggy getting away from him for that. Coffee and pastry and the company of men, and how those things are likely gone forever. Till yesterday his father was still driving. He'd surely found a coffee shop in Thomasville. Did he find a new band of veterans as well? Robert hopes so. He kept his father's actual secret through the years. Peggy would have nagged a stop to those afternoons as surely as if they'd been filled with a mistress.

Seated now, he leans toward his father. The initial covert working of the past in him – the phone conversation with Peggy and his shadowing of his father – is done. But the memory of the New Orleans coffee shop emanates on. As Robert stood in the doorway, he thought to turn and vanish. Simply, quietly.

But instead he stepped in and sat down at a table near the four men, with his father's back still to him. Robert ordered a coffee with chicory and sipped at it, hearing fragments of their talk. They spoke of the weather and the Saints and their aching joints and Obama and al-Qaeda and eventually they arrived at Patton and Eisenhower and at how they lost the peace by letting the Russians into Berlin. And then Robert's coffee was gone and he'd pushed his luck already, not really wanting his father to catch him here, and not really wanting an answer to the question that had lately gnawed its way into the center of his brain. Which was: Would his father get around to the story of a small, doomed house in Bingen? Robert's thoughts were getting ragged enough for him even to wonder if Dad would have his Good War cronies start counting, *One Mississippi, Two Mississippi.*

Robert left money on the table and went out into the street, thinking: *No. That's the stuff he and his pals take for granted. Bingen was a story made for fucking with the minds of a couple of little boys.*

You share a war in one way. You pass it on in another. All this swifts through Robert, though in his father's room at Archbold Memorial Hospital he is washed by its wake.

But small talk prevails for the moment. He says, 'How do you feel?'

William snorts. 'Better a few hours ago.' He groans and

gingerly shifts his shattered arm, which lies between them. 'For the first time in my life I'm beginning to understand drug addicts.'

'Impossible,' Robert says, and he hears a taint of anger in this. He softens his voice. 'How'd that come about?'

'Twenty-four hours on morphine and four hours off it,' his father says.

Robert has had, for some years, two modes of conversation with his father. Most of the time he listens, unchallenging, serious of manner, letting his father set the conversational agenda and its tone. Or, occasionally, when he reaches his limit of tolerance for the man's hypertraditional thinking and rightveering politics and blue-collar attitudinizing, Robert becomes ironic, contrapuntal, engaging with his father but in a manner that tugs at the man's points as if he could be pulled to the left.

Robert knows he should let this conversation roll out in the most comfortable way for a very old man in a hospital bed with a broken hip and a shattered arm. But he does not. He says, 'A little morphine in all the air. It would be wonderfully refreshing for everyone.'

'Are you quoting or just selfishly getting sassy with a badly injured old man?'

'D. H. Lawrence.'

'Was he an addict?'

'I don't think so.'

'I was always an addict,' his father says. 'For the caffeine and the sugar.'

Robert is a little surprised to hear this admission in those terms, even if his father is in a mood to sling the irony back at him. 'That's a serious confession.'

William snorts at this. 'Don't be flip about that. Your mother wanted to get a goddamn priest in here.'

'I take it you said no.' Robert tries to twinkle this. Not very successfully.

William looks at him as if he's being goaded. Which is closer to the truth. 'I told her if she let one in, I'd beat him to death with my cast.'

At this he tries to gesture with his broken arm and barks in pain and then coughs deeply and grindingly, which clenches his body, which further agitates his arm and now even his hip.

Robert puts his hand on his father's shoulder. 'Easy,' he says. The gesture is futile and the coughing and clenching go on, though Robert keeps his hand where it is. 'It'll pass,' he says. 'You're a tough guy,' he says. And finally, 'Should I get the nurse?'

William manages a sharp shake of the head. *No.*

Finally the coughing stops. His body calms. Tears are streaming down William's face.

He seems unaware of them.

'Fuck,' he says.

Robert finds his hand still on his father's shoulder. He gives him a gentle squeeze there and withdraws.

'I wouldn't even be able do it,' his father says. 'Goddamn cast isn't hard enough.'

Things shift in Robert. But to a complicated place. Not to banter. Not to an encouragement to rest. Not to soothing palaver. His father is indeed a tough guy. That Robert believes. But his father may soon be dead.

Robert sits back in his chair.

William is quiet now. He blinks his eyes. His good hand comes up quickly to his face and wipes at the tears. He sees

Robert noticing. 'From the pain,' he says.

'You shouldn't let yourself get worked up over her.'

'That's our life.'

'She's probably going to try again to get the priest in here.'

'She thinks I'm going to die,' William says, but almost gently. 'She says she won't know who she is without me.'

'Are you beginning to understand her?'

'Drug addicts are easier.' William turns his face away, toward the window.

Then he turns back.

He holds his gaze steadily on Robert. His eyes seem heavylidded, as if he's struggling to keep them open. But the impression is not weariness. These strike Robert as the heavy eyes of sadness. And he feels himself to be the object of the look.

Robert does not ask what's behind this. Instead, he says, 'Were you still a Catholic in Germany?'

William snorts softly. His eyes relax. 'You mean, "There are no atheists in foxholes"?'

'Something like that.'

'Whoever thought that up was full of shit. Either they were never in a war or were in the priest's pocket to start with.' William begins carefully to rearrange himself at the shoulders. 'Not that I'm an atheist. That's just another religion.'

He stops arranging. He sucks up the pain.

'Should I get a nurse?' Robert says.

William shakes his head sharply *No*. He takes a deep breath, and pulling from the shoulder he adjusts his broken arm just a little. He closes his eyes to the pain.

Robert stifles his hands, his voice. He will offer no help. Pops has to be Pops.

When the pain has passed, his father says, 'What was it for, my Good War? And what was our national humiliation for?'

He means, by the latter, Robert's Bad War.

William says, 'It only brought us to this fucking world.'

Robert says, softly, 'There it is.' The phrase catches him by surprise. He hasn't used it in decades. It was a meme among the enlisted men in Vietnam. Its meaning slid upon a long continuum from *I am content* to *We're all fucked*. In this case: *You said it, brother.*

William begins to cough again.

But he stops it. With a sharp intake of breath and a brief flinch of his body and a sneer. A sneer at the cough and at the pain. He takes a moment to let out the breath, fight off a little after-tremor of hacking, and he says, 'Who wouldn't be happy to die tonight? Give me the political wars of the twentieth century any old day. At least your communist or your fascist gave a shit about this present life. The religious wars are going to take us all down. Behead the other guys and blow yourselves up. Sure. If you really read the holy book they believe in – that we *all* supposedly believe in; the first part of it for all of us is the *same book* – then what they're doing makes perfect sense. That book's full of genocide, on direct order from the Commander in Chief in the Sky. With Moses himself leading the dirty work. Every holy battle gets around to it. Not just by the punks in the ski masks. Even the New Testament believers get around to it. The Catholics and the Pilgrims both had the stake and the torch.'

William falls silent.

Robert has never heard any of this from his father. Was it new? Did it take the breaking of his body for him to come to this? Or did his little band of brothers look up over their coffee and beignets one afternoon and know?

Robert has to work hard now not to put his hand on his father's hand. The man wouldn't recognize the gesture, so he dare not. But Pops's words have fallen upon Robert like a shared thing. Like an understanding between them. Even like a backdoor expression of fatherly pride. Pops went to war. Robert went to war. Both of them came to this.

Robert embraces this understanding. And with it returns the moment at a corner table in the bar on Magazine Street when it was late enough and they both were lubricated enough and the lights in the place were localized enough and dim enough that he and his father seemed all alone in a dark recess, but there was still enough light from somewhere that when his father turned his face slightly, Robert saw the man's eyes beginning to fill and he thought to reassure him, even though Pops surely understood already, from his own war and from what Robert had just said about his job and duties in Vietnam, but Robert was moved by his father's worry, and he added, 'It's all right. I've got a job inside the wire. I'll be safe in Vietnam. It'll be like research. I'll get home safe.' His father did not speak, did not turn back to him, and the tears that had come to his eyes began to fall. Robert had never seen his father weep. Robert could easily have wept then as well, but he was keenly aware that the pride and appreciation in his father's tears would be diminished by tears of his own. Robert needed to maintain the composure of a soldier. And he did. He cut the tears off, and he waited for his father to be himself again. Which, slowly, silently, the man became, and they drank some more and then some more, and they did not speak to each other again of war. Not on that evening. Not ever. Not about their personal experience of it.

But now.

As a seventy-year-old Robert finds himself as needy and eager to please this man as an adolescent. So he edges his chair as close to the bed as he can. He leans toward his father. He says, 'Whether it's over politics or over religion, it all comes down to whatever nasty gene humans carry that makes us go to war. But once a war's on, it takes warfare to stop it. From a distance both sides on a battlefield look alike. That doesn't mean one of them isn't justified in being there.'

Though animated by his teenage self, Robert has spoken in the voice of the man he is. And he has heard himself. He thinks: *I don't believe half of that. Not in the way it came out.* And his fuller belief hurtles through him, that the very waging of a righteous war, even the very winning of that war, can trigger the dark gene. So the winners go on to fight unrighteous wars. And maybe that's the real gene that causes all the trouble. The one encoded for righteousness. Politics and religion and just the pure waging and winning of wars all share that.

But it makes no difference. The Robert who edged his chair toward his father didn't want to make a nuanced point. His intention was deeper and simpler. Two men. Sharing what they did, what they are. *That* Robert finds his voice now: 'Pops, it's okay. For us both. We had to go to war. You and I did what we could.'

And this turns Pops's face back to him.

They look at each other.

Robert waits.

William struggles with something. Then he says, 'I've held this inside for a long time.'

He pauses.

Robert quickens.

And William says, 'I lost one son utterly.'

Jimmy.

Robert regrets that it has to be in contrast to his brother, but he longs for what's next so much that he puts this regret aside. He even draws a good breath now at how Jimmy has made him even more important to his father.

And William says, 'So I've held my tongue. But the truth is you didn't go to war. You went through the motions. But you turned it into graduate school. You contrived a comfortable place on the edge of the action to go study. You didn't even let the army decide your fate. You wangled your safe little job with a pre-enlistment deal and avoided the real thing. You told all the others who manned up, "Better you do the dirty work, not me. Better your blood than mine."'

Robert falls back in his chair in enervated stillness. He would rise, he would go, but he remains.

His father says, 'And look where you put me. What could I have said to you? How could I argue for my son to risk death? How could I do that to your mother? And what would it say about you, that I should have to talk you into it? You already chose.'

William stops talking.

He keeps his eyes on Robert.

Robert is looking at the distant tops of the pines.

'I probably should have taken this to my grave,' William says.

Robert does not reply. He thinks he sees the trees quaking. Even from this distance. The wind must be strong today.

'It's all over anyway,' William says.

Robert turns to his father. 'I'm sorry I disappointed you.' He regrets saying this. He should argue the point. Or he should rise and go without speaking. He should not give a damn what his father thinks. They are both old men. But he has said it. And now, though he regrets this even more, he waits for his father to dispute him: *No, Robert. No not at all. I'm not disappointed. I've come to be glad. Glad you're alive. Your brother's act is my only shame. You did go to Vietnam, after all. I'm proud of you.*

But his father says nothing of the sort. He has already made himself clear.

Tet comes to mind.

But Robert has never said a word about what haunts him. His father would only be critical of that. Of course the scholar, having tried to create his comfortable little place, would be haunted by an act that any real soldier, any real man, would have understood as necessary, inevitable, righteous. Would have done proudly.

When Hue was secure and the men queued through one long night for a phone call home, Robert told his parents only that he was okay. MACV was not overrun. He was safe.

And later, when the family was safely reunited in America, there were no Vietnam war stories. None offered. None sought. As it had been, mostly, for his father and his war. Robert convinced himself that his own silence was another thing that bound him to his father, that made the man proud.

And now Robert's words hang in the air between them. Robert looks away from this man. Back to the trees, the sky.

William isn't speaking.

Robert finally looks at him.

His father's eyes are squeezed shut. He is writhing minutely in physical pain. Silently.

'I'll get the nurse,' Robert says.

He rises. He walks out of the room. He stops at the nurses'

station and tells the first nurse who looks at him that William Quinlan is hurting.

Then he goes down in the elevator and crosses the lobby and pushes through the door and finds his car and gets in.

He sits for a moment quaking like the tops of the pines all around him.

And he drives away.

~

Darla sits at her desk, fingers poising over her keyboard and then falling away, again and again, trying to signify with her words what it was that she felt before the Confederate monument yesterday, what it was that she understood; but trying first to distinguish her understanding from her feeling; and as she fails at that, trying to decide whether trying to distinguish understanding from feeling isn't, in fact, a fallacy, whether the very act of intellectualizing what was signified by the monument doesn't, in fact, miss the whole point. Which brings her to the kiss. The kiss she gave her husband this morning.

She parted her lips to him. But she placed the kiss on his cheek. Would she have preferred his lips? Yes. Is that preference associated with her fingertips poised but inoperative once again over the keyboard? Perhaps. Yes. After her communion yesterday with the fair and faithful ladies of nineteenth-century Florida, the ardor of her lips longed this morning for Robert's mouth. But she understood him: With his father on his mind, it was hardly the right moment. Her thought trumped her feeling.

Her hands fall.

Still, if she'd kissed him on the lips would she have the

right words now for this thing her ladies built?

She lifts her hands once more, curls her fingers over the keys.

The front door latch clacks. He's home.

She has left her office door open for this. An invitation to him.

The rustle of him now in the foyer.

She puts her hands on the desktop.

She waits.

She hears nothing.

She turns in her chair.

He has not silently appeared. Perhaps he assumed the open door of her office meant that she was elsewhere.

Or perhaps he needs to be alone. This is an interpretation she expects to wish to be true. She shouldn't want to hear about his hospitalized father, a man she has always found insufferable. But, in fact, she wishes Robert had understood the open door and rushed to it.

He has done no such thing.

And her mind, following along in its own path, yields this: *William Quinlan is the product of a* victorious *army, its monuments boilerplated with conventional self-congratulation.*

She turns back to her computer. But she looks beyond its monitor, through the window, out to the live oak. This tree was already massive when her ladies were composing their words. She invites them. She arranges them beneath her oak, their skirts spread out around them, basket lunches at hand.

Unexpectedly, they turn their faces to her.

And she rises to look for her husband. She steps from her office. She moves along the hallway, past the foyer, and she stops at the bottom of the staircase. She listens upward.

But the sound that catches her attention is the ricochet chirp of a cardinal. Distant, but not a sound to be heard from where she is standing.

She steps into the living room.

At the far end a French door is open. Robert is framed there, his back to her. He stands very still, looking out to the oak.

She remains still as well. She watches him for what feels like a long time.

Then his head dips abruptly down. Something has finished in him. He turns and starts at her presence.

'Sorry,' she says, moving toward him.

He steps in. 'I didn't know where you were,' he says. They approach each other but stop short, not touching for a moment as she tries to read him and he tries to collect himself. She looks him carefully in the eyes, his green eyes, which she resolved to do night before last in the bed, in the dark, drawn into a long-set-aside memory. How deep their color seemed to her when they first met, but they are paler to her now, green but not Monet green at all. Were they ever? Have they diminished over the years, gradually, she simply never noticing? Were they never what she thought? Or is this grief she sees in them?

She steps into her husband, putting her arms around him, turning her face and laying her head against his shoulder, telling the ladies beneath the oak to hush.

He pulls her gently close.

The two of them say nothing till they pull apart just as gently.

She looks again into his eyes. They are saturated but unblinking, refusing to express a tear.

'What's happened?' she asks, instead of asking more directly, *Has he died?*

Robert's eyes stay fixed on hers but his head twitches ever so slightly to the right. She takes this as: *Happened? He broke his hip is what happened.* What he's really thought does not, of course, occur to Darla: *Happened? How do you know? Has he said these things about me to you?*

She tries to clarify. 'I thought perhaps he took a turn for the worse.'

'He's bad enough.'

'I understand,' she says, feeling clumsy, caught in the implication that Robert's sadness could be caused only by his father having died. She assumed that mere suffering would simply bring out the abrasive worst in William Quinlan, a worst that would primarily irritate Robert. 'He must be in a lot of pain,' she says.

Robert simply shrugs.

Something has *happened*, she decides. *Just not death.* Now she assumes it's something William has said. But other than expressions of quotidian grumpiness or reflex jingoism – none of which, surely, would affect Robert like this – she cannot imagine what.

Robert turns away, wishing to sit down. Only once, many years ago, did he voice his delusion to Darla. He submitted to her his father's pride in his Vietnam service to help explain how he ended up a soldier in the war that this beautiful and righteously impassioned woman despised. And he submitted it along with a manifestly mature clearheadedness about his need for his father's approval, which allowed the delusion to be unquestioningly shared by them both.

His first impulse is to sit in his reading chair. It's angled away from everything in the room except the French doors. It faces the oak, which is on his mind. He has never said a word to Darla about killing the man in the dark. He has never said a word to anyone. He is weary and he wants his chair for the privacy of his present thoughts. But he does not want to snub his wife. So he moves to the sofa, which also faces the veranda, and he sits there at one end.

Darla has watched him make this choice. She senses he's made it to acknowledge her presence. But he does so without looking her way, without saying a word, and he has placed his back to her. So she circles the sofa but stops at the far end. 'Would you prefer some privacy?' she asks.

He looks at her. 'No,' he says. 'Sorry. I just needed to rest.'

She sits too. Not next to him but not quite apart.

They say nothing.

Darla will not press him for words.

Robert's mind is full of them: *It would be better if I'd fully earned his scorn in the way he pictured me. If I'd stayed behind the walls of MACV that night and never killed. Or simply killed from there in an indeterminate way, as I may have done sometime during the next few days, spraying rifle fire with others into trees and building facades and down the street, aiming at muzzle flash. It would even be better if I'd not gotten lucky that first night: not found my way to the gates of MACV; not arrived in the middle of a battle lull with the right cries and somebody to hear them so I could make a dash to the gate; not dodged, at the last moments, some surprised enemy fire. Better if I'd simply died that first night trying to get back. Would my father, to his surprise, have perceived some sort of courage in a dead body in the street with a pistol in its hand? Would he? Of course he wouldn't. Of course not. He would have known my actions for what they were: headlong flight into cover, more proof of my instinctive cowardice. But at least*

153

I never would have heard about it. Fuck you, Pops. Fuck you.

And in the lull from a heartfelt fuck-you, Robert becomes aware of his wife next to him. He turns his face to her.

Gazing beyond the veranda as a pair of mated cardinals spanks across the yard, Darla senses Robert at once and looks at him.

And the lull in him ceases. He looks away from her, but she has replaced his father in his head. *It wasn't until we'd had sex, until we were quiet at last and slick with sweat, that I explained my work in Vietnam, my work so like research, my work so unlike that of a man who was ready to kill for his country. But when she'd finally asked how it was for me there, my carefully arranged job was all I spoke of. All she wished to know. She was relieved. I was no killer but I was no coward. I was perfect for her. She was glad I was alive. What would she have thought if I'd gone on to tell her about my man in the dark? If I'd told her how I killed a man when he might have been anyone? How he frightened me, so I shot the man down. Decades later she would bitterly criticize two high-profile Florida cases of men acquitted of murder for standing their ground. Back then, at the beginning for us, in her antiwar passion, would she have gotten up at once and gone to the bathroom and closed the door and washed me off her body forever? Or because she was already falling in love with me would she have been glad I hadn't taken the risk?*

Something in Robert fillips a perverse little impulse into his mind: *Tell her. Tell her now. Tell her you killed this man. But tell her as if this were your old man sitting here next to you. Give it to her with the spin he might actually respect, a spin I fervently wish were true: I was alone on what constituted a battlefield in Vietnam. So I did what men do on a battlefield. I may have gone to Vietnam to minimize my risks, but when the real war came to me, I stood in the dark alone and raised a steady hand and I killed and I'm content with that.*

The impulse lingers in Robert for a few beats. If in response she flares at him, if she throws aside her supportive concern for him, even as his father is dying, and vociferates the politics of pragmatic pacifism, if she declares her deep disappointment in him and vanishes into her office for the night, then Robert would know: By the same tale his father might soften; his father might approve; his father might reconsider.

And all of this suddenly sounds crazy to him. Crazy that he still gives a goddamn about his father's regard. Crazy that he'd even fantasize about saying something that risks his wife's love. Crazy that his obsession over the first man he killed – with such mitigating circumstances – should have renewed itself all these decades later. Crazy to think that the twenty-three-year-old in 1968 has anything whatsoever to do with the man he is in 2015. And this last thought instantly seems crazy to him the other way round as well, that the twenty-three-year-old should have anything but a deep connection to the seventy-year-old. He is a historian, after all.

This facile chaos of thoughts beclouds a simpler truth he has ignored for decades: He could never have won the respect – never have won the love – of both his wife and his father. He always had to choose.

He lifts his arm, presses his wrist hard against his forehead. Darla watches. She edges closer to Robert and arrives at the wrong conclusion about the gesture: He is moved by his father's suffering.

Robert is wrong about her, as well. If he were to say what he thought to say a few moments ago, even spun for his father's approval, he would not have risked her love. Would not even have done so in 1968. She did not ask for the details of his military service – though she knew she must eventually – until she could sleep with him at least once.

She wanted him strong-handed and even rough and she wanted to feel in the midst of it that this man might have been a killer. Wanted him that way but it was okay because it was by her desire, by her initiation, by her permission that he was fucking her. She was in control of the pounding of him inside her. It was she clutching him tight and it was she crying out for more and for harder and so it was okay, she was the boss. And she could assume he'd been a killer, but that was in another country, and here and now, in this bed in America, she had the power to reform him. She had the power to forgive him, a man who killed and maybe killed some more and killed and killed. Dangerous as he was, he needed her. He needed her to bring him back even from that.

Not that all this was conscious in her. It resided in her breathlessness, it was in her hands that took his and closed the bedroom door and drew him to the bed and stripped his clothes from him and allowed him to strip the clothes from her, and it was in her hands that ran over the stubble of his whitewalled hair, that grabbed him down there, grabbed the part of him that may even have known Vietnamese women like this, that hurt these women and left them, women she could forgive him for, women she could forgive.

None of this was in her conscious mind. Not then, not since. But the first time they made love it was certainly present in her hands and her breath and in the tremors of her and the grinding in her and in the rushing and release in her and in her sweat afterward and in the lull.

On that night, after she and Robert had sex, when she was

led to ask him what he'd actually done in Vietnam, when she heard how his job had been like research, how he was in a safe place counting and assessing men and weapons, how it was so very unlike combat, after she heard these things and then showered and dressed and came back to him and sat beside him on the bed and hooked her arm in his, after all that, she lied to him. And to herself. She said, 'I'm so glad.'

Not entirely a lie. Her rational mind was glad. If she was to be with this man forever, as she already felt she might, and if she believed in the righteous cause of her generation, it was better that he had not taken part in the fundamental act that makes war evil. Her mind was content with that. Even grateful.

But she had expected the answer to be different. In her body, something was let down, something had lessened. Her body feared – her body knew – that even though her love for him would grow, having sex with this man would never again be as good.

His wrist falls from his forehead.

He looks away, out through the French doors.

Darla says, 'Is he giving up?'

'I don't think so.' Robert turns to her.

'How's your mother?'

'Wallowing in it.'

Darla holds her tongue. About both of Robert's parents.

'I spoke with Jimmy,' he says.

Darla gapes. 'What?'

'My mother found his number.'

'You actually talked with him?'

'I did.'

'Wow.'

'She loves her melodrama.'

'But you called him?'

'I did.'

'For her?'

'*He* made the break permanent. Not me.'

She grunts softly in assent. 'And he actually talked with you?'

'Talked. Some. It ended as you might expect.'

'He has his father in him. I can't see him ever forgiving.'

Robert snags on this, though not about Jimmy. He masks it from Darla by turning his face away toward the veranda. He stays silent.

'You don't think so?' she says.

He still doesn't speak.

'I know it's ironic,' she says.

'But true,' he says. 'He'll never forgive me for going to Vietnam.'

'And your father will always love you for it,' Darla says, overexplaining the irony to reassure him.

Robert rises abruptly, crosses to the French doors.

'You don't need Jimmy's forgiveness,' Darla says, thinking she's read his gesture.

Robert turns back to her.

She cannot see his face with the afternoon sun in the trees behind him.

He braces himself to let go of his father. It's easier to start with his brother, so he answers her, 'I know that. I don't even miss him, is the truth of it,' thinking, *Nor will I miss Pops.* Pops: The word belies his assertion. *I won't,* he insists. But the man won't let him go. Maybe when he's dead. Surely when he's dead it'll all be over.

And Robert has another impulse. No. Not an impulse.

More considered than that. When his father is dead, what is unfinished will not die with him, it will simply stay unfinished. Robert thinks: *Tell him. Whatever the outcome. Go to him. Tomorrow. Tell him about the man in the dark. And tell him the truth. Tell him you can't get over it.*

~

Jimmy despises napping in the daytime. It is, for him, a lying down to a small death. But after Linda has made her announcement and made her suggestion and they have fallen silent, and after she has risen and bent to him and tried to kiss him lightly on lips that he will not lift to her, and after she has, instead, pecked him on the forehead and gone out of the break room and stopped at Jimmy's worktable and put on her quilted coat and knit cap, and after she has closed the barn door behind her and, no doubt, gotten into her car and driven away to either Paul or Becca, Jimmy finds his eyes bloated with the wish to close. He lifts his feet and turns and stretches out on the sofa. Expecting sleep, he sees before him a vast expanse of meadowed snow, the tree line etched thinly at the far horizon, the sun low behind it, setting there he realizes, and he turns and turns and it is the same in all directions: He is alone; he is utterly alone. So he turns and turns and when he is once again facing the setting sun he can see something, far off, tiny still but recognizable as three figures against the snow. At first he is lifted by the sight of them, but then he knows who they are and he cannot imagine how they have come to be here, in this landscape of snow, in his Canada, but here they are, his mother and his father and his brother, and they're coming this way. He thrashes. He sits up.

Mavis's face is before him, her brow furrowed, her gray gaze gone sad.

She waits in silence as he squeezes his eyes shut briefly, clamps his two temples between thumb and fingers, waits for the wooziness of daytime sleep to fade. Finally he lifts his face again, looks at her.

'Are you okay?' she asks.

'Just the effects of the nap.'

'I mean otherwise,' she says.

Her manner with him over the past weeks, particularly when Linda was the seemingly routine subject between them, finally clarifies itself. 'You knew,' he says.

She looks at him for a few beats, filling in the unspoken words between them. 'Only guessed,' she says.

'This won't affect any of you,' he says.

'I'm not worried about that.'

'I'm all right,' he says.

She nods, minutely, as if she's doubtful.

'It's an understanding,' he says.

'I don't mean to intrude,' she says.

'Thanks.'

They stare quietly at each other for a moment.

Then he asks, 'How was the stew?'

She flickers a smile. 'I brought you some.'

'Good,' he says. 'I'll have enough for two nights.'

She puts her hand on his shoulder, squeezes it gently, and she goes.

He rises.

He crosses to the coffeepot, pours a cup, drinks. It's no longer fresh. At the pay phone in Buffalo in July of 1968, after the click of disconnection from his father, Jimmy hung up the receiver, turned his back on the phone, and he looked at his watch. He didn't need to know the time to know it was time to go. In the break room Jimmy does not consciously remember that gesture, but it and the reflex that animated it, that propelled him to the life he's lived all the years since, is the same now: He looks at his watch. It is five minutes to one. He can be on Baldwin Street in three hours. Before the shop closes and Heather goes home. It is time to go.

Less than three hours later, Jimmy steps into his shop, the entry door's retro brass bells jangling above him, the smell of mellowed-down leather filling him, two things that always give him a surge of pleasure, this space he has created, these things he has made. And the long drive has done him good. He quickly ceased thinking about Linda and instead revisited all of Heather's knowing looks and admiring words, compressing them into an underlying narrative that reassures him he's not about to make a fool of himself.

The shop is empty, including the checkout counter. He moves along the center aisle with a sudden and acute sense of Heather: In a place empty where he expected her to be, he misses her.

Then she appears in the doorway to the back room. She's wearing her sales-floor outfit, a jacket off the rack – today a lambskin bomber – over a black crewneck T-shirt. Black on black makes her dark eyes even darker, her skin even whiter. She brightens. His narrative falls apart. He will make a fool of himself.

She comes to him.

She stops just beyond reach. A bad sign.

'I didn't expect you,' she says.

All he has is small talk. 'Things seem slow, eh?' he says.

'Winter Wednesdays. I let Greta go home. She's working up a cold.'

'Good,' he says. He hears the ambiguity. He quickly adds, 'That you let her go.'

She smiles at the correction. Then she softens the smile at the edges and lifts her chin. An inquiry. A prompt.

Such things were part of the Highway 400 narrative. She is saying but she is not saying.

An insistent part of him wants simply to thank her vaguely and claim that he only dropped in to see how things are and he's meeting somebody down the street and has to leave.

So he tries to drag himself in the other direction by the improbable strategy of nodding at her chest. He means to indicate the bomber jacket. He says, 'You're modeling today.'

'I sold its mate this morning. The lady took one look and said, "I want what you're wearing."'

'On a Winter Wednesday to boot.' He knows he sounds lame.

But, generously, she laughs.

Overloaded with prompts, Jimmy is mystified why this should be so difficult for him. He's never been awkward approaching a woman. And he offers himself an explanation: *It's too important, is why. This is different.*

'You look beautiful,' he says.

Heather soughs, as if she's been holding her breath. She gathers herself and says softly, 'Thank you.'

And he finds himself needing to explain. To her. To himself. 'You've admired how my spirit seems free,' he says.

He has more words but the effort of just these makes him pause.

She fills the pause, again softly: 'Yes.'

'Free by ideology,' he says. 'Free by protocol. Free by...' He searches for a word now. '... devaluing it,' he says. '*Thus.* Thus it's devalued, the freedom.'

He stops. Tries to clear his head.

'I'm having trouble,' he says. 'Putting it into words.'

'Do you have to?' she says.

Another invitation. He won't ignore it, but he trusts it will stay valid for a few more moments. 'I have to,' he says. 'I think I understand. I was free because what my wife and I decided we were free to have wasn't worth all that much.'

He finds that Heather has moved closer to him.

They are in each other's arms.

And in the room above his shop Jimmy lies on his side, the fern frost on the window jaundiced by street-light, Heather spooned into him, her arm draped around his chest. He closes his eyes, discerns the soft touch of her nipples just beneath his shoulder blades.

He and Heather are quilted over, the room still cold. He'll have her call someone to look at the furnace.

It seems to have been such a long long while since he had that thought yesterday. The flex of time.

And he thinks of dark matter, dark energy. How astrophysicists now understand that all visible matter – from the galaxies to our bodies to the strands of our DNA – makes up only a tiny percentage of the mass of the universe. How all of the rest of the matter and energy – unobservable, unrecordable, the dark 95 percent – somehow resides in the spaces formerly thought to be empty. How quantum physicists are beginning to theorize the existence of parallel worlds to explain the bizarre mechanics of matter in its smallest particles. How, as well, it's known that our bodies are made up of atoms, electrons orbiting nuclei, with empty space in between, that our bodies themselves are mostly empty space. And so if dark matter and dark energy exist in the empty space between the stars, why should they not exist inside our very bodies? Are we not ourselves mostly dark matter and dark energy? And what if that's where those parallel worlds reside?

Linda was wrong. Being with Heather won't stop me thinking about what's next. Linda was stupidly wrong: It's not worry. For millennia we've all been thinking there's a place for us other than the one we're in, this savage place where we fight each other, consume each other. This place we must escape. From the sun to the moon to the earth, from Heather's nipples to my shoulder blades, from her atoms to mine. In all the empty space within and between, there is consciousness, there is existence. Impervious to war and betrayal and hardness of heart. It's the place we all will run to.

'Are you awake?' Heather whispers.

'I am,' Jimmy says.

'What are you thinking?'

Only in his wish to answer her does he realize: 'How it was I came to Canada.'

Heather tightens her arm around his chest. 'I can't hold you close enough,' she says.

~

The next morning Heather and Jimmy rise late, her daughter having spent the night with the grandmother, who is accustomed to sending the girl off to school. They have to rush to get ready to open the shop on time, tussling for first use of the bathroom basin, pausing to laugh at feeling like a couple already. Robert and Darla rise in their usual manner, having gone to sleep in their usual manner, Robert distracted, this time by his intention to speak to his father, and Darla sublimating with Bach. She is to go for her run and drive to the hospital on her own in the late morning. Robert will head up earlier, though after Darla has left the house he lingers for another bean-grinding and brewing and a second slow sipping of Ethiopian coffee, in his reading chair facing his oak. Peggy sleeps late in her one-bedroom assisted living apartment at Longleaf Village, exhausted by her husband's pain, sorry the twin bed next to her is empty, dreading when it will not be. Bob is up early from his bunk bed at the Mercy Mild Shelter. He's happy that North Florida is behaving in the way it often suddenly can, throwing off the cold, warming the morning. He makes his way to the woods near Munson Slough, where he will spend a couple of hours dry-firing his Glock, getting back his trigger control.

And a physical therapist at Archbold Memorial named Tammy, a former softball star at the University of Georgia, uncovers William with encouraging chatter about how tough he looks and how he's going to muscle through this little episode. She unwraps his compression leggings and she straps a thick cloth belt around him, and she starts to get him up, get him vertical, get him on his feet with her help, just for a little bit, to prime his body to heal, to engage him in staying alive, to get him used to the cost. This is her specialty. She is a champ at this.

William is grumpy but compliant. He might think this is a good time in history to die, given what the world has come to, but he's too pissed about it to succumb. So he is vertical now. And he feels something begin in the middle of the calf of his right leg. A pulling loose. Like an adhesive bandage that's been on for too long being stripped off, beginning there in his calf and running now upward, behind his knee, and then curving to the inside of his thigh. It's a good feeling. A letting go. But the rushing changes, as if the bandage finishes breaking away and something emerges from beneath it, a goddamn night crawler burrowing its way past his broken hip and up his spine, and William thinks, *What the hell is that doing inside me?* but it moves too fast for a worm way too fast and the blood clot hits his heart and the engine seizes *in Papa's Ford Runabout pickup, which is as old as me, and maybe this is when it finally dies, on this dirt road along Bayou Bernard and Papa has stripped off his shirt and has the hood up and he's cussing like Mama won't stand for, and now we're sitting beside the bayou letting the Ford cool off and Papa cool off, and I'm a little behind him and sneaking peeks as usual at the slash of a scar below his left shoulder blade, and I been warned by Mama since I was toddling not to ask him, since the scar was from the Big War and full of bad memories, but today I do ask and he turns on me and his hands come up but he doesn't hit me, he just gets quiet and he gets sad and he takes me by the shirt and pushes me over backward, but not hard not to hurt me just to tell me to shut up, and he's weeping like a baby with me at the train station and I'm in my uniform and there's another Big War, and as I put my duffel over my shoulder it hits me like a rifle shot in the brain what it is that he's been carrying around all this time, the fact that his battle scar is in his back, it's in his goddamn back, he turned his back, and so I turn my back on him, I turn my own goddamn back and I run away from this man and I'm going up the stairs in a house in Mainz, and it's just mop-up, we haven't yet found a living soul on this whole block, it's only us Patton boys tidying up with the Third Army that's about to cross the Rhine, and I'm checking the second floor, just for procedure's sake, and I'm at the top of the stairs and there's a doorway to my left and I step into it and across the room the window is bright behind him and he's sitting tall there and I can't see his face, I can't read his face for the shadow but his Schmeisser is crosswise in his lap and his hands are down but I don't check where they are I just know they're down but I don't check if his shooting hand is near the grip and it's all fast and my M1 is up and I'm squeezing and squeezing and the Kraut's chest blows open and he flies back and he's dead, and then I notice some little thing, no I don't, not then, I just see it but I don't really notice it, not then while I'm rushing inside over killing the enemy, rushing sweetly at that moment, sweetly like happens in a war, and it's only years later, when my sons are about ten, about the age I was myself in the dying Ford, and it's hot summer in the Ninth Ward and the afternoon thunderstorm has just passed and my boys take off their shoes to run barefoot in the wet grass, it's then that I really notice the German soldier's boots, which are sitting there beside him, the two boots straightened up side by side and his socks draped over them, his feet hurt, this guy, his feet hurt and he took off his shoes and socks so whatever is going to happen to him on this day at least his feet won't hurt him so bad, and I turn away from my sons so there's no chance they'll glance back at me and see my eyes filling with tears, and not a week goes by for the rest of my years that I don't think about that man and I squeeze the trigger and I squeeze and there is no rushing in me, no fucking sweet thing, my own chest cracks open and my heart seizes, and I come up the stairs and I step into the doorway and I see him sitting there and I notice his boots, and I take my hand off the trigger, I don't squeeze the trigger, and the light behind him gets brighter but the shadow on his face fades away, and we look each other in the eyes, and it's just two fellas in a sunny room*

And William Quinlan is dead.

~

When the phone rings in the foyer, Robert is still sitting in his reading chair, his coffee mug empty for a while now. He's not actively dreading his father. He's not wavering in his intention to tell him. He's just inert. Intending to overcome that. The dread driven deep. The wavering converted to dozy distraction: wondering if this lot of coffee beans is depleted yet at the roaster; watching the flash of cardinals beyond the veranda; thinking the room too warm and suspecting the weather has changed overnight. It takes a second ring of the phone to make him rise, and still there is no urgency in him, no sense of dread. Just the phone ringing.

Doctor Tyler himself. Very sorry. A saddle embolism is not uncommon in spite of doing everything possible. Death certificate signed. In the hospital mortuary awaiting instructions. Have you done this before? Do you have a funeral home?

'No,' Robert is finally saying, 'I'll have to see about one.'

'Not a problem. Call here and tell us when you decide. The home will take care of everything from this point on.'

'All right,' Robert says.

'I'm very sorry,' Doctor Tyler says.

'Yes,' Robert says. 'Thank you.'

'He didn't suffer.'

'That's good.'

And the conversation is over.

Robert puts the phone down.

168

He finds himself inert again.

He does not miss his father.

But something got misplaced.

He looks around him. 'Darla?' he calls.

No answer. Again, louder: 'Darla?'

Nothing. She's not back. She sometimes gets inspired and runs a long time. He understands that. She has to go up to the hospital afterward and she wants to run thoroughly first.

No.

She won't have to go to the hospital.

There's a beeping. Distant. But nearby.

He looks. It's the cordless phone. He's forgotten to push the off button. He picks up the phone. He pushes the button. He puts it down.

He drifts back into the living room, looks at the French doors, moves to them, opens them, steps into a morning that feels almost warm.

He looks to the live oak standing massively before and above him. He walks to it, turns his back to it, and sits heavily down in the crotch of two roots. He presses against his tree even as his limbs feel their tone fading. They waver, and he wills his legs to stretch flat and he lets his arms fall to his sides.

The oak's trunk is rough, touching him hard in the back in long, uprunning ridges. He is glad for its hardness against him and he is glad to smell the sudden Florida warmth in the air. He is glad he is in his own country now and did not die. But he aches. He aches for the dead. For one man he did not know at all. For one man he knows too well.

He sits like this until he hears Darla calling for him from inside the house.

'Out here.' He does not move.

169

She appears in the open French door, sweating in her running clothes, a towel around her neck. 'What is it?' she says.

'He's dead,' Robert says.

She steps to the edge of the veranda, but pauses.

She doesn't want to force him to stand by coming too near the tree. He seems propped there as if after a beating in a ring. 'Are you okay?'

He rouses himself, flails a little with his arms, drags at his legs.

She presents a palm. 'You don't have to...'

'I'm fine,' he says, making it to his feet.

She steps closer, ready to hold him but not initiating it, regretting her sweat.

He's not ready for the ritual of this. He holds still, looks down to the space between them.

The phone rings, a small sound from the foyer but it lifts Robert's eyes to hers.

He knows who it is, and from his look, she knows. Darla says, 'Would you like me to talk with her?'

He considers this.

The phone rings again.

'Thanks,' he says. 'But I better.'

He moves past her.

She remains.

Not just in the small of her back, the touch of his hand; not just in her chest, the press of his; but in her conscious memory now, his arms come around her in the darkness of their bedroom with both her parents laid out in a hospital morgue a thousand miles away, and he pulls her close. She should have done that for him just now, instantly, as he did it for her, not pausing in the doorway or on the veranda. But he surprised her, the tableau of him and the tree. She did not expect him to be stricken by the death of such a difficult man, a man who would no longer be able to disappoint him. She'd needed a few moments to get over her surprise. Then the phone intervened.

Darla needs to be close to him now.

She turns, steps through the French doors, crosses the living room toward his voice in the foyer: 'Of course, Mom... Of course... Try to be calm till I'm with you... Say a prayer. Say a rosary.'

Darla hears these last few words trying to stick in his throat. She stops before she becomes visible in the living room doorway.

'Soon,' he says. 'Yes.'

He listens. He says, 'Of course. Very safe.'

Moments after this she hears the phone clack into its cradle. She steps into the foyer and he turns to her. She comes to him and puts her arms around him.

He draws her close, but only briefly, and he gently pulls away. 'I have to go up there now.'

'I'll follow as soon as I can,' she says.

An hour later Robert is sitting on his mother's sofa, his arm around her, her head on his shoulder as she weeps. Across the room the leg rest of his father's overstuffed brown velvet recliner remains raised from the last time he sat there, barely more than forty-eight hours ago. Whenever Peggy's tears swell into sobs, Robert murmurs *I know, I know* until they ebb. She has not reminisced or eulogized or criticized but has simply wept, which makes her grief seem to him unadulterated and keeps his arm around her, gentles his grip on her shoulder, which makes him long for his mother to show this part of her more often. He wonders if Darla's arrival, the expansion

171

of the audience, will put her back onstage.

He tightens his hold on her as if to prevent that.

As he does, Robert grows conscious again of the leg rest on the recliner. Whenever the old man figured he was returning soon, he kept it raised and worked his way out of the chair at an angle. He'd hobble then. He never spoke of them, but surely those knees hurt him. Most likely arthritis. They hurt him to push against the leg rest to lower it, though they probably hurt him as much climbing from the chair so awkwardly. But he'd gotten it into his head that this was the best way to do it, so by damn he'd do it this way forever. The last time he sat here he struggled to extend one leg off the chair and to drag his butt on the cushion till he could get the other leg over and then to drag some more to put both his feet flat on the floor and then he braced himself and he rose. He'd done this thousands of times and he thought he'd be right back. He was wrong. He'd be dead before he could do it again.

Robert finds his eyes filling with tears.

He does not feel as if they're for the man himself exactly. Maybe some. Maybe for the father Robert wished he'd been. But these tears seem mostly about knowing this small, commonplace thing. How his father got out of a chair. True to his character. Stubbornly. Hurting himself trying not to hurt himself. Someone Robert comprehends in this small but telling way has vanished from the world: That's what these incipient tears are about. And he raises his free arm, drags his wrist across his eyes, refuses to shed them.

He feels his mother's face turn upward toward his.

She will get this all wrong.

That pisses him off.

He abruptly drops his arm. He does not look at her. He says nothing.

He feels her face turn downward again.

Good.

Peggy Quinlan gently disengages her son's arm from around her, raises the handkerchief she's been fisting, and dabs at her eyes, wipes her nose.

She tucks the handkerchief into a pocket of her sweater. Robert is still not looking at her. Not looking at the chair either. His eyes have drifted to a Currier and Ives print of a sleigh in the foreground of a snowy countryside, its pair of horses in a synchronized trot, the sleigh holding a mother and father and two children. This print has hung on his parents' living room walls through his whole lifetime. Robert long ago stopped even seeing it. He sees it now. And he remembers that as a child he took the two children, bundled similarly, to be brothers. They are not. One is a girl.

'He loved you,' she says.

Damn.

Robert regards her. He wishes he could offer the reflex reassurance that has been so easy for the past half hour. Just one *I know* and she might refrain from making the case for William's love. In the absence of any overt avowals from the man, Robert made his own faulty case for that over the years. Those tears in the bar, for instance. And none of it carries weight anymore. Not after yesterday. He tells himself: *After yesterday I can't lie about this even to say those two words.*

But he considers the alternative.

She is brimming with bullshit reassurances.

'I know,' he says.

And he thinks: *Fuck me. I'm your son. So there's the lie we can agree to between us, so we can just go on.*

She lays her head on his shoulder again.

She does not resume crying. Robert feels her working up to more words, though this intervening silence makes him hopeful they won't be intended proofs of his father's love for him.

But before she speaks there's a knock at the door.

She rises and moves off.

Robert flexes the ache out of his mother-hugging arm, rolls the kink out of his shoulder. As his mother and his wife linger just inside the door to embrace and murmur, Robert rises from the sofa and steps to his father's recliner. He looks for a moment at the man's indent in the backrest and seat cushion. Then he lifts his foot and pushes the leg rest down till it snaps into place.

He cannot imagine how they will all get through the next several hours. But Darla squeezes Robert at the elbow and sits with Peggy on the sofa for a time, and soon enough things grow as much practical as mournful, seeing as William waits in the basement of Archbold. He needs a funeral home to carry him away and this leads to Peggy's entreaty that they bury him in Tallahassee so that when she joins him they will both be nearer to Robert and Darla. This leads them to a choice of a funeral home and a cemetery and then to details of a wake and a service and then to a locating of Peggy's desk copy of the will and of papers for insurance and Social Security and, in the process, the finding of a box of family photographs and the consequent reminiscences and criticisms cast as endearments and Peggy weeps some more and grows weary from weeping. Darla tucks her in for a late-afternoon nap while Robert wanders into the living room, weary himself. He stares at his father's recliner and sees no reason why he shouldn't sit there and put his feet up, but he finds no capacity to do so. And then Darla is beside him.

'Why don't you go on home,' she says softly.

She puts her head against his shoulder. The same spot that has been occupied for a long while already on this day.

She says, 'I suspect this is harder on you than you realize.' He puts his arm around her, squeezes her gently, and lets go.

'I'll work on her papers,' she says.

'Thanks,' he says.

'We need to make some calls.'

'Yes.'

'Shall I do them?'

'No. I'm fine.'

'Let's divide up the close ones,' she says.

Robert nods.

Darla suggests she call their daughter and Robert their son. He speaks what suddenly strikes him: 'We're getting to this late.'

'We needed some arrangements first so they could make plans.' Again she speaks softly.

She's being patient with him.

Robert takes Darla in his arms, kisses her on the top of the head.

She turns her head, lays it on his chest, and exhales deeply. She says, 'In his own way, I'm sure he loved you.'

He makes himself wait for a few moments before ending the embrace so she won't suspect anything is suddenly amiss. He thinks of something to say: 'I really appreciate what you're doing here.' And he goes out of the apartment and fumbles with the key in the door lock of his Mercedes.

On the Florida-Georgia Parkway he places a call to his son in Atlanta. Kevin's voice sounds cheery on the answering machine. Robert simply asks him to call back. He hangs up. He turns his headlights on in the thickening twilight. He decides to stop at the New Leaf Co-op for a quick dinner.

~

Bob sits at an outside table in front of the New Leaf, watching the sky darken. He won't let it sneak up on him this time, the dark. If it wants to come he will wait for it and he will own it. He is strong enough. Till a woman's voice. Rushing by Bob, a woman talking rapidly on a cellphone, a fluttering jabber beating outward like something you're planning to shoot, flushed from a plum thicket. Then she stops at the curb, invisible to him behind a support column on the arcade over the front of the co-op. She talks, she laughs, unseen. Laughs. Sapping him. Through a thin wall a woman's talk, a woman's laughter. Bob is fifteen. He is naked. Against this sound, from the past and from the present, he crosses his two arms before him at the wrists, pounds his chest once and again, hard, but the woman yammers on into her cellphone and Bob knows he can't just get up and step out beside her on the curb to deal with her, he has to let her be and take care of it in his own head, and so he sings, he grabs a few words from the first song that comes to him and he sings them over and over – *There's something happening here* – at first only inside his head but then they find their way into his mouth and into the chill of the dark, looping over and over *There's something happening here* and the voice of the woman at the curb before the New Leaf abruptly moves off and fades away. The words slide back

176

into Bob's head. He listens outward while they play, and he realizes they can stop and he stops them.

All around, the darkness has taken over but he didn't let it catch him off guard. He should go inside now. He has some coins. But he finds he cannot move. Somebody has turned the flame up inside the knot on his forehead. The pain has his full conscious attention, but inside him, coming upon him while he's distracted, like the night overtaking the day, he is still fifteen but he's not yet naked, it's earlier in the evening and he's staring at the flicker of the TV screen in the living room, and beyond the kitchen, at the far end of the single-wide, from behind the closed door of his parents' bedroom, their two voices are grappling fiercely and then they stop and all that's left is his mother weeping and now his father emerges and slams the door and Bob steels himself, waits for it all to turn against him. But his father stops in the kitchen, and beyond the thin wall his mother weeps on and Bob wants to go to her and try to help her stop, but his father is between him and the bedroom and so he stays where he is, keeping his eyes on the TV screen, seeing nothing. The refrigerator door opens and closes. A bottle cap hisses off and falls. And another.

And now Calvin looms over Bob. Bob keeps his eyes where they are. He braces himself. But the man simply stands there. Waiting. Bob looks up. *Here*, his father says. He's holding two Blue Labels and he extends one of them to him. His father's in that middle ground he sometimes can get into when he's buzzing with beer and not hard stuff. His mother's weeping has faded. Bob takes the beer, and as quick as that, he knows *this* is what he wants. His father sitting down in his chair nearby and the two of them drinking a beer together. It's happened a couple of times before, and this is what Bob wants.

And when their beers are done, his father rises and says, *It's time for you, boy.* Bob does not ask what that means. They go out of their trailer and the night has come on. It's July, a few days after the Fourth, which Calvin celebrated in places unknown. Then they're in his pickup running south on 119, and after a long while he actually talks. *It's still Independence Day for you, boy. You're with me and I can draw the day on out. Fourth of July is my Christmas and Thanksgiving and fucking Arbor Day all in one, 'cause of what I went through for this country. We still got some fireworks to shoot off, you and me. I went through shit for this country and you know what it was all for? Five days. Five fucking days by the seaside. The US Army can blow your mind. They put you in a jungle to kill and be killed and then by God they pluck you right out of there for five days and nights and they put you in a pretty little city right there in-country, right on the South China Sea, and it's like Jesus himself went down into Hell with His winnowing fork and nicked you out of there and put you in Heaven where you belong and you're walking down a street and it's not paved with gold, it's better than that, it's paved with pussy, in bars and in massage parlors, and this pussy isn't mama-san pussy, it's the real pretty ones, even though the day before, if you see girls like this in a village you're clearing, you can't trust to turn your back on them much less drop your pants. The day before, you might have to blow their pretty asses away. But now you go right on in for a massage and more, and you just fuck your brains out, you fuck your fears out, you fuck your goddamn blood-and-gore memories out, and you're doing it with the enemy – that's the thing – you're doing it with the prettiest little* Co Cong *in the whole shithole country.*

And Calvin Weber stops talking. He just drives. And what he does not say to his son, though it is the feeling he has just come to, unexpectedly, what he could not even shape into words in his own head is this: It has never been the same since. Not sex. Not intimacy of any kind. With a woman. With a buddy later, the two of you drinking and trying to laugh off the experience, trying to crude it down but failing and falling silent and sitting in that silence in a bar in Vung Tau, Vietnam, knowing the same thing, that being with a woman, being with a buddy, being with anyone, will never be as good as that again. And the price isn't worth it. Not for what you have to go through. Not for what you're left with.

But for Bob the next thing is his father whooping softly and pulling off the highway toward a crimson neon sign through the trees: **MASSAGE**. Calvin says, *See what we got now, right here in West Virginia? You'll finally be a man tonight, Private Weber.* Then Bob is with a woman and he's naked. And his father is in the next room. Even as Bob finds himself naked with a naked woman and finds himself ready for her, he can hear his father's voice through the thin wall. He can hear his father talking big and laughing big and he can hear the woman in there laughing with him. And Bob knows what's about to happen to himself will not be good. Knows nothing will ever be good.

And a figure is emerging from the dark in front of the New Leaf a tall and rangy figure and it's almost upon him and Bob knows all too well who it is and he might as well get this over with and his hand starts to move, though his reflexes aren't so quick anymore, his hand is moving toward the rightside pocket of his overcoat, moving too slow but moving for goddamn sure and he knows once it's there at least he's got his trigger control back, he can end this thing between him and the old man once and for all, but a voice comes from the figure *Hello Bob* and Bob knows the voice and he can make out the figure now and he recognizes this man and Bob's hand wants to keep on going anyway, wants to pay somebody back for something, but it comes to him that this isn't the right place or the right time or the right man, and he stops his hand, and it's the other Bob standing over him now, and Bob answers him: 'Hello, Bob.'

~

As Robert approaches the New Leaf in the early dark he does not immediately recognize the shapeless hulk sitting at a table near the door. Robert's old man is too much with him, though his overt thoughts have taken refuge in the trivial: how chilled he feels though the air is mild; how fragile his eyes have been this past year or so, with the lights inside the co-op seeming far brighter than they likely are. But as the hulk becomes a man and clarifies its face, Robert's recognition of him instantly evokes a recollection of Bob's parting question three days ago: *You know my old man?*

Perhaps this should make Robert keep on walking. Perhaps he should avoid Bob this time. But only his mind engages this option. His body veers at once toward the man of hard times, the man a decade too young for Vietnam, the man of responsibilities in Charleston, the man whose father can come sharply and unbidden to his mind. Robert stops before him and says, 'Hello, Bob.'

'Hello, Bob,' the man says.

Bob's bandaged forehead fully registers now on Robert. 'Are you all right?' he asks.

Bob pulls back tight at the chest, as if the question is out of line.

'Your head,' Robert says.

Bob loosens, humphs. 'My head. My head got assaulted by a mystery man with a shovel.'

'Damn. How'd it happen?'

'Not worth saying.'

'You got help?'

'With my head. Not with the son of a bitch.'

'You need anything for it?' Robert figures to buy him something for the pain.

'Revenge would be good,' Bob says.

He sounds serious. Robert hesitates, recognizing the need for caution in replying to this, though nothing comes to mind. He's saved by his cellphone ringing.

'Sorry,' he says to Bob, pulling the phone from his pocket and lofting it in explanation of his apology. He turns, paces a few feet away in the direction of the parking lot.

The cellphone screen says: Kevin Quinlan.

As often happens with grandfathers, William was warmer with his grandson than he'd ever been with his sons. As Robert is well aware. Kevin and the old man were close. Robert should have planned this out. How to say it.

The phone rings again. He answers. 'Kevin?'

'Dad. What's the news?'

How even to begin? Here at the end of this difficult day, it eludes Robert for a moment that Darla already talked to the kids, right after the accident. 'Your grandfather fell,' he says.

'Mom said. We've been Googling broken hips.'

It's going on three weeks since Kevin last spoke with Robert, normally a weekly Sunday tradition. His son has been busy with work, no doubt. Which is very good. As a boy more a Lego kid than a book kid, as a man Kevin saved his small architectural firm in the recession by guiding it into associated general contracting. Robert longs simply to ask him about that, about how his work is going, about how busy he must be. Robert knows he can't. And for what he *must* say, he's far from having *any* words, much less the right ones.

'Looks serious,' Kevin says.

'Yes.'

'Did the surgery go okay?'

'The surgery itself went fine.' Robert hesitates.

'Itself?'

Restless with his clumsiness, Robert rolls his shoulders, turns around. 'He's dead.'

Robert is now facing Bob but is unaware of him. Bob is quite aware of Robert. This abrupt announcement has rung clearly in the dark. Someone is dead.

Kevin is silent for a moment. And a moment more.

Robert turns around again, faces the parking lot. 'I'm sorry. Sorry for your loss. Sorry for just blurting it.'

'No,' Kevin says. 'It's okay. I know this must be hitting you hard. Harder than me. Your Pops.'

Now Robert goes silent.

'What happened?' Kevin asks.

'A blood clot, as I understand it. First time they stood him up, it went straight from his leg to his heart.'

'Jesus.'

More silence. Robert grows restless again, paces the edge of the sidewalk in front of the New Leaf.

Kevin says, 'How's Grandma?'

'Being Grandma.'

'Holding up then?'

'Holding up.'

Robert hears sounds on Kevin's end of the phone: a door

slam; sharp voices, recognizably his grandson and daughter-in-law.

'Excuse me,' Kevin says to Robert, and then, muffled, 'Jake. I'm talking. It's important.'

Jacob lately turned twenty. And yes, as grandfathers can be, Robert is unreservedly warm with him, though in this case he has nothing to make up for, as he has always been warm with his son as well. For most of Jake's life, however, the warmth has flowed mostly from a distance. For those years, Kevin and his family have lived a long day's drive away, which in practical terms has meant Sunday phone calls and four visits a year, diminishing in the past decade to two.

Kevin returns to Robert. 'Sorry,' he says.

'Jake is home?' After two years at a community college, he's been away on a construction job.

'Temporarily,' Kevin says in a voice fraught with something it isn't ready to get into.

In the following beat of silence Robert stops pacing.

He prefers to talk now about his grandson.

But Kevin says, 'When's the visitation?'

Robert's restlessness returns, propels him in the direction of Bob. 'Monday evening. The funeral's Tuesday.'

'Where?'

'Tallahassee.'

'I've got a crucial meeting Monday morning. We may have to come straight to see him.'

'Tillotson Funeral Home on Apalachee,' Robert says. Bob hears this too.

Robert becomes vaguely aware he's within earshot. He stops, turns away again as he adds, 'Anytime after six. There'll be food. Your grandmother wants it to feel like a real wake.'

'Granddad won't like that,' Kevin says, though Robert hears no irony in his voice, only sadness.

'No he won't.'

'I won't be telling funny anecdotes about him,' Kevin says.

'He'll appreciate that.' Robert hears his son puff at this, no doubt ready to weep. He thinks Kevin will want to do that privately; he'll want to keep the tears from his voice. So Robert says, 'Sorry to be abrupt but I have to go now. I love you. See you Monday.' And he ends the call.

Robert puffs too.

He stares sightlessly into the parking lot for a few moments, puts the phone in his pocket, remembers Bob, and turns back toward the man, half expecting him to be gone.

But Bob is there.

Robert approaches again, stops before him.

Bob raises his face. 'Someone's dead?' he says.

'My father,' Robert says.

Bob feels a rising in his brain like the first rise of gorge, a dizzying bloat, but he forces it down. Far down, without even identifying it.

'Have you eaten?' Robert asks.

'Not for a while. Not tonight.'

'I haven't either. Shall we?'

Sometimes when Bob's next meal is certain; sometimes when an Upstander acts natural around him, like this one is acting, with nothing even vaguely resembling *that look* going on in his face; sometimes when Bob has just struggled for a while with the way his life has gone and the poison that recently wanted to rise has been pushed back down; sometimes when any of these things happen but especially when they all happen at more or less the same time, Bob can find himself suddenly thinking straight like he used to and having acceptable words to speak and making a pretty good impression on somebody. This is one of those times.

Bob says, 'It's my turn to pick up the tab. But I'm afraid that'll make for slim pickings tonight.'

Robert is surprised at Bob's banter, but Robert's consequent smile contains no incredulity, no irony, no patronage. For Bob, his banter has carried a risk: Making an unexpected good impression on an Upstander can also provoke a version of *that look*. But the other Bob shows no trace of it, only a smile like he'd give anybody, and Bob is grateful for that.

'I've got it covered,' Robert says.

As Bob rises from his chair, something occurs to Robert. When the man is standing, Robert extends his hand. 'We never got past "Bob." I'm Bob Quinlan.'

'I'm Bob Weber.'

They shake on this.

So the two Bobs find their way to a corner table inside the New Leaf, well away from the handful of other diners, and they sit with beans and rice before both of them.

'I'm glad you made me think of this,' Robert says, nodding at his plate, though he chose it out of sympathetic deference to Bob's teeth. 'I used to love beans and rice.'

Bob has never loved it. 'When was that?' he asks.

'You'd think it'd be growing up in New Orleans. But my mother was more potatoes than beans. It was in the army. Basic training.'

He's army. Bob's straight thinking suffers a little blip. This man before him has already blurred, now and then, into Calvin.

Robert says, 'Of course in basic, you can fall in love with a tepid shower and dry socks and sharing a cigarette, though you don't even like to smoke.'

185

Bob is working hard now to keep straight. He's got a little litany for this from some counselor or other. *This is this; this isn't that. This is now; this isn't then. It seems the same but it's different.*

Okay.

He thinks he has a grasp on things and he can move on. But he hears himself lingering. 'So you were in the army?'

Robert nods. 'Fort Polk, Louisiana.'

Bob looks hard into Robert's face. This is not his old man. This is another guy. He's not even an Upstander but an actual stand-up guy. They're eating food together. They're talking straight. Bob can ask this thing. 'Did you go to war?'

Robert falters, briefly, but long enough for his voice to thicken and sadden and soften from the past twenty-four hours. 'I went to Vietnam,' Robert says.

And Bob, who still fears dark hints about unspeakable secrets, instead has just heard a tone in this voice he never expected, hears this other Bob clearly going: *Let's not make a big thing of it.* And going: *There may be guys who get fierce over this but it sure ain't me.* And going: *I'm just fucking sad about the whole fucking thing.*

Bob is fucking sad too. And Bob feels his mind straighten. He says, 'Your father died?'

The man hesitates again. Bob clutches up. Maybe he shouldn't have asked. And though he expected his own father to show up a few moments ago over Vietnam, it's now that Calvin steps into the room and strides this way. He stops just behind Bob's shoulder, and Bob is afraid this sad man before him will suddenly see Calvin and he'll go holy shit and he'll bolt. But instead the man says, 'He died this morning.'

Now it's Bob who goes holy shit. He thinks: *So what are you doing having beans and rice tonight with the likes of me?* But he asks, 'How?'

'A blood clot to the heart. He was in the hospital.' Calvin vanishes. *Fucking poof.*

'I don't trust hospitals,' Bob says.

'That's probably smart.'

For a time now, they eat their food in silence. Robert feels odd. Finally he has spoken of his service today, though spoken to a stranger, to a man of hard times, to a man who could not have known Vietnam directly. Though Robert has spoken of small things. But small things bind men at war as well, bind them just as certainly as they are bound by spilled blood. The man he has spoken to: Did he serve in another war perhaps? Unlikely. By the look of him, he was of the wrong generation for Afghanistan or for either Iraq, unless he was a lifer. Robert almost asks, but he doesn't.

The two men go on eating. And Robert goes on wondering about Bob. The way Bob's father came upon him a few days ago, Robert figures his neglected responsibilities in Charleston might have to do with his old man.

Robert works at his basic-training food for a few bites, trying to put all this aside. But he knows Bob is a man of suffering, of wrong choices, of lost chances. Also a man with limited options. Robert is keenly aware that no one's options to redeem a lost chance are more limited than his own. He does not quite think of it this way, he simply follows the impulse, but the effect is the same: To deal with your own problem, meddle with somebody else's.

Sensing, however, that the meddling needs tact, Robert begins, 'So you're from Charleston?'

'Yes.'

'Been gone a long time?'

'Years.'

'Any folks back there?'

That is a sore point for Bob right now. A sore point anytime. He shrugs.

'Your father still alive?' Robert asks.

Okay. Okay. This other Bob's own father died just this morning. Bob is still thinking straight enough to see that. But he wants to stay straight and the question is starting to drag him aside. He realizes time is passing. He realizes he's not saying anything. He touches his forehead, where the sizzle has resumed.

Robert finds himself ready to buy Bob a bus ticket. Send him back to Charleston to find his father. Advise him to use the bus trip to figure out everything he's got to say to the old man before it's too late. Even if it's *Fuck you*.

But Bob's still not talking. He's flailing in his head for things to think about other than what the other Bob and his dead father would have him think, and the oil drum fire in his forehead gives him something: Maybe on the next cold night he'll take a little walk to check out the groundskeeper's storage room at the Blood of the Lamb Full Gospel Church. Check to see who might have returned to the scene of the crime.

Robert senses the shift in Bob. He senses his mistake. Pressing about a father is wrong. The bus ticket is wrong. But the impulse to fund Bob suggests another plan. A way to actually help. 'Have you got a place to sleep tonight, Bob?' he asks.

Bob's reflexes on matters of food and shelter are strong. This question, in that tone of voice, from a stand-up guy, casts off, for the moment, both Calvin and revenge. 'No I don't, Bob,' he says.

'Can you make good use of a week in a motel?'

The answer to that, for Bob, can be a little complicated. But on balance, yes. 'Yes,' he says.

Instantly a practical problem presents itself to Robert. He hesitates, recognizes a likely expert sitting before him, but doesn't know how to ask. 'Do you have a place in mind...'

He gets this far and realizes he could have just made that the question. Unfortunately his tone kept the thing open-ended.

Bob understands. He finishes, declaratively: '... that will take a guy like me.' Before the other Bob can feel awkward for asking, Bob goes on, 'Sure. You know the Prince Murat Motel?'

Through this day, from his awakening to the revelation of his father's death to the hours with his mother to this unexpected dinner, Robert, unawares, has been winding tight inside. Now it all seems to snap loose and he nearly gasps with relief as his safely scholarly mind seizes on something familiar. 'I do,' he says, leaning toward Bob. 'It's my favorite business establishment in Tallahassee. Prince Achille Murat was a nephew of Napoleon Bonaparte and the son of the King of Naples. He was exiled with his family to Vienna after Napoleon's final defeat, and then he emigrated to Florida. By the age of twenty-four he was the mayor of Tallahassee. He was a Jacksonian Democrat, though he never really made much of a political career outside the area. He became a bosom pal of the young Ralph Waldo Emerson, who called Tallahassee in 1826 a "grotesque place," by the way. But Murat eventually was known mostly for his eccentricities.'

The first of these that comes to Robert's mind is Murat's reputation for washing his feet only after he wore out his shoes. Robert leaves this unspoken. He's beginning to hear himself.

Bob has no idea what Robert is talking about. Bob has even begun to wonder if Robert has troubles like his own.

After a moment of silence between them, Robert says, as if to explain his little lecture, 'I do know the Murat.'

Still silence.

'I teach history.'

'They'll let me in there,' Bob says.

'Then it's the Murat,' Robert says, and he says no more. What seemed to loosen in him is again wrung taut.

~

After Robert leaves his wife and mother on the day his father died, as the January late afternoon wanes into darkness and Darla works in the next room sorting through papers and arranging the wake, Peggy finds herself unable to sleep. She turns her face to the ribbon of parking lot light edging her window blind. She closes her eyes. And she is standing very still, trying not to sweat, not to swoon from all the cheap perfume – like hers – on all the bodies of all the girls as they wait – like her – along the platform of the inbound track, wait for the troop train, wait for the long wait to be over. Their men will return to them on this day. Bill will return. The rest of Peggy's life will begin. She is wearing her daisyprint sundress. Her arms are bare, and her hair falls to her shoulders in long curls and mounts high above her forehead in a pompadour. Little Bobby is elsewhere. He is up and running already, at thirteen months, always running, and talking as well, babbling an hour at a time to a framed photo of his father, he and the image sitting together in the center of the living room floor, the glass perpetually smudged with Bobby's fingerprints. He was conceived on Peggy and

Bill's wedding night, which was also their last night together. Bill has never seen his son. But he won't see him on this night either. The boy is at Mama's and Papa's, where the four of them have lived these two years. And Uncle Joe is happy to go on a bender for a few days with his buddies at the Industrial Canal so Peggy and Bill can have some time alone in Joe's shotgun on Constance Street. So they can make love for the second time.

Peggy opens her eyes. She has turned and is facing her husband's empty bed, barely visible in the dim room, as if this is the memory and the train platform is her life in the moment.

She closes her eyes again. Briefly she watches the splash of phosphenes there, the color of street-light. Then there is only bright New Orleans sunlight beyond the shade of the railroad shed. And now cries at the far end of the platform. Someone sees the train. The bodies around her begin to move, to surge. She holds still. He will find her. She has always known he will return and he will find her.

And she says to her nineteen-year-old self: *Oh, baby, don't get your hopes up. He's been off fighting a holy war against the legions of evil, an evil so pitiless that it would have one day crossed the ocean and come to our own front porch. He has seen things and done things that required a bravery beyond your imagining. You have been faithful to him. You have trusted in the noble cause he fought for and you must make him feel how proud you are. You must try to hold him close. But don't be surprised at the things you both have sacrificed. This night will be one of them. And the next. And the next. Try not to be disappointed in him.*

~

Later this same evening, Jimmy turns off Harrison Trail and into his Twelve Mile Bay property. He has returned to pack his bags. He will stay in Toronto till the future is arranged with Linda. Heather is beside him. She becomes abruptly quiet as they enter the half-mile approach to the house. In the city, when he told her he needed to come up here for his things and it was best to do it right away, she did not speak of the reason but she insisted on coming along. She stirs now, leans toward the lights they push before them.

'She won't be here,' Jimmy says, offering a hand.

He has read her correctly. She grasps his, holds on tight. They emerge from the pines. The house is lit by the moon.

There are no lights within. No car in the driveway. Heather lets go of his hand.

Barely through the front door, she brings the two of them to a stop.

'Sorry,' she says.

'Why?'

'Cold feet.'

'No need…'

'I know the place is yours too,' she says. 'But it feels like *her*.'

'Then you should wait. I have to go upstairs.'

She looks at him.

Outside it's January in Canada.

Jimmy nods to the nearby door. 'The parlor. You won't find much of her there.'

Heather steps before him, squares him at the shoulders, pulls him to her. They kiss.

'Soon,' he says.

And soon he descends the stairs with two large leather Pullmans. By the time he reaches the bottom, Heather appears in the parlor doorway. She has not turned on the light.

She steps from the room as Jimmy approaches. He puts the suitcases on the floor.

'What?' she says.

'I just want to kiss you once more. The last thing I do in this house tonight.'

Before they can move, the phone rings.

They both look toward the parlor door, then back to each other.

'Do you think it's her?' Heather says.

'No.'

'I want that kiss,' she says.

The phone rings again.

Jimmy starts to explain that it has an answering machine. That to do the kiss they will have to listen to whoever it is. But he does not have time even to shape the words. Apparently there is another message already on the machine because it kicks in now, after the second ring.

And a woman's voice begins to speak in the parlor. 'Hello, darling.'

Even before Heather can flinch, the voice says. 'It's your mother.'

Peggy pauses.

'Come on,' Jimmy says.

And Peggy says, 'Your father died this morning.'

She pauses again.

Jimmy picks up his suitcases.

Heather touches him on the arm. 'Wait, baby.' He explained his family to Heather last night, in the long rush of shared backstories between them.

Peggy says, 'I know your feelings about him.'

She hesitates once more.

'At least listen,' Heather says.

'I don't blame you,' Peggy says. 'I'm free to say that now. I don't blame you at all. For anything. You had to deal with his feelings about you.'

Jimmy sets the bags down.

'They weren't *my* feelings. You have always been my son, who I love. You always will be. But I was married to your father, who I loved. I was his wife.'

Peggy begins to weep.

Her tears are for the man she loved, for his vanishing from this earth and from her life, for that loss. They are also in release – they are even in relief – at his vanishing from her life, for that loss. They are in guilt for that relief. The tears are also for the love of him, for the thrill that faded but never vanished at his unexpected smile and at the trailing of his fingertips along her neck whenever he passed unexpectedly behind her, though she always feigned a leap of ticklish discomfort, knowing that was necessary to induce him to continue the gesture through the years. The tears are for that necessity too. And the tears are from the belief that there is a next life as the Holy Catholic Church describes it and that he won't do so well in that regard. They are also for herself, for having to lie and manipulate to maintain the coherence and happiness of the family; for having to do these venial sins on so many occasions that she has consequently neglected to sufficiently acknowledge them, much less reconcile them, in the sacrament of confession; that she will not do so well herself, therefore, in the next life. The tears are for the possibility that in the place where those sins must be dealt with, she will find herself once again wed to William Quinlan, and the struggle will resume in much the same way. And the tears are for Jimmy as well. So he can understand that things have changed. That he can come home. That he has always been her son, whom she loves. Because she does truly love him. Which is to say, in part, that her happiness is not fully possible without his being happy, though she cannot rest assured he is happy unless it is in a way she herself can recognize. And manage. So as she weeps, she does not hang up. She does not take the phone away from her mouth. And she takes care to weep loudly enough that the phone message will not cut off.

Heather is moved by her tears. 'Can't you speak to her?' she says.

'No,' Jimmy says. Though he recognizes how drastically things have changed in the past thirty-six hours. How in this chosen country of his, a vast and leveling snow has fallen over his convictions about family, about connectedness. He awoke to that yesterday. He dreamt of it and he woke to it. Convictions constructed and refined again over five decades have been overwhelmed as if overnight. And a new conviction, seemingly as strong, has bloomed over the same night: his love for this woman before him who was not even born when he exiled himself from the United States. He has either been something of a self-delusional fool through most of his life or he has suddenly become a fool of an old man; or both; or neither.

Heather says, 'So many of her generation were loyal wives before everything else.'

Jimmy thinks: *So many of mine accept instant love. With no exclusions, age included.*

He wants to hold Heather close.

Peggy's tears are snubbing to a stop.

195

Jimmy opens his arms and Heather falls into them.

Peggy says, 'I'm sorry. I'm so sorry. This is a difficult time. But if some good can come of this. If I could see you. Wouldn't it be a closure for you as well? For us all.'

She pauses.

'Whatever you decide, my darling,' Heather says. Jimmy does not move.

'Just in case,' Peggy says. 'Tillotson's Funeral Home in Tallahassee. The wake begins at six Monday evening. The funeral's at ten on Tuesday morning. Please think about it.'

She pauses one last time.

Jimmy waits for more drama from his mother. More tears. Effusive avowals of love, in spite of her sticking by the man who rejected Jimmy to his dying day. But instead she says, 'Let's put him in the ground, my son. Together. We both need that.'

And she hangs up.

~

Peggy has made her phone call to Jimmy from the kitchen, with Darla sitting at the dining table beneath the pass-through. She'd emerged from the bedroom a few minutes before, after sleeping for several hours.

'I'm glad you could rest,' Darla said.

'I feel clearer about things,' Peggy said.

'I ordered Chinese while you were sleeping. Plenty of it. Can I warm some for you?'

'No, honey. I'm fine.'

'Tea?'

'I have a call to make before anything,' Peggy said. The second phone was in the bedroom from which she'd just emerged, but she moved past Darla and into the kitchen.

Darla handled the papers in front of her but did not see a thing. Naturally she listened. Till Peggy suggested to her long-lost son that they put William in the ground together and hung up.

Darla sets the papers down. No faking. She waits.

A cabinet door opens. Pots clatter. The door closes. Water runs. A pot lands on a metal stove burner. 'I've changed my mind about tea,' Peggy says. 'You want some?'

'Thanks,' Darla says. 'Yes.'

A few minutes later Peggy emerges with a tea service on a tray and she leads Darla to the couch, putting the tray before them on the coffee table.

In this quotidian matter they are equally imprinted by the old school of female propriety, so they hold both saucer and cup to eliminate the unseemly stretch to the coffee table. They sip and sip again in silence.

Darla has never felt particularly close to Peggy. She has witnessed the woman's poses and dramas – experienced them, indeed, as lies and manipulations – for as long as they've known each other. But Peggy's words to Jimmy and her clear intention for Darla to overhear them and now simply her silence over tea somehow don't feel like manipulations. This feels like a different Peggy.

So Darla puts her cup and saucer on the coffee table, and she says, 'Why did you let me hear that conversation?'

As the woman's face turns to her, Darla still expects the old Peggy. A look of faux surprise perhaps. *Did I? I'm so stricken I wasn't even thinking.*

Instead, Peggy offers Darla a quick but restrained smile. 'I wanted to share my clarity with you,' she says.

Darla's surprise is genuine. She masks it, and says nothing.

Peggy stretches to the coffee table, puts down her own cup and saucer, and sits back. She lays her hands side by side on her lap, as if this revelation was expected and what follows has been thought out.

She says, 'I hope I didn't sound harsh. I loved Bill. I'm going to cry over him again and again in the coming weeks. Please don't doubt the sincerity of those tears. But Jimmy needed to hear this other part of it.'

'I understand,' Darla says.

'Men have their ways,' Peggy says. 'How they communicate with each other. How they bond. My husband and yours, for instance. Their father-and-son bond was so strong. But after all, they both went to war. Is this why men make wars, do you suppose? To share something like that? Is it the only way they can truly feel close to each other?'

Peggy pauses, as if she wants Darla's opinion on this. Darla sees her Confederate men sitting around the barbershop through a long, hot summer afternoon, getting drunk on Old Forester and war stories, as their women sit in a parlor, sipping blueberry shrub and writing their impassioned prose.

But before Darla can say *Yes, you may be right*, Peggy says, 'Jimmy never had that. As a man, he had to know instinctively what he was giving up when he went to Canada. That may have been the hardest thing about what he did. I feel free now to fully respect him. For his courage to walk away from what sons usually want.'

This all strikes Darla as sincere. She covers one of Peggy's hands with her own.

Peggy looks Darla in the eyes, holds the gaze quietly. Then she says, 'I feel like I've always been held back from you as well. You're my daughter. Truly you are.'

Even as the woman invokes a newly liberated self, a frank and direct self, Darla hears this as the old Peggy, hears a lie crafted to serve a false image of the family. A newly revised, freshly reconstructed image, sans patriarch. But then she thinks *No*. Peggy's eyes do not waver in the following silence. The woman may well feel this way about her. But to Darla, Peggy has never felt like a mother. Not even close. And now Peggy's unwavering eyes themselves – the very sincerity of them, if sincere they be – seem like a mode of manipulation. These eyes expect Darla to proclaim a corresponding daughterly feeling about her. Even if it's a lie.

Darla does find this to say about her daughterhood: 'I intend to be a good one.' Not that this isn't also more or less a lie, knowing, as she does, Peggy's standards for a good daughter.

Peggy turns her hand to Darla's, palm to palm, meshes their fingers. She chuckles. A willed chuckle, brittle with rue. And she says, 'Why did God choose to surround me with men all my life? Gracious me. I would have been such a good mother to a daughter.' She lets that sit between them for a moment. Then she gently squeezes their entwined hands and says, 'I feel ever so close to you, my dear.'

Darla has exerted her own will to keep from imagining a lifetime as Peggy's actual daughter. And she doesn't believe this climactic declaration for a moment. But she accepts it with her own little squeeze.

Peggy doesn't need belief, doesn't even try to assess that. Acceptance of her assertion is all she seeks. But she does hear the plunk of one more venial sin dropping into her bucket. *Ah well*, she thinks. *It can't be helped.*

~

When Darla finds Robert, he is sitting in his office, in his desk chair, before his computer showing an Apple icon doing an endless Pong bounce. After calling for him from the foyer and hearing his answer from up here, she has approached quietly. His door was open. Before he knows she's there, she stands for a long moment, feeling tender about the back of his head, his overcast-gray hair going shaggy at the collar.

Finally, she says, 'Hey.'

He looks over his shoulder, turns a little in his swivel chair. 'Hey. How is she?'

Darla crosses to him.

He stays seated.

'She's doing remarkably well,' she says.

'Good.'

She nods at the screen saver. 'You've been like this for a while.'

He turns back to the bounce of the bitten apple, as if to confirm what she's said. 'It's been a long day.'

He stares for a few more moments.

'I'm so sorry,' she says.

She lays her hand on his shoulder.

'Thanks,' he says.

He doesn't move.

'Better to sleep in bed,' she says. 'With your eyes closed.'

He rises.

They say little else until they are beside each other beneath the covers.

No Kindle.

No iPod.

Darla's lingering tenderness for Robert stops the grating in her, leads her quickly to the cusp of sleep. As her longing drifts into vagueness on its way to unconsciousness, it offers a final, spoken 'If there's anything I can do' even as she sees her own dead father's face pause over his lifted soup spoon, his vast and shaggy brows rising, and he says, *You will grow old simply canvassing for Democrats and bloviating at dinner parties, doing far less for the world than the manufacture of a fine sausage*, and she remains mute before him, mute but eloquent on the red fields of sausage, a woman fair and faithful, and Robert, his head shaved into whitewalls, takes her in his arms for the first time and there are so many things she does not know about him, so many things she need not know in order to love him.

'You've already done it,' Robert says, in answer to her sleepy-voiced offer. 'Thank you.' And he turns onto his side, away from his wife, falling toward sleep himself, and the homeless man sits across the table and he asks, *Did you go to war*, and Robert answers, *I went to Vietnam*, and the man says, *Show me your scars*, and Robert raises his hand to his forehead and he finds a bandage there and he works his fingertips under its edge and he rips it away.

~

The handouts bite Bob on the ass. That and the Murat being closed for refurbishing into a Budgetel. The other Vietnam vet had to put him in The Sojourner, near the bus station, a sizable step down from the Murat, it being the only other place that would take him. Which might've been okay, for the sake of warmth and a sure bed, except for the handouts. Only yesterday Bob acquired new blood-of-the-lamb clothes from skin outward and a full-gospel shower and even a coating of goddamn talcum powder, so after he walks into this room and hangs up his Goodwill coat and sweater on the clothes rack and places his Glock on the nightstand and stacks the pillows for his head and takes off his shoes and lies down beside the pistol and looks up at the ceiling, Bob discovers that the shower and the clothes and the talcum have separated him from his own stink sufficiently so he can smell the stink of the motel – the musty smell of roaches and air conditioner mold in the air, and a couple decades of cigarette smoke and spilled food and spilled spunk and women smells in the carpet and drapes and bedspreads – and all this puts him in another motel room and he's sixteen years old and he's traveling with his father because his mother has had enough, which she's had a couple of times already, and she's gone off to Wheeling to see her sister for an indefinite period and Calvin has decided he and Private Weber need to get out of town, need to go hunting up in the mountains, and on the way they find this cheap motel room, but it's got one beat-up luxury, a television, and Calvin makes the mistake of turning it on. A big mistake, because it's April 30, 1975. The picture flickers and flips into focus just in time for Harry Reasoner to say, *The Viet Cong flag is flying over the Presidential Palace in Saigon today just a few hours after the South Vietnamese government announced its unconditional surrender.* And Calvin jumps up from where he's sitting on the foot of the bed and he says, just once, real low: *Motherfuck.* After that he's just pacing and glancing at the screen and not making a sound, which backs Bob up against the headboard and tucks him tight and scares the shit out of him more than if his old man was raging full-voiced, because once more it's all about the things he's not saying, the things he knows that men have to face down, and Bob understands that it's got to do with killing and being killed and your buddies being killed, of course, but it's not that simple and maybe what makes it complicated *can't* be said, *has* to stay a secret, so it's forever a black hole you carry in the center of you, swallowing everything, not just the killing and the being killed but the living on, swallowing your whole fucking life as well, it's about voices and laughter through a wall when you damn well know there's nothing to laugh about and there are no words to say, and so the old man is pacing back and forth saying nothing while on the TV Americans in civvies and Vietnamese with their women and children are crowding into buses and then running to helicopters and then a door gunner on a chopper is looking down on the roofs of Saigon and then it's roofs along a beach and then it's the sea and a voice on the TV is saying, *The helicopter passed over small fleets of boats leaving the coastal city of Vung Tau* and Calvin stops pacing abruptly at this and whirls to the screen and then he backs away from it and now he's across the room and he's got his Winchester 70 and he squares around to the TV and it's nighttime on the screen and a tall man in a suit and sunglasses with his hair flying shakes hands with admirals in ball caps and the voice is saying it's Ambassador Graham Martin stepping from a Marine helicopter onto the deck of the command ship *Blue Ridge* and he's closing the final chapter on America in Vietnam and Calvin works the bolt on his Winchester, chambering a round, and the voice from the TV says, *When this correspondent asked what his feelings were, Martin would only say that he was hungry,* and Calvin whips the rifle up on his shoulder and Bob turns his face away and the room explodes. And how long does he go on after that, the old man? A little over two years. Quieter than ever, even when drunk. So quiet that Bob's mother, who's come back, seems almost happy. So quiet that Bob feels it's okay to slip out one night and hit the road and end up in Texas for day labor and landscaping and restaurant work, okay to be a West Virginia wetback. And one night the old man himself slips out. He heads into the pines behind the trailer park and chambers a round in his Winchester and sticks the muzzle in his mouth and blows off the back of his head and all his secrets with it.

~

Framed tastefully in brick and Portland pilasters, Tillotson Funeral Home's floodlit marquee beacons into the evening dark:

William Quinlan
Husband, Father, Veteran
Visitation 6 to 9 PM

Two hundred feet away, up the landscaped parking lot, Tillotson's wide, double-winged, hip-roofed Georgian house is similarly lit. In the front foyer a grandfather clock begins to strike six.

As it does: In the visitation extension behind the main house, Peggy is alone at last. She stands before the buffet table, the caterers for casseroles and cold cuts just departed through the rear porte cochere, and her church-lady friends busy cleaning up out of sight in the Tillotson kitchen. They have chatteringly helped her with the Irish stew and the Irish potato soup, which steam now in their own special row of food warmers. Peggy thanks Mary the Holy Mother of God for this moment of quiet. Robert and Darla turn in at the marquee. Darla thinks of those very women – Peggy and her friends from church – and that very row of food warmers, with Peggy putting on her

birthname-is-Pegeen persona to make Irish food; and she thinks
how much Peggy wanted her to be part of that project, the two
of them bonding in the Quinlan family's reconfiguration, with
the church ladies as witness; and Darla thinks how she should
probably feel guilty at having declined Peggy's invitation but
how, in fact, she does not. Not in the least. Robert focuses his
thoughts on the Georgian house itself, built in 1922 by Horace
Naylor in the Great Florida Land Boom, lost by Horace Naylor
in 1926 in the Great Florida Land Bust, restored for the benefit
of the dead and their kin by Howard Tillotson in 1934, and
repeatedly expanded and modernized by two generations of
Tillotsons to follow. Robert is, of course, a historian. And he
happens to live in the middle of a city that sits in the middle of
many of his interests. But even as he sees the personal excesses
of the house's speculator builder in the half dozen two-story
Corinthian front columns, Robert recognizes that his mind
is simply trying to avoid his father's face as it waits for him in
an open casket inside. A mile away, heading east on Apalachee
Parkway, Jimmy is driving a rented Impala to the funeral home
from a room in the downtown DoubleTree. Heather is beside
him. Just before stepping out of their hotel room, Jimmy stopped
Heather and suggested they simply close the door, have an ironic
night of sex and HBO, and then go back to Canada; and Heather
reminded Jimmy of the conclusion they'd struggled to together
in Toronto, that he's seeking closure not renewal and if things go
badly they can escape at any time. Jimmy knows that conclusion
was grossly oversimplified, but he can't begin to say what the
full truth is, except that even though it brought him here, it is
now urging him to turn around and go home. They have been
silent in the car. Heather lays her hand on Jimmy's thigh. He
puts his hand on top of hers. And they pass Bob, a dark and

bundled figure striding along the sidewalk, also heading east, silhouetted against the neon of a liquor store. Sometime in the deep predawn dark of this morning Tallahassee turned cold, and it's been cold all day long, and it is cold tonight, and Bob has a score to settle. So he pushes his aching knees and he accepts the radiating pain from knee to back to mouth, his remaining teeth throbbing with each step. He accepts this pain on the way to the Blood of the Lamb Full Gospel Church, accepts it because he wants to be waiting in the groundskeeper's storage room when the nameless faceless coward returns. Bob has something more effective than a garden tool for him. Bob touches just below and to the side of his heart, touches his coat where, inside, his Glock waits.

Robert and Darla step between the center columns, past Cracker Barrel rockers deployed along the portico right and left, through the front doors, and into the hushed, condoling greeting of two black-suited Tillotsons tanned like winter corpses. One of them breaks off and leads Robert and Darla across the welcome foyer, past a spiral staircase, through a doorway, and into the visitation room foyer. Here they cross a dense Oriental rug toward an open double-wide doorway as William Quinlan floats brightly, unsettlingly out of the dark at Jimmy, who averts his eyes. He steadies himself in the empty lane ahead of him and then glances up the long, dim expanse of parking lot to the funeral home. There seem to be very few cars. He does not pull in but accelerates past.

'We're too early,' he says. 'I don't want to be the center of attention.'

'That'll be hard to avoid,' Heather says.

'Not in a crowd.'

'So we'll take a little drive,' she says.

They rush on along the parkway as the accompanying Tillotson discreetly falls away and Robert and Darla step through the doors of the visitation room. They stop. Robert scans the place. It's large and could be made larger. To the right, an accordion wall creates a doorway into a somewhat smaller, separated space, where trays of cold cuts and sides wait on a table whose other end, out of sight from Robert's angle of vision, holds the Irish food before the tranquil-at-last gaze of Pegeen Quinlan. Informal settings of chairs and divans are arrayed all about, most of them facing to the left, where Robert has so far declined to look, though Darla's head is already turned that way. The chairs and divans are empty but for two elderly women in hats on a chesterfield in the center of the floor. But it's barely six o'clock. Kevin and his family are still on the way from the airport. Robert's daughter Kimberly is arguing a case before the Connecticut supreme court in the morning. Peggy is nowhere visible, probably overseeing the food. That's it for the immediate family, who are the only ones, by the protocol, you'd really expect to be here at the opening bell.

Robert needs to get this out of the way before all the others begin to arrive. He turns toward the left-hand wall, where Corinthian half columns flank the casket and ceiling spotlights shine softly down on its contents in what the Tillotsons no doubt have in mind as the gaze from Heaven. The contents at six o'clock, however, are presently blocked from view by the backs of two old men in dark suits. Not Quinlans. Not likely to be Tillotsons. Still. So be it. Get it over with.

Robert touches Darla on the arm. 'Give me a minute,' he says.

'Of course,' she says.

He moves off in the direction of the casket, and as he

approaches, the two men begin to turn. He realizes who they must be. These veteran faces are different in detail from the beignet boys, but they are the same in wizened ethos. These are Bill's coffee buddies from the Thomasville chapter of the Greatest Generation.

'You must be his son,' one of them says.

Robert takes the man's offered hand and says, 'Yes, Robert,' thinking, *He didn't say 'One of his sons.' Of course not. Jimmy never existed.*

But it surprises him that his father acknowledged *his* existence to these men, given the recent revelation.

He has missed hearing the name of the first veteran and finds himself shaking the hand of the second as the man finishes the last couple of syllables of his. '… field.'

The first vet says, 'Harley and me served on the Western Front the same time your dad did.'

'We all had coffee and Dunkin' Donuts pretty near every week,' Harley says.

'In Thomasville?'

'Yep. He loved his Glazed and his Original Joe.'

'He was very proud of you,' the first man says.

This flips Robert's face sharply back to him.

Confident he understands the look in Robert's eyes, the man says: 'Not that he said much about your experience. He respected your silence.'

And the second vet says, 'But the little he did say… Well, we all understand the tough job and the short life span of infantry lieutenants in Vietnam.' He gives Robert a knowing nod and offers his hand for another shake. 'Thank you for your service.'

Robert does not take the hand. If the refusal hurts the man's feelings, it's his donut buddy's lying fucking fault. *That wasn't the service I rendered. I was a cowardly specialist fourth class hiding in a bunker counting beans.*

But the man thinks he understands Robert's hesitation. He straightens up, withdraws the offered shake, and turns it into a salute, holding a strack pose. 'Sergeant Harlan Summerfield offers his gratitude, sir.'

Shit. Shit. Robert can't keep up the rebuff. It's not this man's fault. But neither can he explain. So Robert returns the goddamn salute, forced to buy into the lie of his humiliated father, whose body Robert is suddenly, acutely aware of. It's presently reduced to a chest-to-crotch view by the frame of intervening vets, laid out in his one wearable but outdated suit, a dark gray pinstripe with padded shoulders and wide lapels, his hands crossed over his bowels.

The two men pick up on the shift of Robert's attention. 'We'll leave you with him now,' the first one says.

'Just wanted to pay our respects,' the second one says. Robert is clenching in the chest as if he were about to step out of a banyan tree in the dark.

'Good to meet you,' one or the other of them says.

And the two men step aside and vanish.

Robert moves forward into an aura of dry cleaner perc and mortuary pancake, and he stands alone now in front of his dead father.

Beneath the veneer of a Tillotson tan, William Quinlan's dumb Sunday-doze face is fixed for eternity, the face that always seemed to Robert, in its own parsimonious way, to allow that nothing was terribly wrong between the two of them. The face that said, without actually saying it: *Even though I don't offer any details, you're sufficiently okay by me that I can simply sleep in your presence in this apparently unperturbed way.*

The old man sleeps that way now. Couched in that lie. But even if he were suddenly to wake, brought back for just a few climactic moments, and if he were to look Robert in the eyes and say to him, *I know what you really want to do, so okay, go ahead, punch me in the face if you got the balls, take your best shot*, Robert would not be able to lift an arm or make a fist, would not even be able to lift a lip into a sneer. All he has is a handful of words: *Go back to sleep, Pops.* Robert feels weary. Deeply weary. Simply weary. He feels seventy fucking years old. *Go back to sleep.*

A hand on his shoulder and he starts.

He's done with the casket anyway.

He turns.

It's his mother.

She opens her arms.

He is as little inclined to accept this gesture as he was Sergeant Summerfield's salute. But he is even less capable of brushing it aside. He puts his arms around her, telling himself, *This embrace isn't about my feelings for him. It's about her. It's just for her. That's her dead husband in the casket and she loved him, in her own way. In her own way she loved him very much, so I can hold her and kiss her now on the cheek.* Which he does, and he says, 'I'm so sorry, Mom.'

'I know,' she says.

She kisses his cheek in return. Then she brings her mouth very near his ear and whispers, 'Who are those people?'

Robert whispers in return, 'A couple of his World War Two buddies.'

'Really,' she says, with a thump of a tone, meaning *How come he never mentioned them to me?*

She lets Robert gently disengage the embrace.

'They're casual coffee buddies,' he says.

Darla has drawn near.

Robert sees her over Peggy's shoulder, turns his face to her. Darla, however, is focused on her mother-in-law. The back of Peggy's head; her ashen hair rolled plain and tight; her arms falling from the embrace of her son into a slump of her narrow shoulders; her usual wiry vigorousness transformed abruptly into a bony dwindling, like a twenty-something cat. And she thinks of all the recent mother-daughter words. All the grief words. And the riddance words. And the Irish food prep. These things suddenly signify for Darla. Signify in a way that can, in a century-old monument, elicit her compassion for women long dead. So why not here, for this flesh-and-blood woman?

'Peggy,' she says, the consideration of using *Mom* having flashed into her and out again in a nanosecond. *Maybe another time.*

Peggy turns to her, brightens, throws open her arms, embraces her, pats her.

'I'm so glad you're with me tonight,' Peggy says.

'I am too,' Darla says.

'Can you help me greet people now and then? Not to monopolize you. Robert needs you too.'

'Of course,' Darla says.

Peggy lets go of Darla, pulls back a bit, looks her in the eyes. 'Thank you,' she says. She lets that register, and then she says, 'Would you like a few moments with Bill now?'

Peggy Peggy Peggy. How do I say No *to that? You have a talent.* Darla says, 'Of course.'

Peggy nods, steps away, revealing Robert still stuck standing where he was, looking at his wife with one side of his mouth and the corresponding curve of his cheek clenched in irony.

'I'll give you a few moments,' he says, and he too moves away.

Darla wants to rap him in the arm with a knuckle as he passes. She wants simply to follow him.

But she steps forward.

Her father-in-law's face is a crude likeness, molded in hand-puppet rubber. But it's him. No doubt. The distortion is simply death. It's the stuff he's pumped full of instead of blood. It's all the makeup. And yet: *I envy Robert.* This thought surprises her. She does envy him. Her own father went face forward through his windshield and into an overpass pier. Darla and her brother, far away from the bodies, made the decision by telephone. It was logical. *Don't wait for us. Close the caskets. Seal them up. We don't need to see our parents in that state. I don't need to see the wrecked face of my wrecked father.* But she did. And she didn't know it until now, as she looks at the face of this boring, emotionally obtuse, river-dock-macho, son-bullying, simplistically jingoistic man lying here dead. As altered as the man's face is, this moment with William Quinlan still feels like a kind of existential intimacy, and much to her surprise and a little to her horror, she ardently wishes she'd had a chance for these concluding moments of closeness with her own father. As bullying and politically knuckleheaded as he could be. As passionate over sausages and conservatism but reticent over her. So why does she long for that lost opportunity, to see his final mask of reticence? Her mind replies: *Perhaps because it would say to you: This is the ultimate him and so it was always him. A him apart from you. A him he would have arrived at whether he felt tenderly about you or not. Whether you ever existed or not. You did not create the chill in him. You did not earn it. If he could give no more in life, it was only because he was destined to die.*

That dark wind was already upon his face. If you'd had these final moments with him, perhaps you could have understood all that for yourself. More than understood. You could have actually felt it.

But as she stands before this other father, these are only thoughts.

And so she aches.

Her eyes fill with tears.

She rues them. Rues they'll be construed as mourning William Quinlan. Rues they could not fall upon her own father's face.

She waits for them to subside.

She glances over her shoulder.

Robert is disappearing through the door into the visitation room foyer. Peggy is approaching two elderly couples Darla does not recognize.

And Peggy reaches these strangers now, the two old men and, apparently, their two wives. The women are rising from the chesterfield.

'Hello,' she says.

The two men turn.

'Thank you for coming.' She speaks with the exaggerated brightness of decorous disdain: These men are the first outsiders to mourn her husband, and she has never heard a word about them.

'I'm Peggy Quinlan,' she says.

At least they seem to recognize who she is. As soon as they all finish fluttering their names and their condolences at her, Peggy ignores the wives and looks from one veteran to the other as she says, 'Remind me where Bill first met you.'

'Over at the American Legion hall.'

Neither has Bill ever mentioned the American Legion, much less its hall.

Peggy certainly has no intention of revealing her ignorance of all this. Fortunately, her three friends from church have finished in the kitchen and are now entering the room through its double door from the back hallway.

Peggy nods in the direction of their arrival. 'You'll excuse me.'

The strangers clamor their understanding.

She takes each of their offered hands and says, 'Please step into the next room and have some food. There's Irish stew. It was Bill's favorite. Perhaps you knew?' She does not pause to have that confirmed or denied. Either way it would piss her off. 'Or there are plenty of other things. Please.'

The veterans and their wives all agree to eat.

Peggy moves off toward her friends from St. Mary's Catholic Church. They've taken a turn toward the casket, but the steps of her pursuit slow as she finds her mind accelerating to a thing she thought she left behind in New Orleans, a thing surely already dead, dead on its own, a thing that certainly has no business in her life now, not with the man himself dead, but it does have a life. It very much does. Because if he moved to Georgia and found these two men for friends and she never heard a word about them, then it proves he was capable of a private life full of people he kept from her. Worse. It proves everything she feared in New Orleans, feared for decades: His going off most every afternoon wasn't simply for a drive and some coffee. It was for a woman. A woman he loved. Loved instead of her.

She has slowed now to a stop.

Ahead of her, the three friends are lined up before Bill. She turns her back on them.

The strangers are heading for the food. Robert has vanished. Darla is in the process of vanishing as well, out the entrance door of the visitation room.

And Jimmy once again nears the Tillotson Funeral Home, featuring William Quinlan like the star of his latest movie – *Husband, Father, Veteran*. Jimmy and Heather have been chased back by the Impala's open fresh air vent. A few miles down Apalachee Parkway it sucked in the nighttime stink of the tree-shrouded Leon County dump, a clear sign to both of them that they should give up the drive.

He pulls into the first empty space, far from the few other cars and the floodlit house.

He turns off the engine but does not move.

Heather says, 'Cold feet?'

'The back of the crowd at the cemetery is one thing. But doing this… I don't know.'

'Baby,' she says. 'You want to put *him* in the ground, not just a casket. You need to see him in it, don't you think?'

Jimmy shrugs in a slow-motion, exaggerated, high-shouldered way.

Heather smiles. She's known him long enough to understand the gesture as pouty assent. She finds it endearing, which makes her suspect she's falling in love.

He says, 'We're still too early.'

'So let's sit here and make out for a while,' she says.

Jimmy barks a laugh at this.

But he turns a little in her direction and regrets the ubiquity of center consoles in modern cars. 'We'd have to climb into the backseat to do it right,' he says.

'So?'

'On the way out,' he says. 'After getting him into the casket.'

Heather laughs and leans across the console to him. She initiates a kiss, which they draw out for a time and end with as much of an embrace – of shoulders and chests – as they can manage. Jimmy's attention drifts up to the funeral home. But it's far enough away that he does not even register the figure silhouetted in the open front doorway.

Robert has only moments ago slipped his cellphone into his pocket, having absentmindedly carried it in his hand from the visitation room to this place in the doorway. The text message that brought him here was sent by his grandson. *Almost there.* The message pleased Robert, and surprised him a little. If they're almost here, there's no reason for Jake to text, except that he's eager to see his granddad.

Far down at the parkway, lights have just turned into the parking lot, but they immediately pull into a spot and go dark. Clearly not Kevin. Nor is it Kevin at the opening and shutting of doors much closer. Figures from school are emerging there.

'Are you okay?' This is Darla's voice from just over his shoulder.

He glances at her. 'Yes. Thanks. I got a text from Jake. They're almost here.'

Darla steps up beside him.

Four FSU colleagues, three of Robert's, one of Darla's, are heading this way.

She feels Robert fidget a little. 'I'll handle them, if you like,' she says.

'Thanks. Yes.'

And after the commiserations, she does, taking them away to the food and alcohol that make this a wake and not a funeral.

More lights turn in now from the parkway and keep approaching until they angle into the nearest parking spot.

Robert goes out into the chill and down the front steps to meet Kevin, who is striding forward, looking young in the dim light, not forty-two, looking like a college boy. He embraces Robert. Grace follows and puts her arms around both of them. A tender woman. Good for Kevin. Robert withdraws one arm from his son to include his daughter-in-law in his embrace.

The death of his father is grieved more simply by these two, who did not know the man, who knew an alternate man. Robert looks beyond this wordless huddle. Molly is on her cellphone; she's eighteen, after all. Jake is standing nearby watching Robert closely. Their eyes meet and the boy nods to his grandfather.

How has this boy gotten so big? This man. Twenty now. He's taller than Robert. Maybe not when Robert was twenty, not before his septuagenarian shrinkage. But tall. A man. And Robert wonders how this is now a surprise. As the hug goes wordlessly on, Robert tries to think of the last time he saw his grandson. A year. Maybe two. Jake's been elsewhere during the family's last couple of visits. Growth spurts have their limits. The last time, Jake surely was some significant fraction of this man who stands before Robert. But it was long enough ago that the near-man has been composted into this present surprise.

Grace begins the exchange of condolences. 'I'm so sorry, Dad,' she says.

The three end the embrace and exchange ardent words as they all gather and turn and move off toward the front door.

Bob cannot distinguish the words but this faint flurry of sound floats down the parking lot to him. He has just stopped abruptly at the foot of the Tillotson driveway. The lights of the marquee have drawn his eyes up from their focus on the sidewalk and have stopped him, and now these distant voices come at him like a past incident that troubles you in the middle of the night but you can't quite remember what it was. And the lights. This sign. William Quinlan. Quinlan. Bob thrashes in his head to understand. Just recently a Quinlan. A handshake. I'm Quinlan. The Vietnam vet. *Vietnam. America's last chapter. Bang. Done.*

Bob's head snaps back at the sign.

Quinlan's dead. *He only just shook my hand. That was quick. Done. Bang. It doesn't make sense.* So Bob tries to do in his head what he can do with his eyes. He squeezes at these thoughts like they're the blur of words in a newspaper. He squeezes till they clarify, just a little, just enough to make them out. The Quinlan who shook his hand was Bob. Not William. He's Bob. A Vietnam vet. In that, too much like the old man. *But this one is Bob like me.*

And now Bob remembers the rest. The father of the other Bob has died. A blood clot in a hospital. Tillotson Funeral Home. Bob looks again at the sign. Tillotson. And this Quinlan: *Husband. Father. Veteran.* Another veteran. This makes Bob stir a little. Too many veterans. But the other Bob is okay. They ate together at New Leaf, the two of them. *But he put me in a hotel with my father. Did the old man arrange it? Did he get his Vietnam buddy to put me in a room with him?*

No.

This is Bob the son of William, who is dead.

Bob looks toward the distant house. Shining.

Dead in this place shining in the dark.

Respects.

Bob can't just walk up to the front door.

He understands that.

Nearby. Twenty yards away. The woods. Bob knows his way through woods. These run up toward the shining house and then past and around back, surrounding the place. Bob heads off. Laurel oak and water oak and sweet gum, dark and dense, and Bob enters them, moving swiftly, silently.

Hushed, Robert and his son's family enter the visitation room. Robert is before them. Kevin steps up now beside him, scans the room, sees the casket at the far wall, keeps on looking around. Robert figures he knows why. When Kevin's gaze arrives at the buffet room, Robert says, 'I suspect they're in there,' meaning Peggy and Darla. When Kevin looks at him, Robert nods back to the partition doorway. 'Serving your grandmother's food.'

Kevin turns to his family and says, softly, 'This is a good time to pay our respects.'

Grace steps beside him, takes his arm. Molly has put her cellphone away and takes her mother's arm. Jake is standing a little apart, and when the others move off toward the casket, he stays put.

'Granddad,' he says in a near-whisper, 'can we have a little talk? I need some advice.'

'Of course,' Robert says, reciprocating the whisper. He nods toward his grandson's retreating family. 'Perhaps a little later.'

Jake understands. 'Thanks.' He follows the others. Robert moves off toward the buffet room thinking how Jake has gotten to age twenty without the two of them ever really sitting down to talk about life in the way a grandfather and grandson often can do. Will this be a night full of ironies? Full of people assuming Robert's unadulterated sorrow, for instance; full of the tender, approving warmth – as one might receive from a loving father – that those assumptions will earn him. And likely this irony as well: The old man has reminded Jacob that families can dissolve, so if you ever want a heart-to-heart connection with your grandfather, you better get it while you can. Not that any of this was William Quinlan's benign intention. He just happened to die.

Robert steps into the partitioned room with his mother's food unfurled on platters and in pots and stainless warmers and with herself stationed behind the row of tables ladling Irish stew and brightly complaining that Tallahassee is muttonless. 'But the lamb is good,' she says, tapping the serving spoon in the air over the filled plate of Darla's colleague. Peggy turns her face at Robert's arrival.

'Kevin and Grace and the kids are here,' he says.

And Bob pushes on through the trees. Why does he feel a rushing in him, why is he beating up his legs and lungs and elbows and shoulders trying to get through a thicket of oak in this big fucking rush? As if something is pursuing him here in the woods. No. He's doing the pursuing. That shifting of the dark up ahead, shaping and shifting and vanishing and shaping again *You can shoot, by God Bobby, you can shoot* and Bob pulls the Glock from inside his coat, snug in palm and crotch of thumb and forefinger, his fingertip lying easy on the trigger, perfectly fitting its curve, perfectly placed for Bobby to be okay by God, a hell of a shot. The old man was worthless in the woods. He was worthless. Maybe he was worthless in the jungles of Vietnam as well, maybe that's what pissed him off so bad at Bob, Bob being okay when the old man wasn't. Maybe Calvin Henry Weber, sergeant – or whatever his rank really was – serial number whatever-the-fuck, was scared of his okay boy Bob. When Bob has a Mossberg or when Bob has a Glock, Calvin Henry Weber is scared. And Bob moves on, dodging the trees, aware, though, that he's not just chasing, aware that he has a destination, aware of a building being sliced into fragments by the trunks of the oaks, a building passing by and passing by and finally vanishing, replaced by the stretch of a sodium-vapor-lit drive, covered along the back edge of the building by a hanging porch. And Bob changes his bearing, which has been north. He now turns east, and the building is passing again through the trees to his right. He has circled behind it and now there is a wide doorway in its rear facade, bright lights inside.

Bob stops.

Things clarify for him.

He has come to pay his respects to a dead man. A father of a Bob. The other Bob. Bob the Vietnam buddy of the father he's been following through the woods.

Keep it straight.

Bob tucks his Glock back inside his inner coat pocket. But the door is opening.

And while Bob has been making his way through the woods to this place behind a particularly large-trunked laurel oak: Peggy and Robert emerge from the buffet and cross the room to wait for Kevin and his wife and his son and his daughter to finish their shoulder-to-shoulder encounter with the corpse of William Quinlan, which they soon do. Kevin and Grace draw their children closer in an embrace and they turn to find Peggy and Robert. They all huddle in condolence. Beyond them the visitation room is beginning to gather visitors, arriving from a flow of cars into the parking lot, including, most recently, a minivan from Longleaf Village. The minivan prompts Jimmy and Heather to look at each other and nod and emerge from their car, though unhurriedly, as they want all these recent arrivals to have a chance to populate the room. Jimmy flexes at his qualms as if they were morning-stiff muscles.

Inside, Peggy abruptly declares to Kevin and his family,

'You're straight from the airport. You must be famished. I've got just the thing.' She steps between Kevin and Grace and arranges herself shoulder to shoulder with them, hooking their arms and conveying them toward the buffet room.

'Come on, kids,' she says over her shoulder.

Molly says, 'I'm famished,' and follows.

Jake glances to Robert, who nods at his grandson and waits for the diners to make some progress toward the partition door. Then Robert says, 'Let's go.' He leads Jake across the visitation room, looking first toward the exit into the foyer. But people are coming in, some of whom he knows, and he looks away to the back wall and the doors there. No one has gathered near them. 'This way,' he says.

Jake follows.

They say nothing to each other as they cross the room and enter the back hallway. It's lit brightly with torchiere floor lamps. Double doors directly before them lead outside.

'Inside or out?' Robert says.

'Out,' Jake says.

'Good man,' Robert says.

Bob has already stopped in the trees across from the back doors of the funeral home. Things have already become clear to him. He has already tucked his Glock away inside his coat.

The door is opening, and he hangs back, fades into the darkness like the ghost of his father that he's been chasing through these woods. No doubt also like his father's ghost, he keeps a careful watch.

Robert and Jake step into the chill air, stop beneath the porte cochere roof, turn to each other, and Jake says at once, 'I've been intending for a while to do this the next time I saw you.' He extends his hand.

Robert accepts Jake's hand and they shake. His grandson's grasp is firm, ardently so but not strained.

Jake says, 'Thank you for your service.'

The puzzlement that Robert felt but did not show when Jake offered his hand must be flickering now in his face because Jake quickly adds, 'For our country. In Vietnam.'

Their hands are still clasped and Jake renews the shake with this.

Robert nods, trying to block out the voice of the corpse just inside the doors, trying to quash the same impulse he'd felt with the old man's donut buddies. He manages: 'That's good of you to say.'

The handshake ends.

Jake says, 'We've never talked about any of that.'

'I tend not to.'

'I respect that,' Jake says. 'But if it's not an absolute thing. "Tend," right? I mean, I've never asked. But I'd like to. I'm older now. I'd like to sit down and talk about war with you. I mean, you're my grandfather and you've been through that and it's crazy I shouldn't find out what you know.'

His grandson's intention, especially now, should rattle Robert. But upon this rush of words, Jake the boy frisks into him, Jake from the few years he lived close by, the three-year-old out with his granddad for a walk but the boy never walking anywhere, always taking off and running ahead.

Not that Robert ever wants to discuss Vietnam, but for now he says, 'Maybe not tonight.'

'No no,' Jake says. 'I understand. We'll make another time.'

'Of course.'

'Soon.'

'Sure.'

The two of them are standing here growing a little chilly now up the sleeves and down the collar and beneath the tie because of Jake and his interest in their talking together. So when his grandson pauses, Robert simply waits, glad he's put off Vietnam. For some years the two households have had ongoing good intentions to get together more often and soon, but it never seems to happen. Robert regrets that but hopes the phenomenon will at least save him from ever having this particular grandfather-and-grandson conversation.

Robert assumes that asking for this was the purpose of tonight's private talk. He expects Jake to take them back inside.

But he doesn't. Jake is working up to something else. He looks away, toward the trees, where Bob is watching closely.

He's spotted me. But Bob doesn't react abruptly, as much as his hand wants to duck inside his coat. Just in case it's okay. Just in case the darkness that Bob is standing in is sufficient, he simply moves backward, deeper into the shadows, but without seeming to move, in minute measures, steadily, his hand ready to leap if necessary. The boy's head turns back to Cal's buddy.

Jake says to Robert, 'There's one other thing. Maybe we can talk now just a bit? They're okay inside without us for a couple more minutes, aren't they?'

Robert hears a different sort of rush in Jake's voice, an urgency, a pressing private need. 'Whatever you need, Jake.'

'I just need to say it. I'm joining the Marines.'

Robert steels himself instantly to show no reaction. Though he's staggered.

Jake rolls on. 'Dad is freaked. But I've made up my mind. He sees me as a child. Always will, probably. At least till I'm forty or something. I'm smart, Granddad. I've been thinking about this for a long time, you know? The war you fought – we can talk about all that another time – but that one was fucked up. Sorry for the language. That's a thing too with Pop. But Jesus. It's just a fucking word. In the Vietnam War we got mixed up with another country that was trying to decide for itself who they were, and they had no intention to make anybody else think the same way. Much less kill you if you disagreed. You know? They weren't about to send the Viet Cong over here to hijack an American Airlines jet and fly it into a New York skyscraper. Hell, how did the dreaded communist Vietnam end up? They're filling clothes racks at Walmart and Target. But this war now is different. The jihadists of the world are cutting off the heads of anyone who disagrees with them. Not just Christians. Even other Muslims. Over what? Over a fourteen-century-old beef about who should carry on Muhammad's work, a cousin or a caliph. And they're coming for us. They say so. They mean it. If they had the technology and a modern country and the governing chops of Adolf Hitler, they'd out-Hitler Hitler. This is a real cause to fight for. If we don't become the new Greatest Generation, then the jihadists will turn us into the Beheaded Generation.'

Bob has stopped retreating into the dark. The boy's voice has risen and it's angry and though it takes too much from Bob to make out the words at this distance, too much squeezing in his head, he knows the boy is telling off his father, standing up to him, and Bob is breathing hard, his right hand is itchy but he keeps it at his side for the moment. Still he owes it to the boy, so he strains to hear, and there's *Viet Cong* and there's *jihad* and there's *Hitler* and there's *beheaded* and Bob can't draw his next breath because there's just too much in his chest to get past.

Jake has stopped talking. He's panting a little.

Robert wants badly to have words now. His life, his work, is about words. None come to mind. Jake *is* smart. Robert has listened to him carefully. He's heard him. He understands how Jake can see the world in this way, how he can see this cause as just. But how to reason a young man out of going to war? As reasonable as Jake's words sound, his decision itself isn't about reason. But now that the babble in Robert's head has quieted, the only words he commands can't begin to address Jake's rush, his passion.

It may be too late anyway.

Robert says, ' Have you already joined?'

'I've taken the aptitude test. And I've passed the medical. I make it official next week.'

'What do you need from me?'

'If you can talk to Dad, help him through this. He's really upset. He won't get off it.'

Kevin is smart too. He's surely said it all. Robert despairs of finding a way to dissuade Jake.

'Your dad isn't making any sense to you?'

Jake shrugs. 'It's not really about sense. He loves me.'

'I love you too, Jake.'

'But you made the same choice when you were my age. For a worse cause.'

Another irony for this night. That was also about a father's love. A worse cause indeed. And Robert suddenly has relevant words: 'Are you sure you're not doing this because he *does* love you? Because you need to be your own man, separate from him?'

Jake turns his face away to the trees. To think this over. Bob straightens sharply. Something's happened across the way. Since he resumed his breathing, Bob has held himself very still, in body and mind, trying to understand what was before him and what he should do about it. But either the words faded or his mind has. And now the boy has looked away again. As if he's been slapped across the face. Things can change quickly. Bob puts his hand inside his coat. Holds the Glock but keeps it inside there for the moment.

Jake turns his face back to Robert. He says, 'I'm sure. Living with what I believe, how I feel, I couldn't bear to watch the future unfold if I don't do what I can.'

Robert does love this boy. Loves this smart, tough, quick Jake, who has not gotten enough of his grandfather in his life. Robert lifts his hands to grasp Jake at the shoulders.

Oh no you don't. Bob slips his Glock from his pocket, takes a breath. *Breath control. Trigger control.*

Robert cups Jake's shoulders and he begins to pull him toward him.

Bob's right hand comes up strong, steady, brings the Glock to bear, tracking the side of Robert's head.

Jake could take one breath more, could have one more flicker of a thought, he could hesitate for the briefest moment to accept from his grandfather what he has resisted over and over in the past few weeks from his father, but Granddad can do this because he was a soldier, because he went to war, Granddad knows what it means because he's been there, and so Jake rushes now, he opens his arms to Robert and they hug.

And one flicker, one breath, one moment away from squeezing the trigger, Bob's right forefinger freezes, and a deep recoil of air rushes into Bob, drops his right arm, pushes him back as if a Viet Cong sniper has been following him through these woods and has squeezed off his own round and shot Bob through the center of his chest. Because this father and this son have embraced.

Bob leans against a tree. Closes his eyes.

Robert and Jake say nothing but hold the embrace for a few more moments. Then they let each other go and they turn and head back through doors, into the hallway.

They pause before entering the visitation room.

'Thanks, Granddad,' Jake says.

Robert reaches out, cuffs his grandson on the shoulder. He fills with a thing too complicated to call *regret*, though his insistently abstracting mind would be content with that. 'What are you going to do for them?' he asks.

'The Marines?'

'Yes.'

'That's what the test was about. Whatever they want. But you know the first thing they teach in the Corps. Every Marine is a rifleman.'

Robert manages a nod.

Jake says, 'Well, time to deploy.' He opens the visitation room door, holds it for his grandfather.

Robert finds himself immovable with the thought that Jake would have made his Grandpa Bill proud.

He flicks his chin to Jake to send him on in. Jake winks and says, 'Cover me.' And he disappears.

The door swings closed.

Robert reboots.

He goes in.

Near the door Peggy is quickly closing in on Jake. She reaches him, hugs him, releases him while giving Robert a tilt-headed frown, and she propels her grandson toward the buffet room.

She does not follow but comes to Robert. 'Where were you two?'

'Jake wanted to talk.'

'Is he okay?'

'He's okay.'

'I'm sure it's hard for him,' Peggy says. 'Losing his Grandpa Bill. He's not experienced death before. That's a blessing, of course. But now he's got to face it.'

'He's fine, Mom.'

'Your father loved that boy.'

'I'm sure he did.'

'He was so *full* of love.'

Robert doesn't have any words for that.

Peggy's eyes are filling with tears. But not about Jake. Or the old man. She's fixed on Robert now. She lifts a hand and touches his cheek.

He accepts it. Waits.

She withdraws the hand, looks over her shoulder. Several dozen visitors are arranged now in small, softly murmuring groups about the room.

Peggy turns back to her son. 'I'm weary of them, Bobby. Can we talk a little?'

'Of course,' he says, hoping she won't speak to him as *Bobby*. 'There's a place through here.'

He leads her into the back hallway. For a moment they pause between the two sets of doors. 'This is nice,' she says.

Beyond the porte cochere doors, beyond the back driveway, in the darkness of the trees, Bob has settled to the ground at the foot of an oak, his back against the trunk. The Glock is still in his hand, though he is presently unaware of it. His head is full of a high metallic whine. It's often there. Words can cover it over. Or other sounds. But he has no words to speak, for the moment, and the woods around him are silent. So he listens to the whine. Idly. An oscillating whine. Though its highs and

229

its lows are very near each other, he can distinguish them. He's smart that way. He begins to count in his head. At each peak. One. Two.

Robert and Peggy step away, toward the end of the hall opposite the kitchen. They stop in the amber bloom of light of a torchiere. They face each other. Peggy initiates a hug, which Robert returns. They hold this for a long moment and then Peggy pulls away, but barely a half step, maintaining the connection of their eyes.

She says, 'I keep thinking of when he came home. You and I were living with Mama and Papa, you know. In that creole cottage in the Irish Channel. You were two years old and he was thunderstruck at the sight of you. He picked you up and put you on his shoulders and that's pretty much where you stayed for a couple of weeks. He'd carry you everywhere from up there. "Let him see far," is what Bill would say. "Let my boy see far."'

Robert has heard this story often enough that any capacity it once had to move him is long gone. Besides, the old man as a young man was already the man he was and forever would be. A toddler son was easy to sling around. Easy to give a damn about when you could overpower him absolutely.

Peggy says, 'He wanted to name you William Junior, you know.'

This is not the first time he's heard this either.

'He loved you that much,' she says.

What Robert wants is to avoid arguing with his mother on this night. However, he says, 'What he wanted was his firstborn son to be just like him.'

She brightens. 'You see?'

He has said this to her as if to disprove his father's love. But he realizes she hears it as a demonstration of that love.

Her bright smile of QED beams on. And the smile suddenly strikes Robert as one of her lies.

Does she know about his father's deep disappointment in him? The man kept it from his son. Did he keep it from his wife?

Robert and his mother look at each other for a long moment in silence. Her brightness fades a little. He struggles, wanting to let this pass but wanting to know if she knows, wanting to ask but wanting to keep the truth strictly between him and the dead man if she doesn't.

So he says, 'But I wasn't just like him.'

He expects a spin now, or an evasion or a lie.

She even hesitates.

Then she surprises him. 'It was me who talked him out of naming you William,' she says.

The family explanation – Robert can't remember the exact moment it was offered him but he's sure it came from her – was that his father realized that his son, to be kept distinct in conversation, would become 'Billy' or even 'Junior,' and he thought both sounded sissified.

Robert narrows his eyes at her. 'You said he talked himself out of it.'

'Did I tell you that?'

'You did.'

'For his sake. He didn't like admitting my influence.'

'You didn't like biting your tongue.'

'I bit it as an act of love.' She squares up before him and doesn't flinch: 'It was me. I told him, "This boy needs to be his own man."'

'Did he understand that?'

'Well, who knows. He was a father, after all, with strong ideas. He gave you a love for books. This soldier and dockworker gave his son that.'

Robert does not really expect to learn if the old man revealed his fatherly disgust over Vietnam. He probably didn't. But she did witness his disappointment in Robert. Listen to her: Your father may not have loved you for what you became but he made you read. That was the substitute from childhood onward. Isn't that an outcome worthy of actual love? Aren't you grateful?

He says, 'He gave me the love of books expecting me to come to the same conclusions from them that he did.'

Her face puckers in puzzlement. 'You seemed to.'

She's right.

'I often bit my tongue,' Robert says.

She smiles at him, half smiles. 'An act of love.'

Well, the act never won his. He catches himself before this comes out of his mouth. She's tried the same tactic all her life long.

Her eyes are fixed on Robert's but restlessly so.

'He loved all of us,' she says.

And he understands. If she can convince Robert of William's love for him, then she might believe that the man loved her as well.

Because she doesn't believe it.

Of course she doesn't.

And it abruptly occurs to him: He hasn't told her what he knows about the old man's secret trysts.

Her priests would nail me for a sin of omission. A big one. Sure it was for his privacy. It was his place to tell her. It was between them. It had been going on for years when I found out. She would

232

have stopped him. She would have nagged him back home if she knew it was something that didn't threaten her so profoundly she preferred the lie. But still. He wasn't worth keeping it from her. He was never worth it. Mea culpa.

'Mom,' he says. 'I'm so sorry. I should have told you sooner. But it wasn't so long ago I found out. All those afternoons, for all those years, that he drove off on his own in New Orleans: It wasn't a woman. It was guys like those you met tonight. It was Dad and his army buddies doing beignets and chicory coffee.'

Peggy's face goes blank. Then she blinks, and for a few moments more she shows nothing. And a few more.

Robert doesn't understand.

So he says, 'He loved you.'

She blinks again. Then she begins to cry.

Oh shit: Robert should have told her long ago. Or he should have figured out a better way to tell her now.

He lifts his hand to touch her shoulder, perhaps pull her to him.

She catches his hand in hers, lifts it, and squeezes it. 'Are you sure?' she says.

'I'm sure.'

'It's time for me to cry a while,' she says. 'Thanks for this.'

'I'm really sorry,' he says. 'I should have told you at once.'

Peggy struggles to manage her voice, hold off the tears.

'You were caught between us. I totally understand, sweetheart. You loved your father too.'

She looks around, lets go of Robert's hand, sits down on an overstuffed chair beneath the torchiere. 'I'll be in soon,' she says.

Robert stands over her for a moment more, but she has lowered her face to weep.

He turns and moves along the hallway.

233

He pauses between the two sets of doors.

He thinks to head outside, to get away from all of this. He faces the porte cochere exit. His hands go to the push bar.

Beneath the tree Bob's eyes are open again. The whining has been fading. It's almost gone. The numbers are gone. He's done these countings before. He wishes he could decide when they happen, could make them happen. The whine, the numbers are better than the voice and the words. *Hello, Private Weber. Let's talk.*

Robert's hand is on the push bar.

But he knows this is futile. There will be no escape tonight. He looks back down the hallway to his mother, her torso, in profile, bent forward, her head bowed, her hands clasped, resting on her knees.

He turns around, crosses to the doors into the visitation room, pushes through.

Darla appears before him.

'Hey,' she says. She must have been standing nearby, expecting him.

'Hey.'

Darla glances over his shoulder, sees that Peggy isn't appearing. 'Is she okay?'

'She's crying alone for a while,' Robert says.

'That's good.'

'I hope.'

'I saw you two go out.'

'There isn't much privacy at a thing like this.'

'It's what a wake's for. So you're not alone.'

'What have you been doing?'

'Serving food.'

'Is it going over?'

'The Irish stew is a big hit.'

'That'll please her.'

'So it will.'

Robert looks away, into the room, whose numbers seem to have increased since he stepped out. Not that he sees anyone in particular. They are all blurring together now.

Darla says, 'Can I make a suggestion?'

'Sure.'

'I never saw my own dad after he died. Did I ever tell you that?'

He looks at her. 'No.'

'Well. I didn't. It was a closed casket. I needed to look at him. It's a good way to get things straight in your head so he won't hang around in there.'

Robert tries to take this in. He's not sure. He stalls by quibbling.

'Still waiting for the suggestion,' he says.

'You weren't with him at the casket for very long,' she says. 'Just make sure you did enough tonight.'

Robert looks off in the direction of the far wall. In the middle of the room, a clump of assisted living visitors with plates of Irish stew blocks his view of the casket beyond. But he's thinking Darla may be right.

She says, 'It's not about good guys. I had as much trouble with my dad as you did with yours. More.'

'Okay,' he says. 'You're right.'

Robert and Darla would both agree: This is one of the paradigms of the two of them at their intellectual best with each other. A difference. A discussion. Patience over a semantic quibble. One sees the other's point. And concurs. Sealed with a moment of contented silence.

That moment ends, but before they part she says, 'Does she need me, do you think?'

'Mom?'

'Yes.'

'Not right now. I think she needs to be alone.'

'I'll go dip some stew.'

'I think you're starting to like it.'

'Please,' she says.

She begins to turn away.

Robert puts his hand on her arm. 'Hey.'

She looks back at him.

'Thanks,' he says.

She nods.

He heads off toward the wall with the casket.

She moves in the other direction, toward the buffet room. But she puts only a few steps of separation between her and the back door of the visitation room before her department chair intercepts her and hugs her as if the dead father were Darla's own. Darla figures the warmth is mostly about department politics, which means a conversation is imminent. She gives up the hope of hiding immediately behind the stew.

Robert veers wide around the group of old women in hats and old men in wide ties from Longleaf Village. He keeps his face averted; he's met a couple of them and this is not a time to chat.

He's past them now and he looks toward the casket.

A man is standing there, his back to Robert.

Robert does not recognize him.

Just a man. A lanky man wearing a leather jacket, his hands clasped behind him, his pewter-gray hair thick-curled and shaggy at the collar.

Robert stops. He'll wait till the man moves off.

Robert looks about to see if anyone else is waiting to view the body.

A few steps off to the left is a pretty, pale-skinned woman, her dark hair spilling from beneath a knit cap. He takes her for an art theory student of Darla's. Perhaps she has a concealed sketchbook, waiting to capture a dead man.

Robert thinks to walk away now.

But he returns his gaze to the man.

He has not moved.

Well, yes. His hands, in their clasp, have begun to twist, have grown fretful.

And now Robert has a thought. This man is not from FSU. Not from assisted living. Not one of Bill's generation. Wearing leather at a funeral home visitation, he's not from Peggy's church. Robert looks at the woman again. Her gaze is fixed on the man. They are here together. And she's older than he thought at first glance. Robert looks closely at her jaw, looking for his father's, his own, his brother's. Looks at her eyes. He's not recognizing a Quinlan, but he's never met Linda. This woman's features could be from Linda's genes. He follows her eyes back to the casket. The man's hands cling to each other to quell their restlessness. Robert suspects his own hands were just as restless when he stood there. *It's him.*

Jimmy has not been here for long. He is still breathless, standing in the presence of death. Not realizing, not quite yet, that its immanence in this casket is a major reason why he's here. All he presently understands is that the face of his dead father is largely an unrecognizable face. Not a man at all. Not even a good caricature. All the features are bloated and blurred and slathered over. Features he last saw forty-six years ago. Features that would have been nearly as unrecognizable last week, when Bill was still walking around, unawares, in death's anteroom. Jimmy once more asks himself the basic question: *What the hell am I doing here?* And since the dead body is not providing an answer at the moment, Jimmy works his way along. *Closure. Sure. But I'm here because Linda left me. I'm here because I found Heather. Here because I found her only very recently and she's not yet enough. Blood ties are overrated. But that's about the inefficacy of blood, not about the need for ties to something. The something was once Linda and Canada. I still have Canada. Oh Canada. Unarmed, universally doctored, killingly polite Canada; grumbling-not-hating Canada; minding-its-own-fucking-business-in-the-community-of-nations Canada. Tolerant, come-find-a-refuge-and-your-own-identity-here Canada. Not enough. I know that. Canada and Heather may eventually be enough. But for some reason I had to come stand here before this man. Only blood connected us. Not part of the real equation. I did dream of him. And my mother. And my brother. But you can dream about an old girlfriend or a high school teacher or a crooked auto mechanic and it doesn't mean you need to seek them out before they go into the ground. Still I came to this man, his corpse waiting to rot. Because he's dead; he's dead so he knows something important, something no one alive knows. Right now. What is it? Is he wedged into the dark matter, pressing his face against mine? Has he run off to be someone else, somewhere else? Or maybe he's nothing at all. Or just made new. Maybe death is like when they knock you out for a colonoscopy. You're counting backwards one second and awake the next and they tell you it's all done and you don't remember a thing. Maybe you die and you wake and this life you lived is utterly forgotten like that lost hour. Life in the USA and life in*

Canada. Life on planet earth. Life is just the camera up your ass that you won't even remember. So what actually happens after death is fucking academic. If there's nothing afterward or if it's something that you'll totally forget, then it's all the same. Okay. What the hell am I doing here? I'm here to look at the bag of bones my father has become so maybe I can stop thinking about this thing I can't stop thinking about. I came to face death.

Another thought, flowing from these, begins to shape itself. About his brother.

And someone is standing next to him.

'Hello, Jimmy.'

Jimmy turns to his brother. Jimmy's impulsive few nights of Googling – yielding images of Dr Robert Quinlan at academic conferences, on a book dust jacket, from the university website – have prepared him only a little for the changes of nearly five decades. The abrupt, palpable presence of Robert's graying and slackening and weathering, his leap from twenty-three years old to seventy: These twist the knife of mortality in Jimmy's brain. His own face in the mirror each day is much the same as this one. But even as he's struggled with the thoughts of death, he could look in the mirror and convince himself, *I'm pretty good for my age. I can put off dying.* But he got to that understanding of his own face gently, gradually. Jimmy regards this man before him, this man of Jimmy's blood, this man in the same pretty good shape as he, and sees him as mortally old.

'Hello, Robert,' he says.

'I didn't expect you.'

'It was last-minute.'

They need a little break from each other already.

They have a corpse for that.

They both look in its direction.

All the possible small talk coming to Robert's head sounds potentially touchy or argumentative: *So what changed your mind? Mom will be very pleased. Is Linda with you? Who's the woman? Well, there he is. Was it worth the trip?*

He resists all of these.

And perhaps for that very reason, perhaps because he refuses to choose one of these superficial, calculated things, what he does say is from quite a different part of him. 'If you want to slap him across the face, feel free.'

They turn and goggle at each other.

Neither can think of a thing to say.

They look back to William.

Robert reboots. 'Well, there he is.'

'There he is.'

'Was it worth the trip?'

'Not yet.'

'Is there anything I can do?' Robert asks this with a little surge of animation, a vague impulse, which he stifles to offer forward his hands. He even finds himself about to say, *I'm glad you came*, but he doesn't want to stir up Jimmy's scorn. He's lived with a bellyful of scorn these past few days and he wants to keep things calm with his brother.

Jimmy says, 'Answer a question if you can, without looking around.'

'All right.'

'Where's our mother?'

'She's taking a few minutes alone. I can get her. She'd be only too glad...'

'No.' Jimmy says it sharply. He softens his tone but with it justifies his sharpness: 'That's why I didn't want you to look around.'

'So *there's* something I can do,' Robert says. 'Help you slip out unnoticed.'

The words could be construed as sarcastic. Would have been in the life they lived together before each went away. But Robert has also softened his tone.

'I haven't decided yet,' Jimmy says. 'I may.'

Still another matter of tone. This fastidious one in Jimmy makes a warmth rise in Robert, from his cheeks and into his temples, replacing sympathy with pissoffedness.

'Look, Jimmy,' he says, but quietly, calmly. 'Why don't *I* just slip away and let you do what you need to do. If Mom appears I'll run interference for you. Distract her so you can get the hell away.'

Jimmy sucks a breath, pulls back ever so slightly.

Robert thinks: *It was the "get the hell away." All right. All right. I'm not in the mood. Let's get it on, brother.*

But Jimmy says, 'I'm sorry. I sounded arrogant. I'm here because I want to be here. But it's complicated.'

Robert feels animated again. He may need to slip away for his own sake, just to stop the mood swings. He says, 'I get it. Not a problem. It's always been complicated.'

He looks at William. It wasn't such a crazy thing to say. About the slap. It was Jimmy's fretfully clasped hands. He says, 'Not long before you appeared, I stood here and I thought about him waking up and daring me to punch him in the face.'

'Did you do it?'

'No.'

'Not even in your head?'

A beat of silence between them now. And another. 'No,' Robert says. 'Wish I could've. But it's just a corpse.' Another silence.

But brief. For Jimmy, this too is spoken from an impulse. 'We should make a pact,' he says. 'We'll fight no fights from the past. If we get angry at each other it needs to be about something right in front of us.'

'Man, I agree with that,' Robert says. 'But the past is all you and I have. If we're going to speak at all, things may come up. But not to argue them.'

'Fair enough,' Jimmy says. 'And this can't be a sentimental agreement. It's not mindless make-nice. You know what I mean?'

'I do.' Robert offers his hand.

Jimmy takes the hand.

They shake.

The thought of adding their other hands to the ones shaking occurs to both men but only in the abstract, only to be recognized as sentimental and set aside.

When they let go of their hands, Jimmy says, 'I'm going to test our pact right away. I came here because of a dead father. But it's not just about him. Maybe not about him very much at all anymore.'

Jimmy hesitates. He hasn't planned this. Never imagined relating it to his brother. But he's glad for the chance. He says, 'You were precocious when we were kids. And I think you had something dark in you. Can I ask? Did you go off to Vietnam to face death? Did you have to get into the very presence of death to figure it out? Is that what I didn't recognize about what you did?'

This is not the question Robert expected. He wants the answer to be *Yes*. To square himself with Jimmy. To put his motives beyond the criticism of his father, who would never understand such a thing. But the answer isn't yes. Isn't even partially yes. He says, 'Since we've agreed not to argue the past, is it possible for us also to be entirely honest?'

Jimmy waggles his head a little at this sudden complexity. 'Good question. At least we need to try. Otherwise you might as well just go ahead and help me get the hell out of here. But perhaps we can have it both ways, eh?'

'Perhaps,' Robert says. 'So then. No. I didn't go off to face death. Not at all.'

And he thinks: *Simply that much honesty may not result in an argument, but it will preserve, everlastingly, the estrangement between us.* And he knows: *I can say the thing that the man lying next to us nearly took to his grave.* A thing Robert would just as soon take to his. *Do I want a brother?* If Robert says no more, he will lose Jimmy forever. If he speaks fully, Jimmy might have a way to understand him, even in light of his own drastic deed of the sixties. *Do I want this man for my brother?*

Perhaps.

Robert says, 'You were right long ago. It was all about Pops. About winning his love. You were smart to give up trying. I can see that now. I didn't go to Vietnam to confront death. I did everything I could to avoid it. Not to see it. Certainly not to inflict it. I voluntarily enlisted so I could choose an army job. A deep-in-a-hole faux research job. And in doing that, I destroyed the thing I wanted most from Pops. I got its opposite. He'd expected me to go off eagerly to the killing, as he had. So he despised me for the rest of his life. Silently. I never knew. Not till he told me himself the afternoon before he died.'

Robert finds himself relieved not to take that to his own grave. Even if Jimmy doesn't get it.

Robert turns his face away, in the only direction possible. To his father. To the death mask of his father. Concerning

243

his brother, Robert thinks, *I don't trust him. But he's the only person alive who can possibly understand. The only other son of my only father.*

'Bobby.'

Robert looks back to his brother. Jimmy stopped calling him that before they were teenagers.

For Jimmy, though what seems to be happening here is new to him, though the army part mitigates his worst assumptions about Robert, his mind could easily swirl on now in its accustomed way. With no mitigations possible once you become part of the war machine. With the established legacy of his father's blows and Robert's silence. But the other part of all this surges in him: their shared father, who betrayed them both. And Jimmy thinks: *Do I want a brother?*

And he says, 'I didn't know any of that. Never imagined.' Then a pause between them.

Long enough for Robert to turn a corner in his head and find another abyss to leap across. *But I did confront death: I inflicted it.*

This he cannot tell his brother.

Jimmy says, 'If I were you – if I were the big brother – I probably would've courted the old man the same way. At least you kept the blood off your hands. I hope I would've been smart enough to do it the way you did.'

Robert struggles now with one more irony: As fine as his brother's reaction is, Robert's remaining secret about Vietnam would've had a better chance for absolution from Pops. If Jimmy were to know, Robert would lose him again.

'Thanks,' Robert says.

But that is the only show of sentimentality between the two brothers, who both turn now to look at their father's dead body.

Together they eye him silently for a few moments. 'Crappy suit,' Robert says.

'He needs leather for the grave,' Jimmy says.

And Bob is standing at the edge of the woods. Calvin is in him. Saying things he hasn't said before. *So Private Weber, you're in the woods tonight and you see the enemy and you're quick like you've always been, quick to lock and load and aim, 'cause you're my boy and you're good at what I'm good at. Yeah, I said good like me. Good like I used to be. I know all you ever saw was how wrecked I was. They fucking beat us down. Not the enemy. The brass. The government. They did it to all of us. They humped our asses through the jungles of Hell, blew us apart, body and mind, and then they just up and quit. Turned the last page. Gave the whole thing away and turned us into chumps. Dead chumps. Maimed chumps. Batshit-crazy chumps. Sure you saw me already broken like that, even with a rifle in my hand, which is a fucking shame. That wasn't me. Not like I was in the heat of it, not while I was waging war. You need to believe that of your old man. You're like the me in Vietnam. But tonight you were quick and ready and then you backed off. Why? A fucking hug. You had your target in your sights and you let him get away because you turned it into this bullshit jungle village scene. A father giving his boy a hug. There's a lot you don't know about life. I can't even begin to tell you. But you walk into the prettiest little village with bananas in the trees and clucking fucking hens in the doorways and you can get your ass blown apart there just like anywhere else. These are tough lessons to learn, boy, things you have to learn for yourself. I can't say I'm sorry I learned them, even as fucked up as it was. That's better than being a chump who stays stupid all his life, thinking things are gonna turn out fine. Go on through those doors over there. You'll see. I'll come with you. We'll see together. I can't give you a hug. Grow up. I seen too much in this world to do a thing like that. But I can slide on inside your head and your heart and your itchy good right hand and ain't that even better?*

And Bob is crossing the driveway.

He feels his Glock lying heavily against his heart.

And he's through the porte cochere doors and it's not what he was ready for. A long room. No, a corridor. Piss-colored light and easy chairs. Just an old woman down the way. Just one old woman. Looking up now. Looking at him. *What's to see here?*

She's looking Bob over. With *that look.*

She rises.

Bob waits for his father to tell him what to do.

She's heading this way.

And Bob hears Calvin again: *I can slide inside your head and your heart.*

He takes a deep breath.

He fills himself up.

Like breathing in a ghost.

The old man.

Bob feels light as air.

And she's before him. Cocking her head. Pursing her lips into a tight line.

But an odd thing. Her eyes are red. From crying. Her cheeks glisten. *Hold your horses, boy. I've seen this in my wife. I didn't mean to hurt her but I have. Hanging with people she doesn't understand. Drinking too much. Getting a little rough. She's not the enemy.*

So Bob is calm.

'Yes?' the old woman says.

'Yes,' Bob says.

'Can I help you?'

'I don't know.'

'This is a funeral home.'

But see how dense she can be sometimes? What the fuck am I supposed to do about that?

'I know that,' Bob says.

She looks at him closely. She uncocks her head. She unpurses her lips, which she has repursed after stating the dumbshit obvious.

'Do you know someone here?' she asks.

Even with Calvin inside his brain, he is still Bob. That's good. So he remembers. 'Bob Quinlan,' he says.

This makes the woman smile. 'Bob?'

'Yes.'

'I see. Where do you know him?'

'From Vietnam,' he says.

And something enters her. That look vanishes. Her eyes soften. 'You're a veteran,' she says, lifting up the word as if she should have known all along.

'Yes,' Bob says.

'Please wait,' she says.

She moves past him. He turns and watches her step to the inner doors.

She pauses before going in. 'I'll find him for you,' she says. 'What's your name?'

'Bob.'

And she changes again. Her face crimps up like that's impossible, the name's already taken. 'Bob,' she says.

'Bob,' he says.

'Why don't you wait here, Bob,' she says. 'I'll get Robert.'

She pushes through one of the doors and it swings shut. He's clearly not wanted in there. *Too fucking bad.*

Peggy pauses. Takes in the room. She was afraid of a visitation space this big. Afraid Bill would look unloved. But there are people. Dozens. He looks loved. If he's nearby, hovering around before finally departing, he'll see.

She has let the man in the hallway slide to the side of her mind. He's probably homeless. He has the clothes, the whiff. But he's a veteran. Of her son's war. She looks to the doorway to her food. She should make the man a plate of food. From this angle she sees the beginning of her special row of warmers, a glimpse of Darla moving, out of sight now, serving Peggy's dishes to Bill's mourners. This is good.

She should find Robert for the veteran. Is Robert helping this man? She scans the crowd, ending at the far wall, the casket. She sees Robert there, talking to a couple. She moves off toward him, thinking, *Bob. You've never been Bob.*

And Bob steps through the doors into the visitation room. The woman has just passed by, not noticing him. Just as well. She's moving briskly. She would have him stand around waiting on her like a bum at the back door.

He turns.

He follows her.

But more slowly. Taking in all the people as he goes. *Look at them. Hats and ties and rouged cheeks and jowls and stubble and crimson lips and scarfs and sweaters and throats and hands, it's that simple, boy, like feathers and fur and claws and hooves, like jungle jackets and rucksacks and pith helmets and VC pajamas, like white faces and black faces and yellow faces, this is what you learned there, all these are the same, people and their bodies and their uniforms and their skin, all of them are a zip of lead or a burst of flame or a tumble of shrapnel away from dead. Or a round of .45 Auto from the Glock in your pocket. You are a walking, talking, swinging dick of a reminder that it's all just a wisp of smoke that the least little puff of air will blow away, and all the politics and all the ideas and all the scheming and raping and robbing and conquering, all the grunting and raving and wailing and weeping by every last one of these creatures is for nothing, because just that simple thing in your pocket there, boy, if you hold it steady and you aim it true, can turn any one of these poor motherfuckers into maggots and bones.*

'Oh my God,' Peggy says, close enough now to recognize the other man, who is turning to her voice. 'Jimmy,' she says. 'Oh Jimmy.'

She rushes and she throws open her arms and Jimmy expected this moment if he came, if he stayed, and he decides to set aside all the years of his mother's loyal-wife silence so that he can go through these motions. He opens his arms too and he takes her up and she embraces him. He looks at Heather, who is smiling the same smile he's seen in quiet moments over coffee in their three breakfasts as a couple – even as Peggy looks at Heather thinking, *I have another granddaughter and I didn't even know she exists* – and Jimmy looks at Robert, expecting from his brother a mutual lift of the eyebrows over this other difficult, shared parent. But Robert is beginning to turn his face away, to look into the room.

And as he draws near, Bob understands. *You see what we've learned? What I gave my life to learn? At every moment, no matter who we are, we are all of us on the brink of being fucked. Nothing to save you from that. Nothing you can do. There it is. I am hugging you close now, my son.*

And Robert sees Bob. Half a dozen strides away.

Their eyes lock.

Bob stops.

They look at each other.

Bob lifts his right hand, moves it up to his chest, and then reaches inside his coat. He pauses. For a moment Robert thinks Bob is feeling his heart. Is he in pain? But Bob's hand is moving again, emerging.

A pistol, in profile against his chest, moving now, turning, the barrel coming round, and Robert is moving too, pushing forward in chest and shoulders sensing in them the placement of mother and brother and brother's lover and of Bob and the vector between and Robert steps and the muzzle appears now and Robert steps again veering right, lunging between Bob and the others, the muzzle stopping, steadying, and Robert stops and squares and centers his chest on the killing black hole at the tip of the pistol.

'Bob,' he says.

They wait for a single breath.

And Bob understands.

He lifts the pistol and puts the barrel in his mouth and he holds his father close and he pulls the trigger.

~

Robert slips into the bed and pulls the covers to his chest. Only his table lamp is lit. Darla is in the bathroom. The door is closed and a thin fluorescent line shows at its base. The water is running. And then it stops. Not a sound from where he knows his wife to be. Not in this moment, not in the next. His limbs quicken. They would have him jump from the bed, rush to her. But now he hears some small sound. Unidentifiable. Perhaps a bottle-click on porcelain. Something. It is enough. The electric clock whines softly from her nightstand. He did not lose her. He did not lose any of them. Except for Bob.

It's been a week.

Bob has appeared each night but one in a dream. His eyes are oddly warm and wide upon Robert even as the back of his head explodes. And each night Robert has awakened in a thrash of regret: *I stopped to take a bullet when I should have lunged onward to take your gun.* Last night, for the first time, Bob did not come to him.

Robert has not dreamt at all of his father. Or he has utterly forgotten him before waking. After all, he and his brother, side by side, watched the box that held the old man vanish into the earth.

But he is keenly aware: *One dead man still lives.*

In the bathroom Darla has cleaned her face and she stares at its nakedness and thinks, *I am old.* She closes her eyes. She saw nothing of the event itself, arriving in the doorway after the gunshot, Robert rushing to her while all around him the crowd surged backward, breaking apart, wailing. Robert took her in his arms, spun her into the buffet room, shielded her from the sight, as witnesses said he shielded his brother and his mother from the gun.

She can still feel his arms upon her.

She will ask Robert to turn out his light before she enters the bedroom. They have held each other every night since, but silently and inertly and only for a few minutes. She opens her eyes. She cannot bear to see herself. She looks away. Her lipstick sits on the cosmetics shelf beside the sink. She reaches out, puts her hand on it, hesitates, picks it up.

After she is ready; after she is all right again in the mirror, looking pretty good for sixty-seven; after she feels his arms around her, turning her away from harm, lifting her with the sound of a gunshot ringing in her head; after she feels his mind working beyond this door, his fine mind that she sometimes senses in his study when she is in hers; after she can picture him sitting alone at the bistro table in the corner of the coffee shop in Baton Rouge; after she is ready, she turns to the door and puts her hand on the knob and she pauses. She has felt this present desire for him often in these past few years, when her hand wished to rise to him, when her body wished to press against him; but then she has paused to consider the moment and her body and his body, to consider the day just passed and the day to come and the lateness of the hour, to consider the words that may have lately been spoken between them over some trivial thing. And she has not acted.

But in this pause now, she thinks of something to do. She grasps her nightgown at the shoulders and lifts it from her body and over her head and she tosses it to the floor.

She opens the door only wide enough for her voice and says to her husband, 'Turn out the light.'

He does.

She does the same with the bathroom light and steps into the darkness.

And she crosses the room feeling like a fool, her body naked but her face made up. But no. It's not foolish. She wants her face as beautiful as possible for him in this present moment even if he can't see it, and she wants him to remember her body from the past, when he first loved her. This present nakedness is for herself: She can't reason herself out of it.

She must stay in her body. She must act.

Darla slips into the bed.

She keeps a small separation between their bodies, letting the dark continue to mask her intention. This is sweet to her, to let that be for a few moments. This imminence.

As for Robert, he is lifting his face from his coffee while protesters are streaming by in the street outside, but one of them, this woman with blue eyes, is standing over him, bantering at him from the start, and he hears himself speak the first words he ever said to her: *I've been away.* And he thinks now of her, of them: *I've always been away.* He turns his face, seeing only a vague shaping of the dark beside him, and he says, 'If I tell you something I did in Vietnam, a thing I deeply regret, will you stop loving me?'

She answers by rising up and moving over him and descending into an embrace.

And as they make love, Darla is very glad to be connected to her husband. She is comfortable, though the parts of her that ache each day are aching now and the parts that once were vivace are now andante. But she is old. She knows him so well. And she senses her Confederate women nearby, perhaps sitting out in the yard, in the dark, perhaps under the live oak tree near the veranda, waiting for her, understanding.

Robert, too, is glad for this connection, glad to be inside his wife once again. And when they are finished making love, he will tell her his secret from Vietnam, about the man he killed in the night, and he knows, from this answer of her nakedness, that she will continue to love him. The only secret he will keep from her forever is what fills him now, unexpectedly, as he moves within her: his first days in the city of Hue, in the autumn, in the midst of a war, the air full of the perfume of fruit blossoms floating downriver, heading for the South China Sea, and the woman he met and loved and lost, and the fear he has carried ever since that the smell of the air and the love of a woman would never again be as good.

About Us

In addition to No Exit Press, Oldcastle Books has a number
of other imprints, including Kamera Books, Creative Essentials,
Pulp! The Classics, Pocket Essentials and High Stakes Publishing
> oldcastlebooks.com

For more information about Crime Books go to > crimetime.co.uk

Check out the kamera film salon for independent, arthouse and world
cinema > kamera.co.uk

For more information, media enquiries and review copies please contact
> marketing@oldcastlebooks.com